RAVE REVIEWS FOR
KAREN WHIDDON AND
POWERFUL MAGIC !

"A mystical, magical time-travel
with a charming cast of characters."
—*Romantic Times*

"A passionate, spellbinding tale
with characters who bewitch and charm!"
—*Rendezvous*

"A rewarding venture into a magical world."
—*Romance Reviews Today*

"A delight!"
—NewandUsedBooks.com

"Karen Whiddon has written a winner
here—love, excitement, and fantasy
all rolled into one fun story!"
—*The Road to Romance*

FREE AT LAST

"The moon's music flows through me and around me, and I travel to other places on its power. I seek to bend it to my will, and in some small things I succeed: a fertile harvest, a minor illness cured, a barren wife's womb brought fruit. What little I have at my command is only used for good, never evil. It is by dancing, by this magic, that I kept my people happy."

Sorrow filled her and she looked away. The golden radiance of Egann's aura suddenly seemed too bright to bear. "Of course, in the end, I could not even save them—so small is my magic. There is naught I can do that will help you find this amulet you seek."

"You are wrong."

His contradiction startled her. The people of the cliffs never spoke to her thus. She'd been revered, cosseted, and set apart. Isolated. For the first time in her entire life, someone was treating her like an equal.

'Twas a strange and exhilarating feeling.

Other *Love Spell* books by Karen Whiddon:
POWERFUL MAGIC

Shadow Magic

KAREN WHIDDON

LOVE SPELL   NEW YORK CITY

LOVE SPELL®

March 2003

Published by

Dorchester Publishing Co., Inc.
276 Fifth Avenue
New York, NY 10001

ISBN 0-505-52491-0

The name "Love Spell" and its logo are trademarks of Dorchester Publishing Co., Inc.

Printed in the United States of America.

Visit us on the web at www.dorchesterpub.com.

Special thanks to:
My editor, Christopher Keeslar,
because he has such great vision
and truly understands my stories;

And Hebby Roman and Patricia Vermeire.
You helped me strengthen and tighten
and clarify my focus.

SHADOW MAGIC

Prologue

Where another man might have felt pride at this, his own king-making, Prince Egann of Rune knew only regret. That, and the disquieting feeling that he had somehow already departed, that only his richly clothed body stood rigid on the ceremonial stage and bravely faced the assembled mass of his people. His spirit had long ago fled.

If not for the lump in his throat and the too-loud pounding of his heart, he might have convinced himself that what he meant to do was necessary and right. As it was, he could only keep his shoulders back, his head high, and pray that his people would one day understand.

Yet how could they, when he did not understand himself?

If only Banan had lived. Though a younger son, all knew his brother had been destined to be king.

Fiallan the Wise stepped forward, the silver-chained Amulet of Gwymyrr dangling heavy in his hand. How the jewels sparkled and glittered, even though the morning light seemed dim, and the ever-present silver mist covered the sun like a thin layer of faded cloth.

"Long has Rune waited for this day." Fiallan lifted the amulet, holding it high so that the people of Rune might see. The collective silence held as Fiallan began to say the arcane words of the spell that would bind the amulet to Egann forever.

Now Egann must interrupt. For if he did not, he would be robbing his people of much more than merely a king. The power of Rune, contained in the amulet, would go with him.

"Hold." His voice rang out, strong and loud and unshakable, despite his inner quaking. "Do not say the words of binding. I cannot accept the Amulet of Gwymyrr, for I cannot sit upon the throne of Rune."

The crowd's silence broke as shock rippled through it. Of everyone, only Fiallan did not appear startled.

"You were born to wear the medallion—"

"Nay," Egann said softly so that no other might hear. " 'Tis what you wanted, not I. Well you know that Banan should have been king."

At the mention of Banan, Fiallan swayed. "Do not speak of your brother. Not now, not today."

"How can I not, when sorrow at his loss is one of the very reasons I must leave?" Egann raised his voice, knowing that each new word would strike at the assembly like a blow. When he had chosen this course, he had known he would break his teacher's heart, and the heart of his people as well.

"You, and you alone were born to lead our people," Fiallan said. "How can you not see that?"

Egann could only gaze sadly at the wise man and shake his head.

"Listen to me." Fiallan's tone took on an urgency that was underscored by the restless movement of the crowd below them. "You have a strength of magic that only comes along once in a millennium. Your voice is a weapon, for with merely a word you can summon the power. With a simple gesture you can build and you can destroy. But I tell you nothing you do not know, except this: You are sorely needed, Egann of Rune, especially now—"

"I will not rule Rune," Egann swore, his voice cracking yet still carrying out over the restless crowd. "I will leave it to you to find another king.

3

Your new king should rightly wear the Amulet of Gwymyrr."

How he had planned this speech, laboring over every word, so that on this coronation day that was not to be, he might strive to make his people understand. But the clever words and pretty phrases had vanished now, and he found that he could remember none of them.

The crowd erupted, surging forward to rush the platform. With a simple gesture, Fiallan halted them. The amulet, glittering and twirling, still hung from his hand. "Listen," Fiallan ordered. Instantly the people quieted, for the amulet began to sing.

The sound was low, a melodic hum that built in intensity until it became both a lament and a hymn. How could any who heard it fail to be beguiled, especially one such as Egann, for whom the spell of binding had nearly been said?

Though it felt uncomfortably like retreat, Egann took a step backward.

Fiallan lifted the amulet higher, as though despite that prince's wishes he still meant to drape the talisman around Egann's neck. "You cannot so easily evade your destiny," the wise one said.

The amulet continued to sing, soft and mournful. 'Twas a powerful lure that Egann knew he must resist.

4

He took another step back. "You know what can happen to one who attempts to wear the amulet for the wrong reasons."

"Aye." Mysterious and full of secrets, Fiallan's smile gave away nothing. "All who touch its magic see what the amulet wants them to see."

Beyond them, unable to hear, the crowd grew agitated.

"Leave us," Fiallan ordered, his normally quiet voice a bellow.

As one the people obeyed, vanishing in the blink of an eye, leaving Egann alone with the man who had guided him all of his life.

"You speak your heart, I see." Fiallan's gray eyes darkened with emotion. "You mean to abandon your people, and the future for which you were born."

Egann opened his mouth to reply, then closed it. He had no ready answer. Cloaked in pretty words or no, it all meant the same.

He would not be king. Could not be king. One who could not even save his own brother could not possibly protect a nation. His people deserved better.

"Will you guard it then?" His words carrying his weighty disappointment, Fiallan held out the silver pendant, which fell silent as though it waited to hear Egann's answer.

How its magic enthralled him. Keeping his gaze fixed on it, Egann shook his head. "I cannot."

" 'Tis a small request I make." The wise one stepped forward, dangling the amulet before him like a lure. "I only ask you to keep the amulet with you until another steps forward to accept the throne."

Suspicious, Egann studied him: this man who had been like a father to him, his confidant and tutor and closest friend. "Put it back in the Hall of Legends."

"The stone door is sealed. I was able only to retrieve the amulet, nothing more."

"Perhaps it will open again now that the amulet has been refused."

With a sad smile, Fiallan said nothing.

Egann glanced once more at the sparkling amulet. Silent now, it seemed nothing more than a pretty bauble. "It does not compel—"

"Nay," Fiallan interrupted, letting Egann know that he had spoken his thought out loud. "Though it contains potent magic, it cannot act of its own accord."

A fierce longing seized Egann: to wear the ancient amulet, to feel its power pulse with each beat of his heart. Longing mingled with guilt and sorrow, and anger as well, for he sensed that he could not escape this final obligation.

6

"How long would you have me guard it?"

"Until one who would be king claims the throne."

Not long then, for how difficult could such a task be?

"I will take it," Egann said gruffly, holding out his hand and bracing himself for the swell of power.

Fiallan's serene expression told Egann the wise man had known all along Egann would do as he was asked. Stepping forward, the sage placed the heavy silver chain around Egann's neck. The metal felt both cool and warm as it came to rest against his heart.

Immediately, the landscape changed. A series of images flashed past his eyes: a harvest moon, ripe and heavy with the season; a woman dancing, her long black hair flowing gracefully as she swayed and spun.

A sensation of longing seized him, coupled with a sense of dread. Egann felt great danger lurking, an impression of betrayal, an awareness of need.

Fiallan's voice, coming as if from a great distance, sounded alarmed, though the words were unintelligible. Egann tried to focus on his friend's face, but Fiallan seemed to spin and his image to waver. Then the sage and Rune vanished, and Egann knew nothing more.

Chapter One

467 AD
The rocky cliffs at Carn Vellan

Long had the dreams come, always unchanging.
Now they were so customary that Deirdre of the
Shadows welcomed them as one might a familiar
friend. *He* walked there always, never in the shadows, for he was the golden one, beloved and as
bright as the forbidden sun.

Though such a man might not exist except in
her dreams, she embraced him gladly as soon as
sleep claimed her.

Far too long had she walked alone, untouchable.
Far too long had she loved only dreams.

Of late the dreams had been more frequent, more vivid, stronger. Since her magic was small, Deirdre knew not what this might mean. Did such a man truly walk the earth—and if so, did he seek only her?

As the time for the full moon and the ritual of the dance drew near, Deirdre prepared as she always did. And wondered.

The haunting cry of an owl awakened him, echoing off the stone cliffs nearby. It was an eerie sound that both haunted and warned. Egann came awake slowly, reluctantly, fighting for awareness. This was unusual for him, since he had been well trained as a warrior and was usually more vigilant and instantly alert.

When he finally bolted up, heart pounding as if from a battle just fought, he knew immediately that he'd been dreaming of *her*. She had come to him again in the night, the sensual caress of her touch wreaking havoc upon his senses, her kisses bringing his body to a state of arousal so violently acute that he could scarcely walk. In the weeks since he'd left Rune, he had been plagued by many such dreams, all of them vivid and—

The amulet was gone.

Clutching at his chest, Egann felt its loss like a sharp sorrow, knew it by the subtle weakening of his strength. For an instant, he could only stand in stunned disbelief.

Gone. The talisman had been taken from him while he slumbered unaware, stolen by some shadowy thief so skilled that Egann hadn't sensed any presence but his own. In the deepest part of the night, while he lay dreaming—

Of her. Then he saw the truth. The woman, the beautiful sorceress with her long dark hair, had stolen the Amulet of Gwymyrr.

Then Fiallan had appeared, spoke a warning—though Egann had not been able to make out the words. Had the wise man's dream appearance been a warning against the woman? Most likely it was she who had beguiled Egann into such depths of slumber that he, even with his strong magic, had not waked; she, a beautiful thief with magic of her own, who now had the Amulet of Gwymyrr.

He had worn it so briefly, that powerful gemstone which was the symbol of his people's legacy, that ageless repository of magic. Once around his neck, he had felt its awesome pulse and power, until its beat became one with his own heart and he no longer noticed its presence.

The nearby owl cried again, though this time the timbre of the sound had changed. More feral than plaintive, it was the cry of a hunter about to triumph over its prey.

Egann smiled grimly. The sound was fitting, since now he must go on a hunt of his own. He had no choice. More than his honor was at stake. Having refused the throne of Rune, he could not rid himself of the guilt that he had failed his people. The loss of the Amulet of Gwymyrr would only compound and confirm it. Nay, he must search this world of mortals, search both here and in the magical realm of Faerie, if necessary. Whether by magic or brute force, he would reclaim the amulet—and when he did, beautiful woman or not, the thief would pay.

The moon hung heavy and ripe, as close to the vivid orange and gold of the sun as Deirdre would ever see. Strolling out into the night, she closed her eyes and lifted her arms, imagining the cool moonlight as something different, even as she felt the siren song of the harvest moon begin to build within her. Conscious of nothing else, she swayed, taking the first sinuous steps that would begin the seductive motions of her shadow dance.

Her people came slowly at first, drawn by her unvoiced music, watching in silence as she invoked three of the elements—earth, wind, and water—and the dizzying current of magic began to build. She called to each of them and none of them, to something essential within and something wild

11

without, and when the man with the golden hair rode slowly into the clearing on a huge horse so white it seemed to glow, none of them was surprised. Such things had been known to happen when a truly powerful Shadow Dancer danced.

Unknowing and uncaring, Deirdre continued her movements, enthralled by the slow swelling of power that never failed to take her with it. She joined with her people, used with their consent their life-energy to help her as she tamed the magic. Her people's sudden withdrawal came like a cold dash of sea water, making her steps falter, causing the spell to waver.

The golden one.

When she opened her eyes to see him, her first reaction was terror that she'd stayed in the spell of the dance too long and failed to hide from the morning. Her second was a strange lurch of her heart, then an all-encompassing relief that he had come at last, the golden man who haunted her dreams.

"Give it to me," he ordered, his voice rough like cliff-stone, and the tone more authoritative than any usually dared use with her.

She smiled, knowing he did not understand who or what she was, or that he had come here because her dance had called him. "Give what to you?"

"That which you stole under cover of darkness." Dismounting easily, he strode over and stood, towering above her in a way that both threatened and thrilled.

Her people, seeing that Deirdre did not evince fear or distress, melted away, back into their cliff caves to wait or to listen to the music of the pounding surf below, leaving her alone with the golden stranger. If she wanted them, she need only to think it and they would return, ready to defend their Shadow Dancer—if necessary with their lives.

Though she sensed his anger, the stranger did not frighten her. After all, she knew him, had met with him daily in her dreams. His next statement only confirmed her thoughts.

"I recognize you." He ran a restless hand through his long, golden hair. "And I want back what you took from me."

His dreams must have been different from hers. Perplexed, she tilted her head and looked up at him, wondering how it would feel to have him take her in his arms in reality rather than fantasy.

"I have taken nothing but that which you gave to me freely." Her face heated, thinking of all the things they'd done in her dreams, things no other man would have dared to do to a High Priestess of the Shadows. She was glad the golden-haired one had been so bold; now she longed to experience his embrace in reality.

"I would like you to kiss me now." She spoke softly, startling herself with her own bluntness. Still, daydreams were short, and if this warrior had stepped out of one of hers, she had no idea how long she would have him.

His eyes, the color of a moonlit ocean on a stormy night, darkened. Still, instead of reaching for her, he crossed his massive arms and frowned.

"No more tricks, woman. Somehow you have haunted my dreams for months, though I spoke the spells that should have kept you away. Your magic must be great to enable you to do such a thing. But my own power is considerable, and while I slept you took the amulet."

"I did not—" she began.

He interrupted her with a sharp gesture. "Enough. Give me that which belongs to me."

Give me that which belongs to me. Words of ancient legend, of prophetic song. She had dreamed of him saying such a phrase to her, but the manner of his speaking had been different. Passionate instead of furious, fire instead of ice. In her dreams, *she* had been that which belonged to him. And he'd known it then, as surely as she knew now that it could still be truth. So what was it that he was implying she'd taken?

"Surely you have not come so far to settle for less than is yours by right," she said.

14

"You have taken that which is rightfully mine," he repeated. Though he did not raise his voice in anger, she sensed this cold rage of his was infinitely more dangerous.

"I have taken nothing," she said. "And I speak only truth. Unless you talk of what has occurred between us in the world of dreams, and then I took only that which you gave to me of your own free will."

For the first time since he'd arrived, hesitation flickered across his hard countenance. "You utter riddles and lies," he accused. "Be warned that I do not suffer thieves lightly. Return my amulet, and you have my vow that you will not be punished."

Had her people heard his words, they would have laughed. Everyone knew that a Shadow Dancer had no interest in stealing petty baubles. In fact, usually a Shadow Dancer had no interest in anything but her dance.

In this, Deirdre was not usual.

"It is plain you do not know who I am or what I am." She spoke with quiet dignity. "If you knew me, you would also know that I have no need of trinkets. I did not take your amulet."

He took a step closer, putting them chest to chest. Her blood thickened; the slow, aching heat that pooled within her brought awareness of the sensual pleasures she had shared with this man for

15

many weeks in her dreams while she slept.

A gentle breeze turned the night air cool, causing her to shiver. Seeing it, one corner of the golden stranger's mouth tugged up in a reluctant smile. "I do not want you to think I would hurt you."

For a moment she could not catch her breath, reeling from the unexpected beauty of his smile. Instead of responding, she took a measured step back, away from the compelling heat of his body.

His smile vanished. "I have said I will not hurt you. I merely seek my amulet. Tell me where it is."

She gave a slow shake of her head, forcing a smile to show that she was not afraid. The breeze pulled at her hair, making the long, straight length of it dance teasingly around her waist.

"You could never hurt me," she told him, again speaking only truth. "And you'd best look elsewhere for your amulet. I do not have it, nor do I know where it might be."

While he stared at her with narrowed eyes, a cloud scudded across the face of the moon, obscuring it and dimming the light. Though Deirdre was not dancing at the moment, the omen was still not a welcome one, and she shivered again.

One by one, she could sense her people creeping back to the clearing. It struck her how rare this was, that such a combination came together—the full moon, the time of her dancing, and the golden stranger, he of her sleeping dreams, he of the sun and daylight.

He was everything she was not, she realized, and the perfect counterpoint to her darkness. Though he did not seem to remember it, they completed each other, if only in her dreams. A perfect circle they were, like the dances she performed.

"My people gather," she said, hoping he would understand. "It is time for the Shadow Dance, before the harvest moon sinks beneath the weight of her fullness. Will you stay and watch, or must you continue to search for your amulet?"

"I go nowhere." His voice seemed to boom in the small clearing. "Until you return what you have stolen."

With an effort of will, she shrugged. The wind blew the clouds skittishly; they cleared away from the heavy moon, whose pale amber light compelled Deirdre to begin the dance again. Lifting her head, she scented the air and sighed. "Then you'd best step away from the clearing and go hold your horse's head."

Moving lightly on the balls of her feet, Deirdre reached inside of herself for the echoing remnants from the first notes of the moon's song. Arching her back, she tossed her head in restless anticipation and waited for the silvery song of the moon to return to her, to claim her, to make her dance. She no longer worried about where she went while she worked; she thought it likely that she became one with the movement and moonbeams and, while so consumed, left her body and soared out with her naked soul into the vast blackness of the velvet sky and twinkling stars. Never before had she or her people allowed a stranger to watch her though—when a Shadow Dancer danced the movements were sacred, the moon tracks of the magic she generated powerful and bendable only to her command. That magic was necessary to her people's survival, and it was only usable by them.

The notes sounded inside Deirdre, one glittering shard of moon music at a time. Her body was a vessel, used as her mother's had been before her, and her mother's mother's, and so on. With each movement she brought water to the crops, fertility to the fields, babies to those with empty wombs, and health to those who harbored sickness. As long as the moon did not wane, she would dance and dance and dance, until the angry sun sought to push the moon from the sky and Deirdre collapsed in an unconscious heap on the ground.

She trusted her people to take care of her then, to carry her from the clearing into her cave, to make ready her resting place in the cool shadowy darkness, and to place her within it so she could hide from the wrathful gaze of the morning sky.

If they did not do this, she would die. And the magic of her people would die along with her.

Now though, she simply danced. Until she could dance no more and all went black.

When she came back to herself, opening her eyes to the blessed darkness, it was with a sense of aching loneliness, of longing. Another day had passed while she slept, and her people had surely attended to their lives as normal people did. And while the sun blazed overhead and the birds sang and dogs barked and children played, their Shadow Dancer slept and dreamed.

Living her life in a world made only of shadows, Deirdre longed to see sunlight. Glaring brightness she wanted; it haunted her dreams, both waking and sleeping. She tried to imagine the eye-squinting brilliance of it and wondered constantly how the kiss of something that sounded as lovely as "sunshine" would feel upon her pale skin. Would it feel like flame, searing her instantly into dusty ashes, or more like a benevolent caress, sensual, like the first bite of fresh honeycomb unfolding in one's mouth?

In a life where everything was viewed in varying shades of gray and black, Deirdre longed to see what others were free to see, what she could only imagine—like her own shadow, sharply defined instead of blurry. But she kept these wishes and fantasies to herself out of necessity, since everyone knew what she dreamed of was impossible. In fact, it was strictly forbidden, taboo. Were she to try, she would undoubtedly suffer the worst punishment possible: a slow, agonizingly painful death.

For thousands of years her kind had been cursed by a dark spell uttered so long ago the sorcerer and the reason had been completely forgotten. She knew only this: that those who were born to dance in the shadows were fostered as infants, sent alone to castle or village, clan or tribe, wherever the need seemed greatest. 'Twas a Shadow Dancer's destiny to dance and make magic, to serve her people willingly, no matter how heavy the burden of loneliness might lie.

Her attendant Liara, sensing her alertness, materialized at her side.

"Water," Deirdre croaked, reaching gratefully for the proffered cup and draining it before she drew another, shuddering breath.

"You completed the dance," the girl told her shyly, keeping her gaze averted. "These last two days the people have made ready to pluck their bounty from the fields."

Deirdre heard only a few words. "Two days?"

"Aye. You have slept for two days and one night."

She sighed. Sometimes it was like this. It told her that the magic she had danced had been great. That, and that she had dreamed, like before. Only this time, her golden warrior had been conspicuously absent.

Had she dreamed too his arrival at the cliffs?

"The stranger?" she asked. Try as she might, she could not keep the urgency from her voice.

"He has not left. Indeed, he stayed at your side for most of the first day and all of this."

No wonder he had not visited her dreams; he had been here in reality, at her side and awake while she slumbered.

"And now?"

"He sleeps, as do the others. The moon hangs but three-quarters full in the sky."

Now began her time of rest, of preparation. She would not be called to dance again until the moon re-swelled, ripe with power.

But she wanted to see the stranger. With a sense of delicious anticipation, she inclined her head. "Take me to him."

Without hesitation, Liara did as she was bid, leading the way through shadowy corridors with the unerring ability of one long accustomed to moving in darkness. As was Deirdre.

They left the temple cave, the rough stone walk giving way to a soft cushion of plump grass. Rel-

21

ishing it, Deirdre paused to feel the welcome energy of the earth pulsing beneath her bare toes.

There was no wind this fair night, and the heady scents of jasmine and new-cut grain filled the meadow. Laced with this, through it and beneath it, she sensed another energy, more primal and elemental.

The golden one.

Unerringly dodging the sharp edge of the rocks that poked from the grass carpet, Deirdre entered the dark curve of a cave that she'd not visited before. Set off from the rest, near the caves of healing, it was small and undecorated. Here the energy seemed to strengthen, causing the air to vibrate around her, reminding her of what she felt when caught up in the spell of her dreams, heavy and burning with desire. Thinking of it made her weak at the knees.

Was it for this that the warrior had been sent to her?

Had the time come for her body to bear fruit, for her to begin the instruction of yet another child of the shadows?

Sorrow filled her. Hers had been a lonely life, lived among the colorless world of night, forever banned from the sun. Did she wish to condemn another to such a life?

Yet, even as she turned the idea around inside her head, examining it the way one might a gift on the anniversary of one's birth, a softer emotion filled her. She knew it as a longtime companion: the need and longing to have someone to share her life with, to laugh with her and to love her, so that she no longer had to be so very alone.

Even though she knew, as had her mother before her, that to birth a child would be to learn the utter pain of abandonment, for once the babe no longer needed to suckle, the mother would have to send her child away to be fostered with another village or tribe. Just as she had not known her own mother, her babe would never know her but would be given over to others to raise so that, once grown and able to dance, the people would benefit. And Deirdre would ache for a glimpse of her child for the rest of her days.

Such was the way among those cursed to dance in the shadows. It had been that way since before time began and would continue that way until a Shadow Dancer was unable to conceive a child.

She and Liara entered a dark alcove where no candles flickered. The only light came from the crescent of moon and the tiny opening cut into the stone wall.

"Here he is, my lady." Bowing once, Liara left her alone with the one who slept.

A moment passed, then another, while Deirdre watched him, drinking in the sight the same way she gulped down cold water after she woke from a successful dance. He slept like he appeared, larger than life, sprawled out on the sleeping pallet like a restless lion. He dreamed, she saw from his choppy movements, though whether he dreamed of her she could not say.

She moved closer, examining him, trying to obtain a detachment that seemed impossible, especially when he made a sound, low in his throat like a big cat's purr. His skin, she saw in the silver light, was golden too; the ripple of the corded muscles made her breath come faster. She flexed her fingers against a sudden urge to touch him, thinking again of the child a man such as he might beget.

A golden child . . . but one condemned to darkness, a child she would never know. She let the hand that she'd reached out fall back to her side. Such a thing would be cruel beyond belief.

Still, she could not make herself leave him.

Ah, how he called to her, this warrior of the daylight. It was not merely his golden beauty, or his muscular, all too masculine form. Nay, she had known him somehow, in some other time, some other place, where perhaps she was not condemned to walk only in moonlight and darkness, and her dances could celebrate the sharp truth of a shadow cast by the bright fire of the sun.

"Shadow Dancer."

Startled, she became aware that he had awakened, that he watched her with eyes that saw as well as her own in the inky darkness.

"You live." His voice, husky and compelling, seemed to draw her closer to his side.

Without question or even conscious thought, she obeyed the unspoken command and knelt next to him, the edge of her thigh nudging his muscular leg.

Neither spoke, each watching the other. Deirdre's breathing caught, came faster, even as his did the same.

"What spell do you cast over me?" he said, sounding as if he clenched his teeth against the same desire that made her heart race and her blood pound.

For the life of her she could not answer. Instead she placed her hand, pale and cool and trembling, on the heated skin of his broad chest.

He sucked in his breath. "Have a care how you touch me."

"Are you injured in some way?" If he were, she could heal him.

"Nay, woman. But you cannot touch a man in such a way and not expect him to—"

"This"—with uncertain movements, she continued to stroke him, her fingers circling around each taut nipple—"is what we shared when you came to me in my dreams."

25

His muscles quivered, bunching together under her fingers. His nipples hardened, and the rough edge of his breathing mingled with her own jagged breath.

"This"—he growled, pulling her on top of him, until the swollen bulge of his arousal pressed against the damp heat of her own need—"is what such a touch does to me."

Echoes of her dreams made her head spin, but as he caught her hair with his hand and trapped her, bringing her mouth down to receive his kiss, she found she could no longer separate the two. Dreams or reality, captive or willing participant, she squirmed against him, gasping as his rigid flesh surged beneath the thin material of the cloth that covered him.

Dimly, she registered the sound of running footsteps.

"Fire!" Panic-stricken, Liara's voice echoed off the stone walls as she burst into the room. "The Riders of the Mist have come with horses. They set fire to the grass. My lady, you must hide."

Deirdre tried to move, but the golden one held her in place with a tight grip.

"Why?"

Shaking, Deirdre could only look at him in blank terror.

"Why must you hide?" he repeated.

It was Liara who answered, even as Deirdre cast her mind outward, seeking the others who came for her. She could not read individual minds, but she could sense emotions if they were strong enough. In an instant she felt a bloodthirsty rage, indicating that those who sought her meant to slay any who stood in their path.

"These men are Maccus, and they come for our Shadow Dancer. They will capture her if they can to use as a sacrifice to their red and angry god. She must hide."

"Hide where?" he asked. "I have toured your cliff caves. This place is connected like a rabbit's warren. The fire will travel on the straw with which you cover your floors, from one cave to another as fast as lightning."

Releasing Deirdre and pushing her away, the stranger stood and turned his back to them, dressing quickly.

"Come." Holding out his hand for her, he moved to the door. "My horse is fleet of foot and strong. I will take you from this place until the danger is past."

From outside Deirdre heard the death cries of her people. Pain and agony radiated to her in waves, and she hesitated.

"We must help them—"

"You are not trained to fight," Liara said, her eyes round with terror. "Listen to this golden one.

Go with him now, and save yourself."

The sounds outside grew louder. Now Deirdre could hear the crackle and roar of the furious fire.

"Come," he urged. "Time grows short."

She moved across the space that separated them, fighting the urge to do as he said, to run, to flee. Sliding her hand in his big grasp, she dug in her heels when he would have pulled her through the cave door.

"We have to help my people!"

"I cannot." Sorrow filled his voice. "I can help, but I cannot harm."

Her heart plummeted. "What kind of warrior—" Swallowing back an oath, she jerked her hand free. "I am Deirdre, Shadow Dancer of the Cliffs," she told him sternly, her voice catching on a gasp of agonized breath. "These are my people, and I cannot let them go undefended."

"No, my lady." Liara threw herself at Deirdre, seeking to block her path. Nimbly, Deirdre dodged, running into the fire and the noise and the death that surrounded them. The moon still shone through the smoky haze, albeit a pale remnant of her earlier ripeness. Surely a skilled Shadow Dancer could find enough magic, somehow, to defend her people when a warrior would not.

She cast him one more look of desperate entreaty.

" 'Tis forbidden!" he cried, his expression as agonized as her own. "I cannot interfere in the matters of mortals."

"Bah," she spat, the smoke making her eyes tear. "Such rules are meant to be broken."

Blinded by the unexpected brilliance of the flames, Deirdre turned in an unseeing circle, hearing naught but agonized cries, the crackle and roar of the fire. She could feel no moon-magic, could feel nothing but the searing heat on her skin and the stark panic-death-terror emotions emanating from her people.

There were shouts outside the cave, feet pounding, then a sharp scream, abruptly cut off.

"My people!" Looking around wildly for a weapon, she spun too close to the fire. Flame licked at her skirt, caught.

Helpless, she stood in the middle of an inferno and knew that death was upon her.

"Foolish woman. I cannot let you die." Suddenly *he* appeared, towering over the flames. He covered her with a blanket, blotting out the fire. "Come with me. I will take you to safety."

Safety? How could she even think of such a thing when all around them her people were dying.

How could she? Yet how could she not? Death would be the honorable choice, but the will to live was stronger. She had no choice but to leave with this man. Here her people died, and she could do nothing to save them. Instead, she was about to run away, like a coward. She would at least know who he was. "By what name are you called?"

He was silent while he watched her, while the flames licked ever closer, burning, burning. Her heart pounded, the roar of the fire and the screams of her dying people bringing agony and grief.

Except for him, she was alone now—she who had never been alone.

"What are you called?" she asked again, shouting to be heard over the cacophony outside.

"I am Egann." With a muttered oath he yanked her hard against him, lifting her in his arms and slinging her over his shoulder. "Egann of Rune."

Then he ran, past the awful sounds of the panicked horses, the howls and the shouts of her people as they fought futilely. Past the fire and the madness and the pain, Egann raced, fleeing for both of their lives.

Chapter Two

Down the stone hallways he fled, the smoke thick and acrid, the woman weighing almost nothing on his shoulder. Two turns, so close to the raging fire he could feel its heat, and they reached the make-shift corral near the edge of the forest where he'd stabled his horse.

Undetected, as of yet.

The horse, aware of the fire, snorted, more than eager to leave this place of dark stone and death. Tossing the woman on the steed before him, Egann opened the gate and gave the powerful beast its head.

The waning moon provided a feeble light, and for this he was glad. They galloped away unnoticed, the smoke and the noise hiding their escape.

Only when they had left the cliffs and the sea far behind did he slow Weylyn to a walk.

Silent until then, Deirdre rode like one born to the saddle, straight and tall and staring blindly ahead. Egann thought it best not to speak to her. Not now, not while images of her people dying still filled her thoughts.

"Egann of Rune," she said finally, her voice pitched low and full of grief. "There is no such place, except in legend."

" 'Tis behind the veil," he told her, wishing he could somehow ease her pain. "And truly Rune is my home. Or was. Now I remain here because I must find the amulet."

If she understood his blatant request, she made no acknowledgment.

He decided to try a different tack. "Tell me of these men who hunt you."

She sighed, flashing a grief-stricken look at him over her shoulder. "They come from the plains below. Long have they hated those of my kind; long have they feared us. I do not know why, since I harm no one. I only shadow dance for my people and seek not to gain power for my own use."

The bewilderment in her voice sounded genuine. Still, he'd do well to remember that this was the wench who'd stolen his amulet.

She said, "If you truly come from Rune, you must have magic as well." Though she phrased it as a statement, Egann heard the unspoken query beneath her words.

"I could not use my magic to help your people."

"Why?"

"The use of magic alters the fabric of the world. If I interfere in a human matter, I can alter time, destiny, and even fate."

"You could have saved their lives."

He heard the bitter accusation in her voice. "Think you so? I could not even save my own brother's life or change the manner of his dying."

She stared at him, hard. "I did not say I thought you a god."

Egann laughed then; he could not help it. "Would that I were, little dancer."

Frowning, she continued to study him.

"You summon magic. As I do when the spell of the moon impels me." Her tone thoughtful, Deirdre met his gaze briefly, then glanced away. "Our powers must be similar."

Did she seek to shoulder the blame for her people's death? This he could not let her do. Yet he did not answer her, not wanting to spoil what few illusions she had left. As a Faerie Prince of Rune, the magic he commanded was vast and powerful. He doubted what little spells she could conjure by

33

dancing under the full moon were anywhere near as strong.

When the salty smell of the sea was well behind them, Egann reined his stallion to a halt. He'd left Rune, throwing off the heavy mantle of the kingship, longing only to experience a life without responsibilities. Now it seemed he had acquired yet another.

"What am I to do with you?"

Expression serious, she shook her head. "I do not know. But the dawn will arrive in a few short hours—already the sky to the east begins to lighten. I must find a cave or some place that is dark."

In his short time with them, her people had alluded to this, that the one they called Shadow Dancer could not exist in the light. Frowning, Egann looked at her again. In his experience, only beings of great evil relished the darkness.

What type of soul did this woman's exceptional beauty hide? Her sensual lure beckoned to him, tempting him to lose himself in the feel and taste of her.

He could see more of her now; indeed she was correct—the eastern sky had lightened to lavender. Though she kept her face averted, he found enough nobility in her profile to wonder at her origins. He had not known there were women outside of Rune as lovely as she. Nor had there ever been another who made him feel such desire.

"Tell me why you fear the day."

She turned to look at him, her expression quizzical. "Truly, you do not know what I am?"

Impatiently he shook his head.

"I am a Shadow Dancer."

"So I have been told. But your title tells me nothing."

She laughed then, a sad little sound, yet so pure and without guile or malice that he froze. A sudden longing for home filled him, for his sisters' joyous laughter and unaffected ways.

"I am sorry." Deirdre's voice made him look at her again. He saw no amusement in the solemn way she gazed at him. "In Rune have you not heard of those who dance in the shadows?"

"Nay." He waved his hand, his impatience causing his horse to sidestep. With a gentle sound he calmed the beast, guiding the reins so the restless animal stood still.

"I live under a curse." Though she stared straight ahead, her expression emotionless, he sensed strong feelings within her. "And as such I must hide in darkness when others walk freely. The sun's bright rays are my enemy—should they touch my skin they will scald me, and I will die a painful and horrible death. It has always been this way for those of my blood."

35

"So daybreak is like evening to you."

"And sunset my dawn." Swallowing, she lifted her chin. "That is why we must seek shelter from the morning."

He saw real terror flash in her amber eyes; he heard it too in the quick catch of breath she made when she glanced again toward the lightening sky. The place where they rode was flat and without caves, endless marshes with twisted trees that offered little shelter from the light.

"Please." She laid one white hand on his sleeve, her voice husky and sensual and terrified, all at once. "Whether you believe me or not, please help me. I must find somewhere to hide before the sun pushes the moon from the sky."

Without a signal from Egann, the stallion broke into a trot, then a gallop. Startled, Egann glanced at the woman, who inclined her head in thanks.

He decided to let the beast have its head.

They pounded over the moor, the horse fleet of foot and strong of heart. Long, dark hair streaming out behind her like a cloak, his companion fell silent, only the urgency of her concentration reminding Egann that they ran against no less a vast and potent foe than the approaching dawn.

Ahead he saw a blocky shape. The ruins of an ancient stone temple, long ago abandoned. Perhaps here they might find enough darkness for her to hide.

Around them, shielded by the long grass and the blunt leaves of the stunted trees, birds began to sing, heralding the slow and stately approach of the sun.

Deirdre began to tremble.

Egann urged the horse into an all-out run, leaning forward to help the sturdy animal. Deirdre did the same. They reached the crumbling stone building as the first faint streamers of magenta began coloring the horizon.

Again unbidden, his horse skidded to a halt.

Dismounting, Egann held out his hand. "Come."

Her small fingers seemed cold as they took his. He felt the tremors that went through her, and he cursed as he pulled her down from his massive steed and into his arms.

Registering dimly how good she felt, even for that brief moment, in two strides he had her inside the temple, where only part of the roof remained to offer any kind of shelter against the sun.

"There." She pointed to what had once been an altar, with a massive stone crypt built behind. "The tomb."

Again he had cause to wonder what kind of woman this was, but she gave him little time as she pushed out of his arms and began trying to move crypt's the heavy stone lid.

"Please . . ." Her voice broke as her desperate struggles brought no results. "Help me. I do not wish to die."

Though the very thought of her lying in someone else's tomb made him shudder, Egann could see that if she wanted to live, she had no other choice. He hoped the crypt would be unoccupied. Egann did not know what he would do if it were not.

He placed both hands on the stone, putting all his strength behind it. The heavy granite grated as it began to move. Behind him, bit by bit, the sky lightened from lavender to palest gray.

Trying to help, her nails scraping as she pushed and pulled, Deirdre made a quiet sound of distress low in her throat.

The sky grew lighter.

Slowly, slowly, the stone slid open.

Deirdre became frantic, scrabbling at the heavy rock until her nails tore and her fingers bled from her efforts. Egann continued to pull until he felt as if his arms would strain from their sockets.

The cover came at last, grudgingly, grindingly away.

With a glad cry Deirdre turned to Egann, uttering a silent thanks from bloodless lips. He could see her clearly now; it was nearly light, and very soon the first golden rays of the morning would streak across the coral sky.

Inside the tomb he saw naught but dusty ashes: the ancient remnants of some long dead soul. No bones, thank the Fates, no rotting flesh or decaying human remains, just simple ashes.

Gripping his hand, Deirdre climbed into the stone coffin.

"Can you close it?" She pleaded with her eyes. "Please?"

Though his muscles screamed, he nodded. If he didn't help this mortal woman, she would die, and it would be the same as if he had killed her with his own hand.

It seemed to take much less effort to slide the stone back in place. He had barely completed his task, wondering how she would breathe, when the sun burst over the eastern horizon in a dazzling display of golden light.

Alone, he let himself sag against the rock altar. How had he come to this? He had once had the simple intention of coming to explore this mortal world, of experiencing anonymity and freedom for a time. Then his people's amulet had been stolen. Surely, recovering it would seem an easy task for one with such magical skill as he. Yet here he stood in the ruins of some ancient human temple without the artifact he sought. Worse, instead of actively seeking it, he was trying to protect the very woman who might have stolen it.

Glumly he wondered if the Fates were enjoying a colossal jest at his expense.

Long before she opened her eyes, Deirdre became aware of the rising moon. Though many days needed to pass before it would swell to fullness, its lunar vibrations never failed to sound within her, even through thick stone.

Lifting her head, she winced as it slammed against the heavy granite top of the tomb. Instant panic flashed through her—she had never been one to suffer confinement of any kind, and this stone prison allowed little room for movement. With a fierce command, she slowed her breathing, knowing from the thick staleness of the air that she had best be careful until Egann moved back the cover and freed her.

Assuming he had not left her here.

Another stab of anxiety came and was swiftly banished. Any man who would go to such lengths to help a woman in trouble would not abandon her to die in a stone coffin.

As if she had summoned him, the granite slab slid away with a loud grinding, opening slowly. A rush of fresh air made Deirdre dizzy. Then Egann's large hands slid under her and lifted her into the night and blessed freedom.

"Are you all right?" His deep voice rumbled against her ear as, her head on his chest, she closed her eyes, breathed deeply, and offered up a silent prayer of thanks.

"I am." When he put her down, her legs wobbled, but she willed them to support her and they did. Even now, faint as it might be, the silver light of the moon gave her strength. She drew upon it hungrily, greedily, trying not to think of her people and all they had sacrificed to save her.

Hiding in such an awful place as some other soul's tomb seemed like a small price to pay compared to what they had given so that she might be spared.

And this man . . . Opening her eyes, she let her gaze drift over him, wondering if he had spoken true, if he really was Faerie, and in fact much more than a mere mortal male. Looking at him now, she could certainly believe it was true. Even in the silver moonlight, he appeared golden. Beautiful. And so tempting that she reached out her hand to touch him without even conscious thought.

Realizing what she was about to do, Deirdre froze. So much in her life had gone wrong; she would not compound her errors by making an even worse mistake. Shaken, she let her hand fall.

41

He didn't seem to notice. "You are covered in ash."

Glancing down, she saw that indeed she was. Her earth-colored gown now matched the rough rock of the temple walls. Attempting to brush herself off, Deirdre only gained an ash-covered hand for her trouble.

"Let me."

Her breath caught. So help her, she couldn't move, watching with a kind of horrified fascination as he caught her skirt with one hand and proceeded to wipe her off with the other.

She closed her eyes, reveling in the feel of his fingers as they skimmed the line of her waist, the curve of her thigh. She remembered those brief moments together before the attack in his sleeping chamber when she'd come so close to acting upon her dreams. Thinking of how aroused he'd been turned her insides to warm, thick, fluid—honey. She felt herself melt.

Because of the strange connection they shared, Egann seemed to sense her jumbled thoughts. His hand slowed; his touch became more exploratory, more sensual. No longer simply brushing away ashes, he grazed her breast, causing her nipple to tighten.

"Give me my amulet," he said, his voice rough.

Opening her eyes, Deirdre stepped away from the hypnotic magnetism of his touch. She felt like a fool. He still had not given up his ridiculous notion that she was a thief!

"You seek to beguile the wrong female," she snapped. "Use your great magic, oh exalted-one-of-Rune. If you would but take a moment to do so, you would see that I do not have your precious trinket."

With a grim smile, he inclined his head. "Very well then."

He did not move, or wave his hands about in strange motions or chant incomprehensible words, but she instantly felt a disturbance in the atmosphere. It rocked her, the shifting of power as it swirled around her, tingled like lightning striking nearby. Most of all she felt a strong sense of rightness, like her body understood and welcomed such a thing—though how that could be she did not know. The paltry magic she created was not one-tenth as powerful as his.

Abruptly as it began, it suddenly ended.

"Morthar's teeth," he cursed, his expression grim. "You speak truth this time. The amulet of Gwymyrr is not here."

Still reeling from the sensation of power shifting her foundation from beneath her, Deirdre dipped one shoulder in agreement with his words. "I have tried to tell you that I did not take it."

"Then who did?"

Goddess help her, she did not know. "Can you not find this out with your magic?"

He shook his head. "I have tried. Yet somehow I am blocked, by someone or something. This other who seeks to keep me out is powerful indeed, stealing my amulet and keeping it so well hidden."

She inhaled a shaky breath. Did this mean he finally believed her?

"I must find it," he said.

Deirdre nodded. "Tell me of this talisman, this amulet you seek so intently."

His expression went cold. For a moment she thought he might refuse to answer. When he finally spoke, it was with a remote voice that sounded, even to her untrained ear, hollow and devoid of emotion.

"The Amulet of Gwymyrr is passed from king to king."

Stifling a gasp, Deirdre kept her face from showing any emotion. Did this Egann of Rune now claim to be a king?

" 'Twas given to me by Fiallan, the Wise One of Rune. Even after I refused to take the throne, he insisted I have it. Even knowing that I meant to leave Rune for this mortal world."

Patiently she waited, though her insides were in turmoil.

It seemed a long while until he spoke again.

"Though I know not when I might return to Rune, I accepted the task of guarding the Amulet of Gwymyrr until a new king could be chosen. If Fiallan comes to me and wants the amulet back . . ."

"I see." The anguish she heard beneath his carefully modulated tones moved her. More than anything she wanted to go to him, to hold him close and murmur soothing words of comfort. But, knowing him only from her dreams, she dared not.

"Will you help me find it?" he asked, his stare bold and openly daring.

"Me?" Astounded, all she could do was gape at him.

"Yes, you." Voice mocking, he gave her a grim smile. "You are connected with all this somehow. In what way, I do not know. But I *will* unearth the truth. You had best tell me what you know."

Back to that again. What did he imagine, that she'd had some sort of accomplice, some assistant who had spirited the amulet away under cover of darkness? To what end?

Taking a deep breath, she lifted her chin. "Egann of Rune, hear my words. You have saved my life, and for such an act I am eternally grateful. But it should be apparent to you that my command of magic is but a sapling to your ancient oak. I could not stay your hand in any way, or block your

45

eyes from seeing whatever you desired. How could I, a lowly mortal who has but one skill, that of my shadow dancing, assist you in finding your magical talisman?"

Though she'd purposely laced her tone with irony, after she'd spoken, she could see the stark truth in some of her words.

Muscular arms folded across his massive chest, Egann cocked his shaggy head, considering.

"You are mortal, 'tis true." His sharp blue gaze raked over her, missing nothing—not the nervous tapping of her foot, or the way her aching nipples still pebbled against the soft material of her gown. "But even though you are no mage or wizard or witch, still you command a sprinkling of magic, as if you were born to it. That is no small feat."

She thought it best to tell him the truth. "I command nothing; rather, the magic enthralls me. I have no choice, you see, not when the moon hangs full and heavy in the sky and the sharp notes of her song prickle at me, like ice shards too exquisite and fragile to touch. It is not to be controlled."

Looking into his beautiful eyes, she thought of how easy it would be to lose herself in them, just as she did in a shadow dance.

"*Anything* can be controlled." His low voice seemed to vibrate with another meaning, one confirmed by his next words. "Or beguiled, or tamed."

Magic. They spoke of magic, she reminded herself. Yet she could not hold her tongue. "Anything, Lord Egann? Even you?"

His gaze narrowed. "Mayhap once. But only once. When I am aware of an enchantment, I become doubly vigilant. As should you—because all magic can be more than splendor, more than radiant perfection. Like everything else, magic has a dark side. Something that perverts and destroys."

This she already knew. " 'Tis deadly and dangerous in the wrong hands, yes. But for me it is not. When the spell of the moon beguiles me, I care for naught but the dance." She smiled sadly, remembering.

"Its music flows through me and around me, and I travel to other places on its power. Yes, I seek to bend it to my will, and in some small things I do succeed: a fertile harvest, a minor illness cured, a barren wife's womb brought fruit. But what little I have at my command is only used for good, never evil. It is by dancing, by this magic, that I kept my people happy."

Sorrow filled her and she looked away. The golden radiance of Egann's aura suddenly seemed too bright to bear. "Of course, in the end, I could not even save them—so small is my magic. There is naught I can do that will help you find this amulet you seek."

47

"You are wrong."

His contradiction startled her. The people of the cliffs never spoke to her thus. She'd been revered, cosseted, and set apart. Isolated. For the first time in her entire life, someone was treating her like an equal.

'Twas a strange and exhilarating feeling.

When she did not dispute his harshly spoken words, Egann flashed a savage smile. "Do as you bade *me* to do, and look for the truth inside yourself. You are connected to this amulet somehow, even if you do not yet admit it."

Deirdre opened her mouth to speak . . . but did not. Something nagged at the edge of her consciousness. When she dreamed of him he had worn an amulet, some sort of charm that had seemed to amplify the sensations they'd experienced.

As if they'd needed any amplification! Merely thinking of the myriad things they'd done together made her grow warm.

"You seem flushed." Egann took a step closer. "What does it mean?"

Though she knew he referred only to her condition's relation to his amulet, she raised her gaze to his so that he could see how he affected her; she knew her thoughts and tumultuous emotions would be revealed to him in her eyes.

His sharp intake of breath confirmed it.

"Enchantment." He spoke the word like a curse, even as he lowered his head and covered her mouth with his. The kiss was savage, elemental, making Deirdre feel like he drank of her essence and, in turn, let her have an intoxicating taste of his.

When he broke away and turned from her, she felt abandoned, bereft.

"What kind of spell is this?" His harsh accusation reminded her that he had only just concluded that she was not a thief, but perhaps still harbored doubts about her character as an enchantress.

"I . . . do not know."

He would not look at her. Fascinated, she watched as he fought for control.

"I will not let some other force guide my actions," he told her, his voice strained. "Not in Rune and not here."

"I am glad you are able to find the strength of will to resist it," she said quietly. "Because I do not think I am quite so strong."

He spun around to face her, his pupils darkening to storm clouds as he took in the import of her words. He actually took a step toward her before realizing what he meant to do.

And, Goddess help her, but having such a potent effect on him thrilled her to the bottom of her soul.

49

She wanted more. Much more.

"What am I to do with you?" he mused, as if he had somehow read her thoughts. "I cannot take you back to Rune with me. What kind of life would you have there?"

What kind of life had she lived before? Alone and set apart, existing only for the benefit of others, never for herself; longing for something she could never have, only truly alive when she danced or dreamed . . . Deirdre ached to tell him the truth, but could not bear to see pity instead of passion in his eyes.

He was all she had now that her people were dead.

She would take what little she could now and worry about the consequences later.

"I would like to see Rune." This time it was she who took the step to bring them closer, she who held out her hand in entreaty. "There is much I would like to do before I find another people to serve. Let me help you search for your amulet, and in return I will ask nothing except that you shield me from the day."

Chapter Three

He didn't deny her outright, she had to give him that. But her heart sank as he slowly shook his head, ignoring her outstretched hand.

"I can make no promises."

Her pulse leapt. Yet it was a start. Lowering her hand, she took another step toward him. "I do not ask for any promises."

His nostrils flared. "You may only travel in darkness?"

"Yes." Holding herself motionless, she waited. The part of her that feared the prospect of this adventure, she ignored. For so long she had lived a life well-regimented and guarded, that to even think of traipsing off to help a golden prince of

Faerie find his magical amulet seemed dangerous and foolhardy. Yet she wanted to do this nearly as much as she wanted to dance when the full moon rose each month. Of course, it didn't hurt matters any that Egann of Rune was so beautiful. Or that she had nowhere else to go.

"There is a connection," he mused out loud. "You and the amulet and the damnable spell that seeks to entrap me—us."

Deirdre thought it wise to say nothing.

Still gazing down at her, he reached out and lifted the heavy mantle of hair from her shoulder, running his fingers through it and making it cascade like a black silken waterfall down his arm. Her heart stuttered, skipped, and she scarcely dared breathe.

"And there are those who seek to capture you." Twining her hair around his hand, he gave a gentle tug, bringing her the final step closer—so close that she could, if she so desired, turn her head and place a kiss on the rippling muscles of his chest. She swallowed and kept still.

"I cannot destroy them for you." His bass voice was a seductive rumble against her ear. "Though," he continued in a more thoughtful tone, "I can promise you if they try again to hurt you, I will use magic to spirit you away."

She looked up at him then, knowing full well that to do so might be a mistake.

"You are as lovely as any woman of Rune," he swore. He ran his thumb caressingly over her bottom lip.

Her mouth fell open as she fought the urge to take his thumb into her mouth and suckle. Where such thoughts came from she couldn't say, as she had never done with any man the things she dreamed of doing with this one.

"I will keep you safe, fair Deirdre of the Cliffs." Though he'd said he could not promise her anything, he gave her this. Though, she mused, as promises went, this one sounded reluctant, as though forced from him through clenched teeth. "For as long as we search for my amulet, I will let no harm come to you."

Though no breeze blew this eve, still Deirdre shivered. The minuscule, buried-deep-inside part of her that was magic wondered if he knew what his low-voiced vow might entail.

But she could not bring herself to tell him, for she did not relish the thought that he might leave her if he knew the truth. Like most truths, this one was not pretty; indeed Egann of Rune would no doubt find it more of a responsibility than he wished to take on. There were those who made it their destiny to destroy Shadow Dancers. For whatever reason, they hated them with a loathing that was nearly palpable. They had made it their lives' work, and that of their sons and daughters, to hunt Shadow Dancers for sacrifice. Why, she had no idea.

Deirdre had always known that one day they would come for her. Their determination and resourcefulness were legendary, and one of the first things taught to any Child of the Shadows was how to recognize them. And this she knew for certain: now that they had found her once, they would not rest until they found her again.

Though kept to a fast walk, the big stallion's stride covered a fair distance. In the course of half a night, Egann and Deirdre traveled far from the moors and rode now near the edge of a vast forest. In front of him on his horse, Egann watched the beautiful mortal woman try to shake off the last remnants of her no doubt restless sleep in the stone tomb. Her long black eyelashes drifted down to rest on creamy cheeks, then fluttered back up as she blinked and turned to peer at him from magnificent, honey-colored eyes.

She did not speak, which he found restful. The women of Rune were always full of endless chatter, never understanding how well a man liked his silences, his chance to turn his thoughts inward, to reflect and to think.

Deirdre seemed most unusual. He sensed the magic in her, that submerged energy those of Rune so often took for granted. She, on the other hand, seemed unaware of it, other than the times when she danced under the spell of the moon.

He found her to be a puzzle, which intrigued him.

And her beauty—he saw in her a comeliness so exquisite that merely watching her made his chest ache with unnamed emotion.

'Twas unexpected that he might find such loveliness here in the barren, often joyless, human world. Disturbing, in fact. But he'd stopped trying to analyze his reaction to her, finding instead relief in the knowledge that, although she'd haunted his dreams, she hadn't stolen his amulet.

What tie she had to the charm, he'd yet to fathom. But it was there, nonetheless, and he sensed she would somehow be instrumental in obtaining its return. It was a bonus that she'd agreed to help him search—though dangerous as well, in a way he had yet to fully understand. To keep her near him, he would have to guard against two things: one, whatever powerful spell made her so irresistible to him and, two, the stifling obligation of yet another responsibility. After all, he'd promised to keep her safe, granting himself one more obligation in addition to the amulet, before he could truly enjoy his hard-won freedom.

Ah, responsibility. To Egann that meant only failure; it brought the memory that he, despite good intentions, could not be counted on. He'd tried—by the stars, how he'd tried—to live up to his position as eldest son, but never would he forget the look on his brother's face before he died. Before Egann had killed him.

That failure had taken its toll—the highest of all, and Egann had come out of it certain of only one thing: He would not take the chance that he might fail again. As a result, he never did anything impetuous, spontaneous, or simply for the joy of it. As Crown Prince of Rune, Egann knew he was not worthy of the throne; to count on him would be to court disaster. Yet the people—who also knew the truth about him—had seemed to forget. He was looked up to, idolized, and revered by many as their future king.

A position of which he was not and would never be worthy. At Fiallan's wishes he had stayed, suffered the false adulation and accolades until he'd thought he might suffocate if he didn't leave Rune.

Thus he had refused to take the throne, even though his refusal had left the land of Faerie without a king.

The guilt of his decision had nearly destroyed him. Yet the unbelievable sense of freedom, the great weight that seemed to have lifted from his shoulders, made the guilt seem a small price to pay.

Accepting Fiallan's charge to protect the amulet would have helped even more. At least it would have if he had been able to manage this one final service for his people, however small.

But he'd woken to find that he'd failed even at that.

Now he felt undeserving even of his coveted freedom. It was all he had now, though, so he would hold on to it with every fiber of his being. He would enjoy that freedom—as soon as he fulfilled his obligations to protect the woman and find the amulet.

Thinking on it, he shivered. It concerned him greatly that he'd found himself so quickly with more responsibility, another life that counted on him for protection when he might only let her down. One whose very presence was a threat to the freedom he'd abandoned everything to attain. The only thing he truly wanted was to find the amulet, discharge his limited duty, and disappear into the anonymity of the human world. But such was not to be. Not yet. The one who called herself a Shadow Dancer asked so little of him—nothing but protection from the sun, and perhaps from the men who had killed her people. He had given his word that he would give her that. The vow had been spoken freely. So now he had two concerns— Deirdre of the Shadows and the missing Amulet of Gwymyrr.

Fitting, how the two were tied together, though in some inexplicable way he did not yet understand. But Egann felt quite certain that once he deciphered the puzzle, he would find the missing talisman.

And then?

Ah—he smiled to himself, though it was a grim smile at best—he would worry about that later. For one of the beautiful advantages about an irresponsible life was the absence of regulations and planning.

The soft hooting of an owl made Deirdre shiver—the sound seemed overly close, given that they skirted the edge of the forest. Glancing over her shoulder at the huge man who rode behind her, she saw nothing in the hard cast of his features to indicate that he felt reason for concern. Still, she could not shake the tingling of premonition when the owl cried again.

"I heard that same sound when I awakened to find the amulet missing." The grim edge in Egann's voice told her that he felt the same sense of warning.

"Think you it is the same bird?"

"I do not know. If it is, he has traveled far from home."

Home. Smiling sadly, Deirdre thought of the cliffs by the sea. For her entire life she had lived there . . . but never had the place felt like a home.

Egann reined his stallion to a halt and faced the forest.

"What—"

"Wait." He held up a hand for silence.

Again the owl cried.

Egann dismounted, then helped her down. He led the horse toward the forest, where the intertwined limbs of towering oaks created a deeper shroud of darkness.

The sound came again, from farther within the woods this time.

Exchanging glances with him, Deirdre moved closer. She knew he thought as she did: the thief who had taken the amulet now taunted them. But they were surely dealing with some sort of enchantment, something the Faerie Prince was better able to counter than she.

They continued deeper into the woods. Once inside the thick forest, the air held the musty scent of fresh earth. Deirdre breathed deeply, letting her eyes adjust to the gloom, glad that the years she had spent moving about in the depths of night had prepared her. The lack of light did not seem to bother Egann, either; he led them forward stealthily, but with a confidence that told her he too could see his path, even though moonlight did not penetrate the canopy of the trees.

59

Various creatures watched them. Though she did not catch sight of them, Deirdre could sense their perusal, their waiting. But for what, she could not ascertain.

"I begin to think we walk into a trap," Egann muttered, slowing his pace.

"I too feel the sense of wrongness." She touched his arm and he halted. "All is not as it should be, though what is out of place I cannot say."

"Those who hunt you—from where do they come?" The tautness of the question told her Egann thought attack might be imminent.

She could answer, though her response would no doubt frustrate him. "From everywhere and nowhere. The Maccus move from village to village in their never-ending search for those who dance in the shadows."

"Why?"

"I do not know." Her voice sounded small as she considered his question. "All my life I have known of them, feared them, and lived in dread of the day they would find me. 'Tis the entire reason for existence, this hunting and killing of Shadow Dancers. The legend speaks of some sort of revenge, though for what sin I know not."

"How many have they killed?"

"I know not," she repeated, feeling both at ease and uncomfortable in the deepening gloom. "I know only this—they are never satisfied by the taking of only one."

Egann cocked his head, as though he pondered this. But then she wondered, as the owl cried again, whether he'd merely listened for the taunting of the bird.

"How much farther do we go?" he muttered, though his step never faltered. "When will this creature reveal itself and tell what payment is required?"

Payment? Did he think the owl held his amulet?

They came to a place where the undergrowth did not seem as dense. Egann stopped in a clearing, turning to search the perimeter in a few abrupt motions.

"Wait here," he said, handing Deirdre the reins to his horse.

Automatically she took them, trying to calm her unease by backing up until her shoulder blades were against the horse's withers, and she could feel every breath taken by the massive animal.

The owl gave another cry, a long, mournful sound.

Egann touched Deirdre's hand lightly, as if to make certain she understood that she was to wait.

She nodded, her heart in her throat, as he turned away.

Pushing back the underbrush, he disappeared silently in the direction of the bird's cry. She noticed that he, a Faerie Prince by his own account, did not even carry a sword for protection. Perhaps he used magic instead.

He vanished into the woods and she waited, alone and unprotected, with the feeling of dread intensifying. The night air felt heavy, charged. Something was amiss, and she liked it not.

"Greetings."

With a gasp she spun to the left, then to the right, seeing nothing and no one.

"What sort of enchantment is this?" she murmured. Egann's horse turned his head to look at her and snorted.

"Up here." Laced with amusement, the voice was also full of mischief. Perched on the lowest branch of the tree was a large owl, its yellow eyes winking merrily.

"He's gone looking for you." Helplessly, Deirdre glanced off in the direction Egann had gone. "At what sort of jest do you play?"

"I?" Sounding insulted, the bird preened, ruffling its mud-colored feathers. "I play at nothing. Rather I like to think of it as helping things along."

She supposed if she could believe in a talking owl, then she could believe its words as well. Still, she kept her back against the solid horse, feeling safer that way.

"Helping what things along?"

"Egann, of course." The bird chuckled, then introduced itself. "I am Fiallan . . . of Rune."

The air shimmered, a thousand tiny stars twinkling. When the glittering faded, a silver-haired man stood in front of the tree, clad in a robe of some rich material that seemed to cast its own light into the gloom.

"You are the one who gave him the amulet." As soon as she'd spoken, Deirdre blushed. What if Fiallan asked about it? Surely Egann did not wish this man to know of the amulet's disappearance.

"Ah yes. The amulet." Stroking a long beard as white as new snow, the ancient one smiled. "You have seen it then? Felt the power pulse in your hand as you held it?"

She could not lie. "Nay, I have never seen it. Only have I heard Egann speak of it."

"With great reverence?" Fiallan's tone sounded sharp.

"Yes." She hurried to add, "He values it highly."

"So highly then, that he suffered when he lost it?"

He knew. Letting her shoulders sag, Deirdre glanced once more in the direction Egann had gone. It was time he returned and found his own answers for Fiallan's questions.

"It seems that he does." She chose her words carefully. "He came to the cliffs by the sea believing I had stolen it."

"And had you?"

"Of course not. Of what use would such a trinket be to a Shadow Dancer?"

Cocking his head, the sage considered her. "Shadow Dancer, eh? Yet one such as you, who feels the ancestral tug of magic in your blood, would recognize the power of the Amulet of Gwymyrr were you to hold it in your palm. And once having done so, perhaps you might covet it?"

Straightening herself, so that she stood tall and true, Deirdre steadily met his gaze. "I have no doubt that I would recognize this amulet, wise man of Rune, if it resonates with magic as you say. But I have never coveted anything in my life."

His smile, though compassionate, seemed slightly mocking. "What of your longing to see the sun?"

She clenched her hands. "See you so deeply into my very soul that you know every secret which resides there? I have told no one of that longing, not even your Egann, who seeks you—or the owl—as we speak."

"I know much. I can tell you of your people's history if you wish."

"The history of my people is known to me."

"Know you then, how the curse came to be?"

Deirdre went still. "No one knows that. You speak of something so far back in the mists of time that it has been forgotten."

"By some. Not by all."

Though she wanted to believe him, she could not. The history of the Shadow Dancers had been told to her by her mother, passed down from generation to generation, sacred and unchanged. How could this Fiallan, even if he truly were a wise man of Rune, know what her own people did not?

"I do not wish to speak of it," she said firmly. "Now tell me, do you seek to hinder or help Egann in his search for this charm of yours?"

Fiallan's yellow eyes twinkled. "You are wiser than you appear."

She supposed she should take offense, but she did not. "Is that so?"

He chuckled. "I find you a worthy adversary for Prince Egann."

"Adversary?" Shaking her head, she began to pray silently that Egann would come back. "You are wrong. We are allies. I travel with him to help search for the amulet."

"To what end?"

She didn't have a ready answer, so she said nothing.

He coughed, hiding what looked to be a smile behind his hand. "Tell me—for what purpose does Egann seek the Amulet of Gwymyrr?"

It was something he hadn't told her. "I think he means to return it to the rightful owner, the one you name as king in your Faerie land of Rune."

Egann's horse snorted.

"Steady, Weylyn," Fiallan said, reaching out with one long-fingered hand to rub the huge beast's nose. "He will soon return, have no fear."

"Weylyn." The idea that the horse could be so named intrigued her. In the time she had known him, never had she heard Egann refer to the horse as such.

"It means Son of the Lion in our tongue."

Shocked, Deirdre could only stare. She looked at the huge beast, so solid, so steady, and then back at the wizened man so full of life he seemed to vibrate with it.

How much of what he said was truth, how much lie?

Seeing the indecision flicker across her face, Fiallan laughed, a cackle that startled a rabbit from its nest in the underbrush. Though the animal seemed to explode from the forest right in front of Weylyn, the horse only shifted his feet and nickered.

"I cannot lie," Fiallan continued. Though he spoke softly, his voice rang with authority. "Like you."

"Another secret of mine that you seem to know."

"None of us is what we seem," the old man warned. "Especially you."

Impatience made Deirdre shift her feet, causing the horse behind her to move sideways.

"Tell me how we may find the amulet," she asked, knowing the answer would be of the most importance to Egann.

"You will find the amulet when it wishes to be found."

"But that—"

"When the time is right." Then, with a mocking laugh, he changed back into an owl, flapped his mighty wings and disappeared into the night.

A heartbeat later Egann returned. He frowned when he saw that Deirdre stood staring at nothing.

"What is wrong?"

Slowly she shook her head. "Your Fiallan was here."

He froze, lifting his shaggy head as if scenting the wind. "Fiallan? When?"

"Soon after you left. He was the owl that so taunted us." Crossing her arms, she waited for the disbelief that such a statement was sure to bring.

"I do not understand." Instead of disbelieving, he sounded bewildered. "Why would Fiallan appear to you instead of me?"

She swallowed, knowing he wouldn't like what she next had to say. "He knows the amulet is missing."

Egann glared at her. "Why did you tell him?"

"I did not. He already knew. Did you not say to me that he is called the Wise One of Rune?"

Bowing his head, Egann groaned. "He is a very powerful mage."

Since Fiallan had been somehow able to see inside her, to the secrets she had always kept so deeply hidden, Deirdre was inclined to agree.

"What else did he speak of?"

"The history of my people, the name of your horse—"

"Does he know where the amulet has been taken?"

"If he does, he did not tell me. Indeed, when I asked him that very question, he said the amulet 'will be found when it wants to be found.' "

"That makes no sense!" Egann exploded, pacing in the small clearing. "Forever does Fiallan speak in cryptic riddles."

"He also said we must go to Rune."

"Impossible. I cannot return until I have recovered the Amulet of Gwymyrr. And until they have chosen another king."

Wisely, Deirdre kept her silence.

"Why would I go to Rune?" Halting in front of her, he crossed his muscular arms and glared. "What purpose would it serve?"

"Mayhap the amulet is there?"

"No. Someone in your world has taken it."

She decided to try a different tactic. "Why did Fiallan entrust the amulet to you, if you would not be the king?"

"Because—" Midsentence he paused, crossing the distance between them with a few strides, lifting her chin with his big hand. "Your eyes—they were golden. Now they are the color of a robin's egg."

She shrugged, trying to pretend that his nearness did not affect her. " 'Tis true. It has always been so. My eyes change color as often as the moon changes her shape. I do not know why or what it means."

He now seemed interested in watching her mouth. "Perhaps there is more magic within you than you realize."

A thought occurred to her. "How is it that you see so well in the darkness?"

"The darkness lessens." Egann's words came at the same time that Deirdre realized what was happening. The dawn drew near, and she needed to find a place to hide from the sun.

"Think you that the light will be able to penetrate the thickness of this forest?"

It seemed like he'd read her mind. Trying to remain calm, she glanced upward, to where the thick canopy of branches blocked much of the sky. Yet there were holes, gaps—small ones, but there

69

nonetheless. "I do not know," she admitted, hearing the quaver in her voice and hating it. "But I would prefer to find a safe place until the sun has passed overhead and vanished."

He glanced around their small clearing, appearing unconcerned. "Perhaps you can find a hollow tree."

"Or you can take me to Rune and hide me there." The instant she spoke the words, Deirdre recoiled in horror. She hadn't meant to say them, hadn't even thought them. Where they had come from she could only guess.

"Rune?"

"Truly I did not mean to say that," she stammered, "Some enchantment perhaps, or—"

The edge of the forest began to lighten. All around them, birds began to sing welcoming songs of joy to the coming day.

'Twas time for her to take shelter.

Swallowing, she moved closer to Egann.

He placed his massive arm across her shoulders, drawing her near. " 'Tis like before," he muttered. "When we found the ancient temple and hid you in the tomb."

While the thought of such utter confinement made her shudder, she would gladly have climbed into the tomb now to hide from the coming sun. There remained possibly a half hour before the dawn, maybe less.

The dawn. With all her heart she longed to see it, but all her life she had heard the stories of what doing so would cost. For apparently she was not the only Shadow Dancer to want to escape the night—others had tried before her, and their deaths had been a horrible and painful torture. Such tales were common knowledge and had been repeated to Deirdre constantly throughout her childhood, in case such a notion might come to her.

So now common sense and a wish to avoid pain tempered her longing to walk in the daylight.

Yet if she had no place to hide . . .

Deirdre broke away from Egann, running toward the heart of the forest. She who wanted to be— who had always been—so strong, fought panic now, because she could see no place in the twisted maze of undergrowth and towering trees for her to hide. The sun would find her somehow and destroy her; she knew it would. The curse her people lived under was clear on the subject.

"Hold." Egann's voice rang out, bringing her to a crashing, shuddering halt. In a moment he had reached her, turning her in a circle so that she might see in every direction.

All looked the same. No caves, no hollow logs, no ruined temples. Nothing but forest and leaves and various small creatures that made ready to greet the morning.

"I will die," she told him, caring not how her voice trembled, or that a silent tear coursed down her cheek. "I am not ready."

He cursed once, a powerful sounding oath, the exact meaning of which she could not tell. Leading her back to where the stallion waited, he took a deep breath. " 'Tis twice now that we have been caught unprepared. We must plan better in the future."

If there was a future. Her heart pounding, Deirdre snuggled close to the man who had saved her life once only to watch it end in some desolate forest.

"Think you"—licking dry lips, she swallowed hard and drew a deep breath for courage—"that dying this way will be painful?" Her voice broke on the last word, which appalled her. Though terrified, she wanted to at least try to die with some sort of dignity.

"You will not die," he promised, his expression fierce.

The tops of the trees began to glow a vibrant green as the sky lightened.

"I have always wanted to see the sun," she confessed, still trembling. "Though it is death to those of my kind. At least I will have done so."

"You will not die," Egann said again, holding her close. "I refuse to let you. We go to Rune. Now."

Rune. Even as he spoke the words of the spell to take them there, Egann felt himself inwardly balking. It had only been weeks since he had left his home and all it represented. Until he spoke to Fiallan, he had meant to keep well hidden, so that there would be no misconceptions of his intentions by his people.

First he sent Weylyn, knowing his faithful stallion would be eager to resume his normal form and romp in the lush meadows of their home. This took a mere blink of the eye, and even as the horse vanished, Egann spoke the spell of sending for Deirdre and himself.

Holding the mortal woman tightly, he felt the familiar shifting of reality. The forest and the approaching day faded, and he and Deirdre hung for a moment in the great empty void between places.

Rune, he thought again, and suddenly he stood in a lush meadow underneath the velvety blackness of a nighttime sky.

Alone . . . ?

Once more—somehow—it would appear that he had failed. His arms were empty—the Shadow Dancer had not crossed into Rune with him.

Chapter Four

Where was she? Since it seemed Egann had somehow lost her, did she even now go to a slow and agonizing death under the rising sun of the human world?

Heart pounding, he closed his eyes. He had to find her—he'd promised to keep her safe. Surely he, who had failed at so much in his lifetime, was not destined to fail at *every*thing. Especially not this, not another life lost because of his incompetence.

Again he tossed out the magical words, again the air buzzed with power and he crossed the icy void. When he reappeared in the clearing where they'd stood, in the blazing sun of a mortal day already well underway, he saw no sign of Deirdre—alive or dead.

"She is not here." A voice spoke behind him. 'Twas a voice he knew well.

"Fiallan." Spinning to face the wise man, Egann let his panic show.

"The Shadow Dancer—I cannot locate her. I tried to take her to Rune and something happened. I don't—"

"She was not permitted entry," Fiallan explained, in sonorous tones he usually reserved for times of great ceremony. "The curse from the ancient spell apparently forbade her entry into Rune. I was unaware of this, or I would not have bade you travel there."

Egann had no patience for riddles, not now. "I know nothing of ancient spells. She cannot be left unshielded—if the sunlight touches her skin, she will die."

"To all things there is a time," Fiallan mused, stroking his grizzled chin. "Though it seems that your Deirdre's is not yet upon her."

"I must find and protect her. I gave her my word that I—"

"Walk with me," the Wise One said. When he used this tone of command, few dared disobey.

Egann dared. Shaking his head, he met Fiallan's steady gaze. "Nay, not now. I must find Deirdre."

75

"She is safe."

Instantly, the fear left him. If Fiallan said it was so, then Egann knew it for truth. The mage could not, like all people of Rune, tell a direct lie. Egann relaxed slightly and when Fiallan began to walk, fell into step beside him.

Dead leaves rustled underfoot as they walked. Above, in the towering treetops, birds sang and squirrels rustled. All the forest watched from a distance, knowing in the way of all beasts that these were not humans and thus, would not harm them.

Finally, Egann could stand the silence no longer. "What know you of all this? No more games."

Fiallan's response was a slight nod. "You ask about the woman?"

"Yes." Egann sighed. "I ask about all of it: the Shadow Dancer, these Maccus, the missing amulet. I think you know well the answer to my question— what tie is it that binds these things together?"

Fiallan did not answer—instead he slanted a narrow look at Egann and continued to walk sedately into the dappled forest.

Knowing from past experience that the ancient one wished him to reach his own conclusion, Egann smiled, though it felt a bit strained.

Seeing his smile, Fiallan answered with one of his own. "I can tell you this, my friend: 'Tis not what the logical chain of thought would seem to suggest."

Egann fought back his annoyance. "As usual, you speak an answer that is not truly an answer."

"Oh?" Fiallan raised one brow, pausing to rest his gnarled hand on the knotty bark of one particularly stately elm. "You do not believe it is possible that the link can simply be *you*?"

"Nay." The answer came readily. "I know it for a certain truth. I knew nothing of the woman—of the Shadow Dancer—or of the Maccus before I went in search of the amulet."

"But what of your dreams?"

Egann refused to acknowledge his dreams. He wouldn't put it past Fiallan, who had once tried to make Egann participate in the sacred ritual that all of Rune invoked when searching for a mate, to have cast the spell that made him recently dream of the lovely Deirdre so often and so . . . pleasantly. Knowing Fiallan well, he also knew that once the Wise Man of Rune got started, he would not waver from his goal. If he wished to keep certain things hidden, then hidden they would remain, no matter how Egann poked and prodded. This talk then, full of arcane facts, riddles and half-truths, could last for hours without Egann learning one useful thing.

It was time to cut to the heart of the matter. "I wish to make certain Deirdre is safe."

"She is unharmed."

Impatient, Egann growled low in his throat. "I would see for myself."

Fiallan stopped so abruptly that Egann nearly continued on without him.

"Care you so much for this woman?"

Jaw set, Egann shook his head. " 'Tis not that. I have given her my word that I will protect her. I must not—*will not*—fail at it."

Since they both knew well the consequences of his previous failure, it was not necessary for Egann to elaborate. Fiallan had known Banan as well, had felt the sting of his brother's passing from life nearly as sharply as Egann himself.

Faeries did not die easily or often.

A silken red fox, braver than most, crept out from under the brush to watch them. Above, a crow cried raucously, once, twice, then a third time before flapping off into the forest.

Time crept by while the two men waged a silent war.

"You cannot see her now even if you use your magic," Fiallan finally admitted. "If you go to her and open her hiding place, you will also let in the deadly sun. You have no choice but to wait until the sun has traveled the sky and sunk below the horizon."

Only years of ingrained manners kept Egann from cursing aloud. Patience had never been one of his virtues.

Fiallan began walking again, this time farther into the heart of the forest, where the trees grew so massive and intertwined that the dappling gold drops of sunlight came few and far between.

"I will have need of Weylyn," Egann mused. "I do not wish to lose mortal time with magical travel." Lifting one hand casually, he began muttering the few words of the spell necessary to bring the beast back to him, become again a fierce equine steed.

"Nay." Grabbing Egann's hand, Fiallan stopped him midspell. "I have given him leave to hunt the plains of Morthar. I do not think he enjoyed his time spent acting as your horse."

Egann shrugged. "I could not ride around the mortal world on a lion, even one as large as Weylyn. But I will let him have his time to hunt. I will summon him back once I find the woman."

"Ah . . . the woman." Fiallan's smile seemed smug and knowing. "She is beautiful, is she not? 'Tis too bad the curse haunts her. An ancient and powerful one."

Though thinking of her loveliness was the last thing he wanted to do, Egann could not help but remember the supple feel of her limbs as he held her in his arms, or the sweet scent of her hair and smooth silk of her skin. His body instantly responded, which infuriated him.

"What know you of this curse?"

"I know it will not be an easy one to break," Fiallan said. "All who dance in the shadows labor under it."

Focusing on the wise man, Egann slowly shook his head. "Who made this spell—mortal or Faerie? I would not think there could be any human wizard or witch so powerful to bespell an entire race of people for so long."

"You are right. It originated in Rune." Fiallan's voice was heavy. "Long before the Hall of Legends was even built or sealed. I have found little on it, but know that your Deirdre and her kind were cursed by our ancestors."

"Faeries?"

"Yes."

At that they both fell silent. A curse was something not done lightly, even by those few faeries inclined to follow the path of darkness.

Despite his resolve not to get any more deeply involved than he had to, Egann's curiosity overrode his inclination to caution. "Have you at least been able to find out why?"

"Nay. The secret will most likely be found within the place where such knowledge is kept when the time is right."

"Has the door to the Hall of Legends unlocked itself and opened once again?"

"Not yet." Fiallan sighed dramatically, reminding Egann that the man had dreamed of entering the revered repository of records for most of his long life. Legend had it that the hall only opened in times of great need—or great joy.

"I am certain the answer will lie within. Now all I need is the door to open and allow me to search for it."

Egann couldn't help smiling at the anticipation in the Wise One's voice. He had hopes that any day now, the heavy oak door would swing wide open, allowing all seekers access to the ancient records. This had been known to happen every so often, though not in Egann's lifetime.

"Think you it will be soon?" Fiallan asked, as though he had plucked the thought from Egann's head.

The absolute cessation of sound from the wildlife alerted Egann a second before he heard the telltale rustle of leaves. In the blink of an eye Fiallan vanished.

"You there, warrior." A man stepped into the clearing, hands up to show he did not bear arms. Clad all in black, his gaunt face and ascetic features belied the sharpness of his gaze. A rough rope of some homespun cloth belted the robe that hung on his lanky frame. All in all, he looked harmless.

Yet Egann knew better than to trust appearances. He gave a mocking smile and inclined his

81

head, wondering how long it would be before the stranger realized that he too wore no sword and was not a warrior of any kind.

Unarmed, it would seem that they were evenly matched—proving again that appearances could deceive.

"I seek a woman in these woods," the stranger said, his tone cordial.

Immediately, Egann's senses sharpened. Still, he maintained his expressionless stance and skirted as close to the edge of the truth as he dared. "You would have better luck in a pub or tavern. There are naught but wild creatures here."

"Nay." Stepping closer, the man's intent gaze tried to peer inside Egann's brain. "I was told that a lost female roamed the forest this very morn, crying out in some distress or agony. It may be that I know her—and I only seek to help her."

It may be that I know her.

The back of Egann's neck tingled. Absently rubbing it with one hand, he kept his gaze on the stranger. The man lied, that much Egann knew. But to what end?

"Who are you?" His voice was cold and blunt, but Egann did not care. He had accepted the charge of protecting Deirdre and would do so no matter the cost.

Blinking at the violence in Egann's voice, the other man spread his hands, palms up, holding them out before him like he sought some benediction. "I carry no weapon and have no wish to fight."

"Your name?"

"My name I give to no man. Most call me Monk."

"But you are not one."

"Nay, I am not."

Monk sounded so agreeable that Egann nearly relaxed. *Nearly.*

"I have seen no woman here on this day," he said. It was not a lie. Since the sun had risen over the forest, he had seen no sign of the missing Deirdre.

"How came you to these woods?" Monk asked, still in his pleasant tone, which began to irritate Egann like the screeching of metal.

"I might ask you the same question."

With a look of infinite patience, the human tilted his head and studied Egann. Slowly, he shook his close-shorn head and then answered.

"I am a seeker of lost souls," he declared. "And I travel where my spirit leads me. Thus have I come to these woods, directed to find this woman and bring her forth into the light."

"Directed? By whom?"

Smiling, Monk moved closer. "By a purpose greater than the sum of this mortal life."

Maccus. This man could be no other. But how had he known that Deirdre was here? Did he have magic of his own, used to aid him in his dark task of hunting hapless Shadow Dancers?

Quietly Egann reached out with his mind, searching for the vague tendrils created by magic, pretending to merely watch the other while he sought information. Finding nothing—indeed less than nothing, for a blank wall of blackness blocked him—he pondered his next move. He could not actually *harm* this Monk, but perhaps he could confuse and enchant him, send him far from where Deirdre slept, hopefully protected in darkness. His people often delighted in playing such tricks on humans, though he had never done so.

Under his breath he began to mutter the words to a simple spell.

Monk straightened, his gaze sharp. "What is this?" he cried. There was no fear, only curiosity ringing in his sharp tone. "I sense the shifting of the veil, so lightly does it part in this place where we stand."

Stunned, Egann broke off his spell. How did this human know of such things? Mayhap this was no mortal who stood before him, but rather one of his own kind.

"Are you human or fae?" Egann demanded. If this Monk were actually some sort of renegade Faerie, there would be nothing to bar the use of magic to vanquish him. Only against mortals was the use of magic forbidden.

"What a curious question." The other man laughed. "And one I might just as easily ask of you."

Twice now had Monk tried to turn questions back on Egann, and once more would Egann refuse to answer. He did not know whether the Maccus hated *all* who had magic, or merely those that danced in shadow.

"Curious, mayhap." Egann fixed the other with an intent glare of his own. "Yet you do not answer. I ask again, are you mortal or fae?"

Monk shook his head. As he opened his mouth to speak, the sound of pounding hoofbeats echoed through the forest.

Wary of both the newcomer and Monk, Egann looked to see who approached. From the corner of his eye, he saw Monk do the same.

A rider burst into the clearing, the dark coat of his horse lathered with sweat. Seeing them, he reined to a sliding halt.

"You must help me," he gasped. He was a young human, his eyes shadowed, exhaustion and pain carving fresh lines in his young face.

Stepping forward, Monk laid a hand on the horse's wet neck. "What has happened?"

"My family . . . my village . . . we were attacked. Riders of the Mist entered in darkness, and by the strength of some dark magic, killed many while we slept. Women, children, animals—it mattered not to these demons. I know not how many still live— I rode away with the roar of the fires and the screams of my people echoing in my ears."

To Egann it sounded like the attack of the Maccus on the people of the cliffs. In a moment the young human confirmed it.

"They came to capture our Shadow Dancer. They invaded and killed my people, all to take our Shadow Dancer prisoner."

Eyes burning, Monk went utterly still. "And did they succeed?"

The sound of Monk's voice sent a jolt of warning through Egann. Monk spoke with the tone of a madman or a fanatic. Egann had no doubt that, if the other man's answer were in the negative, Monk would travel to the man's village and attempt to capture the Shadow Dancer himself.

"Did they succeed?" Monk hissed again, when the rider did not answer.

The rider's horse sidestepped nervously, and it took a moment for the young man to regain control. Looking at the face of the rider, Egann saw that he too regarded Monk with a combination of horror and confusion.

"I do not know," was his answer.

The simplicity of the man's words bespoke their truth. This one, having ridden for aid, had left in the midst of the onslaught; he truly did not know the fate of his Shadow Dancer.

"Will *you* help me?" The plea was directed at Egann.

Monk stepped forward, causing the skittish horse to dance back. "Of course I will," he said. His smile, no doubt meant to be soothing, seemed to Egann false somehow.

Egann stepped forward as well, then squelched the urge. As much as he might wish it, of course he could not help in this fight. 'Twas mortal business.

"I cannot assist you," he said. Speaking with regret, he turned to eye the one who called himself Monk. "And if I were you, I would not allow this one access to your village. He wants only your Shadow Dancer."

With a feral snarl, Monk spun. Something in his hand—a flash of stone—alerted Egann that somehow the man was now armed. "Have a care what you say, stranger." Still a grin, Monk's expression, like the fire in his eyes, radiated madness. "I live under orders from one much higher than yourself."

The man on the horse spoke, perhaps unwisely. "Speak you of the Christian God? Or the red and angry one?"

Monk's answer was a snort of laughter. He tossed the knife from hand to hand, the sharp blade glinting in the light. "I pay homage to no god, nor do I follow this new belief that poisons our land. I am Maccus, and as such am gifted with a lofty mission; to cleanse the stain of evil from the face of this world."

Because he knew that were the foolish mortal to attack him he could destroy him with a single word, Egann decided to question him. "I would know what evil you find in those who dance in shadow."

"Aye," the young human spoke also, his face hard, his own weapon—a battered sword—drawn and held at the ready. "I would know this as well."

Monk glanced from one to the other, disbelief making his brow furrow. He did not seem overly worried by the other's sword, nor by the fact that he was outnumbered two to one.

"You do not understand?" His voice was a harsh whisper, the sound seeming to echo like the low and howling wind that slides through the cracks in a castle wall before a storm.

Neither Egann nor the rider answered. Instead they both stared, waiting.

"Think on it," Monk urged, his eyes glowing. "Have you ever seen a Shadow Dancer move, enthralled under the light of the full moon?"

Neither Egann nor the other man spoke.

"Shadow Dancers call up evil from within the core of the earth—evil magic, to beguile and confuse men so they only think of how they want to lie with the dancers, become their slaves. Thus do they use their evil powers to wreak havoc upon the world."

Egann laughed. "You are wrong, old man. I have seen this dance you speak of, and while the magic generated was of the earth, yes, it was good and pure and whole. It was used to help the Shadow Dancer's people—and because she worked so hard to bring it forth, they honored her by taking care of her and making certain that sunlight did not find her. No slaves were they, but caretakers."

"Lies!" Monk cried. He had stopped the tossing of his knife and now clenched it in his hand. "Hearne has warned us that others would be blind to the righteousness of our mission."

"Maccus, 'tis you who speaks lies," the other human said, shaking his head in disgust. "And I have no time for your mad notions. I need to find those who can help my village *and* my Shadow Dancer."

"None can help those so cursed!" Monk's words carried the ring of prophecy.

"Cursed?" The young rider tensed. "Say you that my village, my family, are under some spell?"

"If they harbor such evil as a Shadow Dancer, then they are tainted by sin. And their deaths are necessary."

With a snarl, the young rider leapt from his horse, sword in hand. "You are wrong! My people do not deserve such a fate."

Instead of reacting to the obvious threat, Monk threw back his head and laughed. The cackling rang out in the small clearing, causing the rider's horse to shy nervously and a cluster of startled birds to take raucous flight from a nearby tree.

The villager attacked.

Pivoting, Monk easily evaded him.

Watching with interest, Egann stepped back, ignoring his own swell of anger. He would have done the same thing, in the mortal's place—but he could not help the boy, for his own life had not been threatened.

The lad raised his sword for another attack.

Monk sang out an unintelligible phrase. The air shimmered with power. And the human—his sword, his horse, and all—disappeared.

Stunned, Egann froze. He had felt the disturbance in the breeze, slight though it had been, and had begun to realize this Maccus had command of a small bit of magic. He had never guessed it was enough to do this! And, as all those who had magic knew, 'twas forbidden to use it against mortals.

Now the mortal was gone, leaving Egann alone with the madman. He had no weapons, at least visible ones. A twinge of curiosity came over Egann as to what the other would do—then Monk lunged forward, deadly stone knife in his hand.

There was no time to prepare a spell, so Egann lifted an arm to defend himself. Monk's knife slashed downward, but Egann blocked it with a blow to the other's arm. He grabbed Monk's wrist, twisting hard, and the man let out a low howl of pain and fury.

"Think before you touch me, evil one." Egann twisted further, harder, and the other's knife fell to the ground. "If you are of my kind, with a few words I can destroy you, though I have little taste for ending a life, even one as worthless as your own."

"Magic?" Monk's eyes darkened, narrowed to slits. "I have—"

And with another tormented laugh, Monk vanished.

Egann staggered, losing his balance. Clutching empty air where seconds before had stood a man, he spun around.

There was indeed magic at work, stronger than Egann had ever seen in the mortal world. Surely not all the Maccus, who seemed to despise the very word magic, possessed such power?

91

This added a whole new layer to the danger that surrounded Deirdre.

Shrugging, Egann left the clearing, moving deeper into the forest. He would use his magic to find Deirdre's hiding place and stand guard until the sun set and she awakened.

Chapter Five

Head spinning, Deirdre glanced around the shadowy glen. Was this Rune? It felt no different than her world. And if it were Rune, where had Egann gone?

She saw no others; no shimmering Faeries watched her with curiosity in their bright eyes. Even the creatures that surely inhabited such an untamed place seemed oddly absent.

For the first time in her life, Deirdre felt totally alone.

Dead leaves crunched under her bare feet as she moved cautiously forward. The air was still, hushed, held an alarming lack of sound. Her skin tingled, and Deirdre smelled the musky odor of rich, damp earth.

Deep within a forest she was, and as her eyes adjusted to the dim gloom, she knew not whether it was day or night.

This could not be Rune. For some reason, Egann had gone without her. Still, she should count herself blessed. She had not been left to the burning blaze of the sun.

Turning, she surveyed her surroundings. If it were day, this grotto, though small, was blessedly dark and cool.

Something or someone was looking out for her.

A wave of drowsiness made her yawn. With a sigh, she curled into a ball and tried to sleep, but she could not get comfortable, ached with an unfamiliar emotion that she soon identified as loneliness. As Shadow Dancer, her people had always surrounded her, protected her, and taken care of her. And briefly Egann, in his quest for his precious amulet, had done the same.

Now, she knew not whether she should relish or regret the novelty of being alone.

At last sleep claimed her. As always, her dreams were vivid and startling.

As they sometimes foretold the future, she had trained herself to remember them, storing them in her mind and trusting her instincts to reveal to her when the time came to use what she had dreamed.

This day she dreamed of the amulet—that which seemed more precious to Egann than anything else. She saw it, all shimmering gold and fire, its gems blue and green and red, the hues of sky and earth and blood. Ancient, it fairly gleamed with power, even as it swung with the movements of the one who wore it.

She tried to see more, a face perhaps, or a landmark that would give a clue as to the location. But in the way of dreams, the amulet faded and another face, both handsome and familiar, took its place.

And so she dreamed of Egann.

He did not speak, but came to her with the savage intensity of passion. She dreamed of his hands on her flesh, the moist heat of his mouth as he tasted her skin, gliding down her throat, finally suckling her breasts and making her arch back and cry out from pleasure. She let him enter her, she who had always avoided such temptations, joined and welcomed the feel of him deep inside her. She thrilled to the ancient dance as their bodies moved together, delighted then enchanted in the way that the full moon enthralled them.

Yet there was heat, a different kind—molten gold instead of cool silver—and when she woke with a start, her body still shuddered with the blossom of its fresh release.

Stunned, Deirdre lay still until her heartbeat slowed and she could catch her breath. The mere thought of Egann could make her feel such things . . . It made her wonder what the reality of his touch would be like. One could become enslaved by such pleasure and, for the first time, she understood why the women of her former village had often sneaked out into the night for moonlit trysts with lovers. If not for the very real possibility of conceiving a child, Deirdre would not now be adverse to such a tryst herself, were Egann her lover. But such a thing, alas, could never be.

No, Egann wanted only to find his amulet, to clear his name, and to escape into this vast mortal world, to experience some prized freedom.

She shook her head. It was time to think about what she, Deirdre of the Cliffs, wanted.

The familiar tug of the moon startled her. Looking instinctively toward the canopy of trees, she counted back to the time of her last Shadow Dance. Not enough days had passed for the full moon to be upon her again, whether it was night now or not.

But, then, who knew how much time magic had stolen; Egann's attempt to bring her to Rune and her subsequent arrival at this dark and empty place might have taken any amount.

And the first notes of the moon's siren song were calling her.

Spinning in the small clearing, she tried to calm the pounding of her pulse, to clear her mind enough to send her thoughts outward, seeking Egann before the moon-magic took control. Her confused senses, overwrought from the intensity of her dream, refused to cooperate.

Drained already, she forced herself to try harder. She must find Egann before she was overwhelmed by the moon, left her body unprotected. Her whirling senses told her that she also should gather her energy to aid her in the dance; but unfortunately, all she could think about at the moment, her body still vibrating with the power of her solitary release, was how badly she wanted Egann.

She knew she should resist such a desire, was halfway toward convincing herself that she could do so without any real effort, when Egann himself appeared. He strode into the grotto, lifted her unresisting body in his arms. As she stared at him in shock, he lowered his head, covered her mouth with his, and kissed her.

It reminded her of a drowning man seeking air, the stark hunger in the way his lips moved over hers—as if he couldn't get enough.

Newly awakened from the sensual haze of her dream, Deirdre reveled in the kiss, her mouth instinctively opening to him, her tongue mating with his in a way that made him pull her closer with a

97

low-voiced growl of approval. Her body vibrated still, increasing the intensity of her need, this time seeking more than a mere dream.

As he continued to hold her close, using his tongue to plunder her mouth, she moved against him again, feeling the tremors of pleasure build inside her, even as the fierce need built for something more. Much more.

What this need might be, she could not voice.

As Shadow Dancer, many men of the cliffs had vied to become her lover. But she had not wanted to share her body with a man, had never known the sweet ache of her own desire. Until Egann.

"You are safe." The passion in his voice made her shiver.

She tried to answer, but found she could not. Gazing up at him, she saw a smoldering heat in his dark gaze that made her burn.

With a sound—of anger or desire, she knew not which—he captured her mouth again. Gladly she met him, thrilling to the power of it, the mindless, vibrant sensuality that now seemed to ooze from her very pores.

His mouth left hers, moved to suckle her breast through the thin cloth she wore. The rough caress of his tongue brought another kind of desperate madness, made her writhe with mindless need.

As she moved he groaned. She arched her back, seeking to bring the caress of his mouth closer.

Still holding her cradled in his arms, he sank to the ground with her, until intertwined they lay on a soft bed of leaves, with only the rising silver moon and the silent animals of the forest to bear witness.

Above them the canopy of branches seemed to part, revealing the inky night sky.

The moon hung full, ripe with power.

She fought it, tried to ignore its siren's magic, but its song called to her, beguiled, and claimed her, far stronger even than the raging desire Egann's touch evoked.

Stiffening, she pulled away. Inexplicably, she felt her eyes fill with tears.

Breathing harshly, he let her go, saying nothing, merely watching her with a shuttered gaze as she bent low to touch the earth, lifted her head to scent the slight breeze that brought the blessed air, and bowed her head to let the silent fall of her tears summon water to the Earth.

Only once did she glance Egann's way. Silhouetted as he was, so sharply in the bright moonlight, it struck her that this golden man was the fourth element—fire. She had felt it in his touch, this caress of a man whom she wanted more than she had ever wanted anything.

For an instant, she knew a sharp pang of regret. Then the soundless song of the moon mesmerized her. She turned away and reluctantly began to move, as she had been born to do.

As she moved, so moved the magic.

Tingling in her blood, rippling across her skin, the swelling of power surprised her—too strong, too much. It came much more rapidly than ever before, its glittering, dizzying current overwhelming her.

She had not long before she lost all sense of who she was, had been, could be.

"Egann . . ." What she had meant to be a shout was spoken as a whisper.

His hand shot out, catching her wrist, then releasing her as she slipped away. He sought to hold her with his gaze instead, the startling blue of his eyes almost succeeding.

Praying that when she returned to her body after the dance, she would awaken cradled in his strong arms, Deirdre managed a smile. Her last conscious thought, before she gave over her body to the music, was of gratitude and joy that she had Egann here to protect her.

Minutes or hours later, she opened her eyes to find that she had gotten her wish. Holding her close, Egann gazed down at her with a mixture of befuddlement and concern.

"I am back," she murmured drowsily. "How long was I gone?"

"Several hours this time. The moon is well on her journey to the horizon."

With a sigh of relief, Deirdre let herself relax. "Despite the strength of the spell, the dance was not so bad then, for I have not missed an entire night."

"Is it continually like this?" The edge in his voice surprised her. "Do you always leave your body when you are claimed by the dance?"

Again she felt tears gather in her eyes, though this time she held them back. It was shameful that she had no control. "I should not be surprised that you understand it so well."

"I am well acquainted with the ways of magic."

With a slight nod she acknowledged the truth of his words. "Then you also know that I have no choice. When the full moon rises, I must dance."

He leaned forward, bringing her close against his chest. With one big hand he smoothed her hair back from her face, the surprising gentleness of the motion causing her throat to ache. No one had touched her thus in all the years she had lived.

"How does it . . . feel?" His voice was a quiet rumble. "Having no choice, being compelled by such an elemental thing as the moon at its zenith?"

The question surprised her. Then again, perhaps their lives were not so different after all.

"How does it feel?" She gave a sad smile, knowing he could not see it. "Probably the same way it felt to you, when you lived under the heavy mantle of princedom: stifling, infuriating—yet exhilarating as well. The music, the dance, the magic—it confines me, yet it liberates me as well."

"How do you know this?"

She raised a brow at him in question.

"How do you know what my life was like in Rune?"

Her answer was simple, and again only the truth. "I have dreamed of you for years. Sometimes it seemed that you confided in me. You did suffer, while waiting to become king, did you not?"

His silence was more telling than any words he might have spoken. Appreciation flashed in his eyes.

Curious, she pressed for an answer. "Did you not have some method of escape, however temporary, from your duties and the responsibilities of a prince?"

He shook his head, the movement rocking her against him. "Nothing. Even now, when I thought I might find freedom . . . I still cannot be free. At least until"—his grim tone spoke of his resolve—"I find my people's amulet and return it to Fiallan."

And then he would be rid of her as well. Yet he touched her with such tenderness!

"What do you want from me?" She had not meant to ask the question, knew he wanted to keep some sort of distance between them—but the words tore from her even as her body continued to react to his nearness. Holding her breath, she could not keep herself from turning her head and pressing one tiny kiss upon his muscular chest.

To his credit, he did not do any of the things he might have done. He did not laugh or mock; he did not even push her away. Instead he continued to hold her, to watch her, though the hand that had stroked her hair so sweetly went still.

"I do not know." Bewilderment colored his deep voice. "This tie between us is strange indeed."

So he too was discomfited by their connection. More than physical, the strength of it frightened Deirdre, as well as arousing her suspicions as to the origin of the tie. Could such an attraction be natural?

"Think you that magic is the cause of it?" she asked.

He cocked his shaggy blond head and pondered.

Shifting against him, Deirdre wondered why she could not seem to summon the strength to move out of his arms, even as he tightened them around her. Held thus, with his body pressed against her, she felt his hard and swollen manhood—proof of his continued desire for her.

"If it is magic"—his breath ticked her ear—"then 'tis powerful magic indeed."

The touch of his mouth on her neck made her shiver.

I am like an empty vessel, waiting to be filled.

As if she had spoken the words out loud, he reacted, cupping her chin with his hand and turning her face toward him. His kiss was savage, punishing—but only at first. As she met his fervor with her own, showed him her own heat, the kiss gentled, slowed.

He touched her—no friendly stroking of hair, but the sensual touch of a man who wants a woman. Gasping against his mouth, stunned by the force of her desire, she let herself touch him back, reveling in the hard, muscular form of him. He captivated her, enchanted her, and all at once she knew that he would be the one with whom she would share her body.

She only prayed she could keep from giving him her soul.

He moved his hands lower, still stroking, and she opened to him. Now nothing came between them, for beneath her skirt she wore naught.

On her knees now, she turned to face him, daring to lower her eyes to see the proof of his arousal jutting from the top of his braes.

Such a sight—frightening and erotic both—thrilled her. Without hesitation she touched him, her small hand closing around his hardness.

At her touch he groaned, moving his mouth to nip at her ear, her neck. She lifted her breasts to him, her nipples pebbled and aching.

He lifted her body, his big hands at her waist, moved her easily until her womanly core, throbbing and wet, moved against him. She rocked, making wordless sounds to express her delight. Such pleasure enveloped her as she had never known, shards of it, as different from the moondance as ice from fire. Liquid heat pooled between her thighs, and she felt the turgid tip of him seek entrance to her. Gladly, hungry and burning, she held herself still and motionless, letting the unfamiliar sensation rock her even as his mouth fastened on one aching breast, then the other.

Now she knew what she had been missing, even in her dreams. She welcomed it, yearned for it, even as she sought—with her hands, her mouth, her body, indeed, with her very soul—to bring him closer. Though she knew not how or why, she realized that this was more than the mere joining of bodies—this was a melding of wholes, like the way she bonded with the moon when she danced. Though this felt much more powerful. Each caress seemed to bring forth a peculiar sort of shivery magic that grew until she could sense the palpitations in the air, the force of their joining making waves both within and outside of the limited reality she had always known.

Then Egann moved, and she forgot to think.

With a cry he pushed deeper inside her. She felt herself tear, a sharp splinter of momentary pain, and he froze.

"You are not—"

Instead of answering she covered his mouth with hers, using her tongue in the way that he had, nibbling and teasing his lips until he opened his mouth in a gasp and she claimed him. She thought to shift against him, sheathing him fully. The movement brought her such silvery sensations of pleasure that she rocked again and again over him, up and down, reaching, reaching . . . until his hands recaptured her waist and held her still once more with him buried deep inside her.

"Nay!" she cried out in protest, moving her head savagely against his mouth, squirming in complaint. Still he held her captive, his breathing harsh against her mouth. Deep inside her she felt the tremors build, moon shivers of ecstasy such as she'd never danced. Like a mad woman she fought him, taking him deeper and moving and clenching and shuddering until she could bear no more. Finally, with a cry, she held him tight inside her and shattered.

Through hooded eyes he watched her, his jaw tight, his corded muscles bearing witness to the strength of his will. So beautiful, she thought wildly, with the moonlight turning the gold of his hair to silver and his eyes so dark she could not read them. She leaned up, touched her mouth to his again, and felt him tense as he fought to keep the passion from claiming him the powerful way it had taken her.

"Don't . . . move," he ground out, his head falling back and away from her as he sought to regain control. But his body, that rigid flesh that she clenched deep inside of her, had a will of its own. She felt him surge again, felt her own body thrum in answer with a rain of hot honey, and watched Egann finally relinquish his tenuous grip on control.

He drove inside her, filling her, thrusting in a tempo too erratic for her to ever attempt in dance, finally joining her in release with a warrior's cry. She felt his essence fill her as he shuddered inside her; she welcomed and embraced it, in full reluctant knowledge of the fruit such an act might someday bear. Regrets? Later she would examine them, if she had regrets at all.

For now, she would take this moment in all its stark earthy beauty, and revel in it—for Egann, Crown Prince of Faerie and its unwilling heir, would not stay long with one such as she.

Yet so tenderly did he hold her, still wrapped within his arms. They lay together in silence while their heartbeats slowed. Finally, when she had caught her breath, she thought she might have enough self-control to speak, to hide the wonder and the joy and the sense of fulfillment that their lovemaking had given her.

Perhaps he had given her a child.

And what, she wondered, could she give to him? He had his own magic, ten times more powerful than any she could summon with her dance. All he wanted was freedom—that and to find the Amulet of Gwymyrr. How could she truly assist him in that?

She thought of her dream and of how it had foreshadowed the beauty of their bodies joining. Perhaps she had also dreamed true, when she'd dreamed of the amulet. Little as the dream might help, she would share it with him.

"This amulet you seek, is it the shape of a star?"

Egann went suddenly still. "Aye," he growled. "It is."

She smiled, glad that this time she had dreamed true. "And do gems of bright colors decorate each point?"

Instead of answering, he pushed her away, rising.

"What game is this you seek to play?" He towered over her, his voice sounding like the ice that coated the cliffs in winter.

Suddenly cold, Deirdre reached for her skirt, pulling it around her as she willed her heartbeat to return to normal. "I play no game. I have dreamed of it." She told him the truth simply, wondering if he, who had just made it clear that he did not trust her, would understand. "Before you found me, on this very day while I slept. I have seen your amulet in my dreams. It hangs around the neck of a powerful man."

"Who?" Egann faced her with clenched fists and the threatening stance of a warrior about to enter battle. His harsh expression should not hurt her with such sharp and vicious pain, but it did.

"I could not see his face. 'Twas but a dream, after all."

"You know more than you tell." His tone was flat.

Aching, she forced herself to hold his gaze. "All I know is what I have dreamed."

"Dreams." He shook his head, his eyes cold and wary. "They are nothing to depend on. I too have dreams, and you plague them. I am beginning to believe you beguiled me the night my amulet was taken from me, and I think now you use your wiles again to distract me from my purpose."

"Use my . . ." *How dare he!* "If anyone was beguiled this night, it was me." Shaking with the force of her anger, she moved away. A distraction. Was that what he thought this had been? Did he not sense the disturbance their lovemaking had

109

created in the very fabric of the world?

She had been waiting for this all her life. This man, this bright warrior, her true mate. Even though she could not have him for very long, she had lacked the strength of will to deny herself the aching beauty of their joining.

Her anger faded as Deirdre realized the enormity of what she had done. She had made love with an immortal Faerie of Rune, one who personified everything she would forever be denied. If she had conceived a child with one such as he . . . She retreated within herself and tried to think. Great Goddess, what had she done?

Chapter Six

Never before had he exhibited such a shameful lack of restraint.

Cursing his traitorous body, Egann covertly watched the bewitching mortal woman. Though he had been tortured by sensuous dreams of her for months before the amulet had been stolen, he had not planned to give in to his base desires. He needed no such complications in his life—especially when he had such an important task to complete. Thus far he had managed to protect Deirdre from the damaging rays of the sun, but it now appeared he would have to protect her from himself as well. If he had managed to impregnate her, the child would be born half-faerie, half-mortal. Such halflings did not live an easy life. Never would he wish such hardship on a child.

He had to find the amulet as quickly as possible. Otherwise he would never be free. The amulet. Did Deirdre know who had taken it? She had dreamed about it, or so she said. She'd told him just enough information to tantalize, yet not enough to help him in his search.

But her assistance, or lack thereof, mattered not to his body—already he burned to touch her again.

Magic! He should have sensed it, felt its power on him. It had to be enchantment, for surely nothing else could distract him so thoroughly and so well.

And it made sense that the one who had stolen the amulet would seek to enchant him, to distract him from his purpose.

Was it Deirdre . . . or another who remained hidden, seeking to move the strings on some shadowy web of manipulation? Was it the one who had stolen the amulet, who now used its great power in this trivial manner?

No matter. He must resist. He could ill afford to let himself be swayed from his quest by simple lust. He must remain determined, focused on a goal that by all rights should be simpler than it was turning out.

The Shadow Dancer was a distraction he did not need.

In the silver moonlight she looked more like a creature of enchantment than any Fae woman—beautiful, ripe, tousled and sensual. Though she was once again fully clothed, the material over her full breasts still bore the damp marks of his mouth, her swollen lips were still red from his kiss. Just the sight of her made his body surge. He cursed silently, even as he felt himself harden.

Turning away from her so that she would not see how she affected him, he hurriedly pulled on his braes and glanced over his shoulder at her, squinting through the darkness.

Reluctantly, he cast a small spell to light his torch, knowing the flickering light would only make her startling beauty more alluring, knowing as well that he had little control over the situation.

No woman, mortal or Fae, had ever affected him like this.

Deirdre of the Cliffs. A woman cursed. What mysterious tie bound him to her and she to him? Each time he looked at her, he found her even more beguiling. The urge to take her again made him fight for control. Surely one more time would sate him—a simple pleasuring, a final release as he plunged his swollen self deep into her moist body over and over . . .

Such erotic thoughts helped matters not at all. If anything, the bulge in the front of his braes grew larger.

"Tell me now—are you also a witch or some kind of magi? Have you cast some sort of powerful spell that makes me desire you so badly?"

Keeping a good distance from her, knowing that the slightest touch could shatter what little control he had, he was startled when she laughed. The sound was light and silvery, nothing like the smoky murmur she had made when she captured his body and took her pleasure from it.

"A witch? Nay. You know all I am—a simple Shadow Dancer, no more. If it is a spell that makes you hunger, then it has ensnared me as well."

Even her voice, the husky thrum of it, seemed beautiful and sensual to him. And her words—the simple way she told him she wanted him again too—had the effect of making the fire of lust inside him burn hotter.

If a spell had been cast, it was a powerful one. He, a prince of Rune, with all the years of magical training on his side, would have the skill to remove it. *But he did not want to.*

The enchantment was potent, indeed.

They had a powerful enemy. To be able to cast such a spell, on one such as he—a Faerie who was resistant to such things . . . This would have to be more than a spell of simple lust, nay—woven within it was an emotional eroticism of such potency that he knew would continue to haunt him as it did even now, when by all rights he should have slaked his body's thirst with the vigorous coupling they had shared.

She made a small sound, making him conscious that she still stood before him in seductive disarray. Though he rose a full head taller than she and no doubt was twice her weight, so untutored was she in the ways of men that she showed no fear, only an artless lack of guile too straightforward to be believed. But then he was not like other men, never would he take her unwilling.

And she had come to him virgin. Unspoiled, sharing herself with only him.

A fresh wave of desire hit him, strong enough to make him stagger backward. Such untamed lust was dangerous in a man, be he warrior or king. With the enemies Deirdre had, distractions could be fatal indeed.

All he'd wanted was to find his people's amulet and return it, so his people could find another king, but this fascination with the mortal woman drove all else from his mind. *Gods' teeth*! Perhaps he would have no choice but to be rid of her. This information would prove dangerous to both of them. And how could he have his freedom if he must protect this woman from more than just the sun and the Maccus, but from himself as well?

Yet how could he leave her unprotected? He owed her that much, to find her another village,

115

another group of people willing to take care of her.

Perhaps he would let her choose herself.

Trying not to remember his earlier panic when he'd lost her, slowly he turned. "I think mayhap we should consider parting. I know not what matter of spell hangs over us, but I fear I am unable to fight it."

"Part?" Surprise and disbelief colored her voice, along with a faint trace of amusement that told him she believed he spoke in jest. "Why would I leave you when I might be able to help you find this amulet you so desperately seek?"

"You do not understand." Clenching his fists, Egann shook his head in a vain attempt to clear it. Passion still thrummed inside him, made his brain hot and sluggish. "There is danger in this, in the way your touch inflames me. Danger and implications that I cannot yet see clearly."

"I have sensed this too," she admitted. "Yet when I think of being apart from you, I . . ." Hand held out, she shook her head, sending her wealth of dark hair flying. She took a step toward him and he felt his body respond, even as he struggled to keep from touching her.

"Think well on what you do. Your life may well depend on it. Depart," he ordered, his voice cracking. "Leave me, and move around in the darkness as you do each night. I will go the opposite way and be content to travel by the light of the day, as I should."

If he'd sought her heart with his verbal arrow, he saw from her stricken expression that he had struck it. Her lovely face crumpled; the gleam of desire he'd seen in her huge golden eyes vanished. He felt a stab of pain, of regret. Not since his brother died had he felt this conflicted, this torn.

A second later, she'd regained control of her features, her cool mask in place once more.

"Promises mean so little to you, then?" Her attempt at a haughty tone fell short, her husky voice breaking. "You gave your word to protect me, and I in turn pledged to help you find the amulet."

Shame washed over him. Shame and regret. She was right, and in his cowardice and infidelity was proof yet again that he could never be king.

"I have changed my mind," he said, meaning to apologize, to tell her that he could not think clearly with her lush body so close, that in truth he did not really want her to leave. But she heard the wrong connotation of his words.

"Is that so?" She dipped a graceful shoulder, the creamy skin there gleaming, her gaze distant, as if she'd already escaped, fled this scene of emotional anguish.

"Since you are of Rune, not human, the giving of an oath must not carry as much weight with you

117

as it does with me. Very well, then, you shall have your wish. I release you. You are no longer bound to help me, nor I to assist you."

With those words, she spun on her heel and went into the woods, fleeing as easily and gracefully as a wild doe.

For one frozen moment Egann could only stare, marking the spot where she'd been with his gaze, his body still aching with need and some other, more elemental emotion. He had done it again, seeking to avoid failure by precipitating its arrival.

"Fool." He named himself harshly, knowing he had let his brain be beguiled along with his sex. This time he would rectify his mistake. If he could.

Striding after her, he caught up before she had gone ten paces into the forest.

"Wait." He reached for her, but she fought him with all the strength of a wounded fawn caught in a trap. Capturing one wrist, he clenched his teeth and tried to think of honor, even as she twisted and turned, each movement a tormenting friction against his overheated body.

"Stop and listen," he shouted, still fighting to restrain her. Finally, seeing that she would not be still long enough to hear reason, he did the only thing he could think of to quiet her, though he knew once he did it he would be like a drowning man going underwater, sinking for the final time.

He covered her mouth with his and kissed her, feeling the possessive thrill that ran through him, dimly realizing that they were both in far worse trouble than even he might have guessed.

Still, once his lips claimed hers, he could not keep from touching her.

As he had known she would, she instantly stilled. Her response to him—fresh, vibrant, immediate— was as heady an aphrodisiac as any drug or spell. Deirdre melted in his arms, opening her arms in invitation.

God's blood, how he wanted her again.

With great reluctance, he tore his mouth from hers. "We cannot do this." He indicated the eastern sky, just beginning to lighten. "Your dance with the moon lasted most of the night, our lovemaking the rest of it. Soon the sun will rise."

Bowing her head, her silence acknowledged the truth of his words.

"I do not wish to leave you," she said. Her voice was low, and she would not look at him. "Not yet."

He sighed, trying to ignore the thrumming of his still-heated desire for her. "Nor I you. I am a fool. Sending you away was my foolish attempt at self-preservation."

Now she raised her head and met his gaze. The tears that streaked her cheeks stunned him. "I can help you find this amulet of yours, truly. Though

119

I know not why, I believe it to be fact. And you can help me as well, in some mysterious way I have not yet been able to determine."

Glancing once more to the east, Egann swallowed. He could not allow her to trust in him so blindly. Now the time had come to inform her of the reality of himself—what he was and what he wasn't and what he would never be. Also, though it would be difficult to speak of it, he would tell her too, the facts of how horribly he'd failed.

He took a deep breath. "We have a few minutes before we must seek shelter. I must quickly tell you the truth of my life. Then you can decide if you truly want *me* to protect you." Somehow, he forced a laugh, a sound without humor. "After hearing my tale, you may determine you would be much safer without Prince Egann of Rune."

For the space of a heartbeat he watched her, unable to breathe. Then she shook her head, coming to him and placing her pale hand on his arm.

"I must find a place to take refuge, so that I might rest. I do not want to be caught again as I was before. When I awaken, you can speak of your sins if you feel that you must." With a tremulous smile she moved forward and rested her cheek against his chest, closed her eyes.

Such a gesture of trust moved him, though Egann refused to allow her to see it. After all, he knew even if she did not, that there was none less deserving of trust than one such as he.

Her shelter was deep, cracked stone steps leading to nothing, a stone cellar long ago covered over by dirt and leaves and time. In this a cave of sorts had formed, and it was this place Deirdre found in which she could hide from the brilliance of the sun.

She knew not what Egann had meant by his words, nor what old wounds caused the pain she'd recognized in his voice. Perhaps the answer might come to her in dreams, as solutions often did.

Her dreams brought her not Egann, but the amulet instead.

The silver of its chain was heavy, the metal cool and smooth. Marveling, she held it in her hand, feeling the stark wonder of its magic sear her fingers so that she nearly dropped it.

In the nonsensical way of dreams she traveled, standing in a crowd of unfamiliar people. Turning, she looked for Egann, to show him how she'd finally located his precious talisman, but she could not find him in the strange faces that surrounded her.

The amulet made a sound, a cry, a song, a lament that became a mournful dirge. Hearing it caused Deirdre such pain that she fell to her knees,

121

hand closing around the necklace, as if her grip might silence it.

Gradually she became aware that the amulet called to Egann. She added her voice to its lamentation, not understanding why she wept, yet feeling the pain like a sharp knife slipped between her ribs.

When she awoke, it was to find her hand fisted so tightly that her palm bled from the press of her nails.

"Egann?" Unable to keep her voice from quavering, Deirdre pushed herself to her feet, brushing off the dirt and crumpled leaves that clung to her.

Egann did not answer.

Blind panic robbed her of reason, and she rushed up the cracked steps, pushing at the thorny brush that blocked the exit to the surface.

Stumbling, she crossed the darkened clearing, peering into the gloomy depths of the forest, the horror of her dream echoing in her head.

"Egann?" She called again, turning in a slow circle and wishing she could wield her magic to find him.

Then she saw him, lying under the base of an ancient oak, his golden head at an awkward angle, his arm flung out before him.

Through a haze of fear she went to him, praying he only slept. Though she knew not if the Fae needed to rest like mankind did, night was the natural time of sleep for all creatures of the sun.

About to search his body for injury, Deirdre froze. Egann opened his brilliant blue eyes and gave her a sleepy, sad smile.

She wanted to kiss him. Instead, she backed away so quickly she nearly fell.

" 'Tis night already?" he asked. His deep bass rumble of a voice made her shiver.

"Yes." Troubled, she swallowed. "Strange dreams plagued me, but once again I beheld your wondrous amulet."

His gaze sharpened at her words, and he rose in one fluid motion. "Tell me what you saw. Did you see enough to learn in which direction we must go?"

Slowly, she shook her head. "Nay, I did not. I was in a place I have never visited, a dark city of made of stone. All around me people gathered in the smoke, but I knew them not. I searched for you and felt your presence, though I could not find your face. I shouted your name, but you did not answer. And I dreamed the amulet called to you as well."

A startled look crossed his rugged features. "Strange."

She waited for him to say more, though he did not appear inclined to do so, peering off into the dark depths of the forest.

123

When he did speak, his voice sounded distant. "Did you see the face of the one around whose neck the amulet lies?"

She shook her head. "Nay, I did not. This time, I did not even see the talisman, only heard it. But you, do you have a suspicion of who that evildoer might be?"

"My thoughts are of the Maccus, the race that hunts those of your kind. But I do not know for certain"

"The Maccus." Bitterness colored her tone as she remembered the fire that had roared through the cliff caves, her people dying. "The Maccus have created their own god, and he is a red and angry one."

"That is the second time I have heard of this." Egann flashed her a grim smile. "When I lost you I encountered a Maccus here in the forest."

Deirdre stiffened. "Why did you not tell me this?" Unable to help herself, she turned and looked behind her, as though a Maccus might suddenly appear.

"I did not wish to frighten you. 'Tis bad enough that you cannot enter Rune—"

"Cannot? What mean you?" For some reason his words struck fear inside of her, a dread that chilled her more completely than her terror of those who'd slain her people.

Ruefully, Egann shook his head. "I know not. Fiallan only said that your people carried some curse."

"But what does the curse of the sunlight have to do with Rune and the Fae?"

Egann frowned. "It seems that long ago, my people placed a curse upon yours. This is all Fiallan told me. Perhaps the reason you must walk in darkness is the same reason you cannot journey to Rune."

Sadness filled her at his words. "Again," she whispered, "you have sought to hide truth from me."

Egann faced her, his stance that of an arrogant warrior. Never had he looked more like a Prince of Fae, with his aristocratic features and golden hair. Never had the distance between them seemed wider.

"I have hidden nothing," he declared. Then he flashed her a sheepish smile that tugged once again at her heart. "We were rather, er, distracted, if you remember."

Flushing, her body wanted him to distract her again.

He must have felt the same, for his smile faded and his gaze darkened. But instead of reaching out to her, he crossed his arms in front of him and frowned.

"I will not be diverted this time. Now I must speak to you of this other matter—so that you might now know what manner of Fae you travel with."

Glancing sideways at him, she saw that his chiseled features had settled into grim lines, and his eyes had turned an icy gray.

"Once I had a brother, as small and as fiery-haired as I am golden. Named Banan, he was given over to my care when he had grown tall enough."

Deirdre smiled, thinking of Egann caring for a younger, red-haired version of himself. "Where is Banan now?" she asked. "I would like to meet him."

"Banan exists no more." Egann's tones carried the weight of years of sorrow. "He perished because of me."

"Perished?" Stunned, Deirdre's breath caught in her lungs. "I did not know that Faeries could die."

Egann also halted, keeping his gaze averted. He might have worn a mask, so expressionless was his face. "There is one way to extinguish our lives. And in this way we do not die easily or well."

Afraid to ask, yet knowing that she must, Deirdre wet her lips with her tongue. "How did Banan die?" she whispered.

He seemed not to have heard her, so caught up was he in the past. When he spoke again, his voice was full of bitter sorrow. "As boys we were often competitive. Often I took him into the world of mortals. We liked to play harmless tricks on human children for fun." He met her gaze finally, his expression dark with pain.

"Some of the children of my people had friends no one ever saw." She herself had longed for such magical friends, but it seemed they only came in the sunlight, not the darkness, which had been her time to play.

"Aye," he said glumly, "and 'twas no different this day. Until we came upon the mortal warrior sleeping off the effects of the previous eve's drink."

Deirdre held her breath, waiting.

"Banan wanted to avoid the man, to return to Rune. I, the older brother who should have known better, would hear none of it. Though now I cannot tell you why, I tormented the mortal warrior, while Banan begged me to stop. Too late did I realize that my actions had provoked the man into a rage. Banan, wanting to join me, thought to hide the mortal's sword so that he could not use the deadly metal to harm us." His voice cracked and broke. "By that sword Banan died."

Deirdre made a comforting sound and reached out instinctively to comfort Egann, but he was lost in the pain of his memories and moved away.

"Too late, I tried to help him. He cried out to me when the metal blade pierced his flesh. The cut

127

would not have harmed a mortal, small and on the shoulder as it were. But this iron is poison to my people, and by the time I carried Banan back to Rune, he had already begun to fade."

"Surely there was something . . ."

"Something. Aye, I believed the same. So I brought him to Fiallan, who has powerful healing skills."

Deirdre's throat ached at the bleakness in Egann's voice. After a moment she asked. "And Fiallan was not able to save him?"

"No. Banan suffered greatly because of me. He died. And all I could do in my agony was place a curse on the knight who harmed him.

Deirdre shook her head. There were no words to ease so great a grief. "I'm sorry," she said. "So sorry."

He seemed not to hear her, swallowing hard before continuing. "In my sorrow I broke an ancient law, cursing that mortal who sought only to defend himself. And none of it brought my brother back. None of it eased my people's sorrow. To this day, they still mourn. Perhaps now that I am gone, they will be able to forget."

More than anything, Deirdre wanted to go to him, to hold him close and give him what little comfort she could. But both of their wills had proven to be weak. Perhaps she could bring him a measure of consolation with careful words instead.

" 'Twas not your fault—"

"Nay? 'Twas not the fault of the poor warrior, who only nicked the boy with his sword. Such a small cut would have barely wounded a mortal lad—how could Mordred know Banan was not human? Nay, my lady, never doubt that the fault is all mine."

Now everything became clear to her. "And this is the reason you will not be king?"

He gave her a grim smile as he nodded. "Do you not see? If I failed my own brother, how could one such as I protect an entire people? They are better off without me."

Chapter Seven

Once the words had been said, Egann continued walking.

He knew not how Deirdre would react to his truth, how she would respond to the knowledge that the one she trusted to keep her safe was and always had been nothing but a failure.

He could not blame her were she to seek another protector.

Yet as he walked, so did she, remaining at his side.

In silence they moved, while a thousand memories went through his mind. He had loved Banan greatly, as had all of his sisters, some of whom had never stopped mourning. He supposed he would carry the grief—and the guilt—for eternity.

For now, he had to deal with the probable rejection of his mortal companion. He deserved, he thought wryly, whatever scorn or disgust she directed at him.

Yet as they continued toward the village, she did not speak. The silence, normally welcome, began to feel oppressive as he waited.

The mist-shrouded moon, a silver orb, traveled slowly across the evening sky. The air, cool and clear, smelled of heather and fern and fresh-cut hay. Though he listened, he heard no sound that anyone followed or approached; indeed it seemed to him that all mankind slept.

Except Deirdre, the nocturnal Shadow Dancer.

When she finally spoke, it was only to call his name. Her voice was soft, reflective, and he had to strain to hear it.

"Egann?"

He could feel her gaze upon him. Because he did not trust his voice, he settled for a brusque nod.

"Misfortune and mishaps occur in the lives of everyone."

Fiallan had said as much, once. But Egann knew better.

131

"The death of your brother was not your fault."

He would not argue the point. What was done was done. Banan had died. He would not shake off his failed responsibility.

"Please look at me."

This request he could not deny. Reluctantly he slowed his steps, halting finally and bringing his gaze down to meet hers. Her eyes were now a brilliant emerald, gleaming in the silver moonlight. She tilted her chin up in obstinate certainty.

"Even if you do not believe me, even if you go through the rest of your years thinking that you and you alone were the cause of Banan's death, hear me now. This time, with me and with the amulet, you will not fail."

His heart stuttered, then began to pound. 'Twas only with the greatest of will that he kept his expression implacable.

"Your confidence, though touching, might well be misplaced." Though he kept his tone light, he hoped she would understand that he gave her a warning. 'Twas only fair that she know he was not be the best choice of a protector.

Their gazes locked and held. Once again he felt the strength of the seductive spell luring him to touch her. This time, he would prove his self-control was stronger. He would prove that he could touch her as any other man, touch her and not give in to the sweet temptation she presented.

"Come." He held out his hand, released breath he had not even realized he held when she took it. Such a little thing, the feel of her small fingers resting so trustingly in his, but it warmed him all the same.

Someday perhaps, he would tell her how much. For now, he kept his tone airy. "Let us continue onward. We will talk no more of this. Instead, tell me of this new dream you had of the Amulet of Gwymyrr."

Her stride did not falter, though she squeezed his hand.

"Yes. 'Tis a powerful talisman, this amulet of yours. Though I did not see the sparkling jewels or the heavy silver chain, I felt the strength of its force even in the mournful song it made."

"The amulet mourns still?" He should not have been surprised. Would not guilt and sorrow haunt him forever?

She nodded. "Aye. Though great crowds of people surrounded me, I heard the mournful song and it seemed that the amulet called out to you. I know not why I felt this."

He did, for the amulet had called to him once before—on the day he'd refused to become king of Rune.

Now however, it called to him no more. He had but touched it briefly before being robbed of its energy. If the talisman were to let him hear it, he could find it and return it to his people, to Rune, where it belonged.

"You say you did not recognize the city?"

"Nay, for never until now have I left the cliffs. Yet there were buildings made of stone, great walled structures that rose into the smoke."

"There are many such cities in the world of men." Disappointed, he could only hope that somehow the amulet would show him where to search.

"It sings so seductively," she mused. "As if it seeks to tempt me, too, with its call."

"Why have I not heard this song?" he asked, letting his bewilderment and anger resonate in his voice. "I do not understand—why has not a vision of the amulet come to *me* in my dreams? Why you?" It was frustrating to be so dependent upon something, especially when finding that something meant an even greater freedom.

The breeze ruffled Deirdre's long black hair, sending silky strands to caress her shoulders as it did when she danced. Watching her, Egann's mouth went dry.

"I cannot fathom the answer," she said, "though I know one exists."

Dragging his gaze away from her with an effort, he shrugged. "In time perhaps the connection between all things will become known." He forced himself to stay focused on the task at hand.

"We must keep on the move if we are ever to find it and avoid the Maccus. Since you have not been told in which direction the amulet lies, we will head west, in the direction of the setting sun."

Deirdre laughed, a sad little sound. "I will have to take your word for that, since I have never seen the sun set. But I must ask you, do we not have need of your horse?"

More relieved than he should be that she would follow his lead and talk of the task at hand—rather than the attraction he felt coursing through him—he gave her a grim smile.

"Not yet, though I too have thought of Weylyn. He is not all that he appears, however, and wearing the form of a horse is not pleasant to him. I have promised him time to hunt and cannot call him yet, though I will summon him when it is time. For now, we will walk."

A quick glance at Deirdre and the stubborn set of her chin told him that she was not pleased. But, though he waited for her to tell him so, she did not, only squeezed his hand once more.

"Where do we go?" she finally asked.

"We head for the village of Bodmin. There, I will question the hunters, to see if they have noticed anything unusual or strange."

"How many days will this take?" Though she kept her tone even, Egann could hear her trepidation to meet strangers.

"We should reach Bodmin before sunrise."

"I see." She nodded, her head held high, breathlessly trudging along at his side. Though he had shortened his stride to match hers, he could see that she would tire rapidly. Perhaps he would have to call for Weylyn sooner than he had thought.

"Can you not keep up?" Once said, he nearly winced, for he had not meant to ask her so bluntly. But she appeared to take no offense, glancing up at him with a half-smile on her full lips, her eyes glowing with amusement.

"I do not think so," she replied. "Though I am trying. I find I am uneasy at traveling so exposed, especially with no place to take shelter when the sun rises."

His heart sank. He could not blame her for believing him unable to watch out for her. Had he not warned her of that just moments ago? Still, he had no intention of letting her believe she might be in imminent danger.

"Worry not, Deirdre of the Shadows. As I have said, we shall arrive at Bodmin long before morning."

She nodded, the faint glow of the moon making silver strands in her midnight hair. After a moment of walking, she turned and asked, "Do you find it so easy to walk among men?"

He halted so suddenly that she, unprepared, continued a pace farther without him, until his grip on her hand yanked her to a stop. "Why do you ask?" Puzzled, he tilted his head to study her. "Do I appear so different than other men?"

It seemed to him she waited entirely too long before she gave him her answer.

"Since my experience has, until now been limited to my small village only, I am not certain how to best reply. But I will try. Are you different, you ask?" She let her green gaze slowly travel over him, heating his blood and making him wish he had continued to walk.

"Though you may desire it not, you *are* unlike other men I have known. You appear noble perhaps—though I believe most of the nobility do not walk, but ride." She said this with a toss of her head, reminding him that she had asked for his horse. "Oh, and you are taller than other men I have seen, and broader of shoulder and chest. Some might find the sheer size of you frightening."

"Nonsense." Though he dismissed her words with a brusque shake of his head, he gave her a small smile to let her know that she had pleased him. " 'Tis only that you have not seen many warriors, in your remote caves there on the cliffs."

137

"True. And never have I seen a warrior of Rune." She smiled back at him, lighting up her small face with such transcendent beauty that his throat began to ache. Wisely, he resumed walking, keeping her hand entwined in his.

This time when they walked, the silence seemed companionable to Egann. Though he should not, he found himself at peace; for the first time, desire for her did not consume him.

In a short while they came to the outskirts of the village. Under the starlit sky, the place lay sleeping. Even the inns had closed, so late—or early—was the hour. Striding with Deirdre down the empty road, Egann felt the back of his neck begin to tingle. He'd learned well to heed this warning; it never failed to precede bad things.

Halting, he held his hand up for silence and listened. Ah, there it was. From a distance, he heard the quiet clop of a metal-shod horse moving steadily toward them. A far-off dog began to bark. Someone approached on the road from the east, from behind them.

"Quickly." Yanking her with him, Egann pulled her around the corner of a deserted church, onto a darkened side road, keeping her close.

"What is it?" Deirdre asked, her voice muffled against his chest.

"I am not certain. I know only that whoever or whatever it is means us no good."

The clattering of the horse's hooves grew louder. Deirdre peered out from under his arm as the riderless horse came into view.

"It's Weylyn!" Excited, she struggled against his grip. "You summoned him after all."

Egann brought up his arm, encircling her with it.

"Why don't you go and greet him?" she hissed.

"Nay." With his grim tone, he warned her. "That creature is not my horse. I have not called him to me. I know not what manner of beast that is, but it is not Weylyn."

Immediately her struggles ceased. "How do you know?" she whispered. "It bears a perfect likeness to your stallion."

"Remember that iron is deadly to my kind and their mounts. That one's hooves are shod in it."

She shifted against him, the restless movement of her lush body against him overwhelming his already overcharged senses. Somehow he found himself cupping the full breast that had been pressed against his arm.

As the massive horse tromped past, Egann found himself caressing Deirdre, stroking and squeezing, despite the warning that sounded in his mind, the absurdity of what he was doing.

The spell . . .

It was clearly affecting her, too; her heart had begun to race. His body quickened as her nipples pebbled and hardened, his own breathing became as shallow and fast as hers.

"The beast is gone." Little more than a gasp were her words. She leaned into him, even as she shook her head in agitation.

"Aye. We should continue." Absently he spoke, even as he bent his head to take her mouth in a deep kiss.

Her response was heady and immediate.

With reluctance, he forced himself to lift his head. "Nay." Hoarse-voiced, he nearly choked as he spoke. "Again the spell seeks to compel us. We need not this distraction, not now. It is dangerous."

"You speak true." She stiffened and moved away from him.

He had to clench his hands to keep from reaching out to her. Inhaling deeply, he focused on the one thing sure to distract them. "Even now the eastern sky grows lighter."

To his surprise she did not panic.

"I know." Her voice as cool as the stream of Rangoine, she looked up at him with an almost impersonal expression. "I suppose we must find a place for me to take shelter and sleep."

"I suppose we must," he agreed. Setting his jaw, he resolved to question her later. "The inns are closed, and we do not want to draw attention to our presence. There are crypts under this church. Let us look there."

* * *

For the first time since Deirdre could remember, sleep did not come easily. Shifting restlessly on the cold stone of the altar she'd made her bed, she pondered the strange changes that seemed to be coming upon her. Not only had the prospect of the approaching morning seemed less threatening, but she sensed a difference in her body as well, a softening that she could only attribute to the continuing temptation of Egann's presence.

Having experienced his lovemaking, she now found that thoughts of his touch, his kiss, of him moving slowly inside her, consumed her, even as she merely walked at his side. Egann had said that he believed it to be some sort of enchantment, though who would cast such a spell she did not know. The one who had stolen the magical amulet was using it to impede its retrieval: that was the only reason that made sense.

Or perhaps, a small voice whispered in her head, *it is not a spell at all.*

Deirdre shivered. How different all of this was from her old existence, her comfortable life with the people of the cliffs. She had longed for adventure, excitement, and had been given it, though she had not foreseen the dire actions of the Maccus. Nor had she predicted her inappropriate longing for a man whom, once their quest had been

141

satisfactorily completed, she would never see again.

Ah, so it was *this* thought that kept her edgy and unsettled instead of slumbering. She had come to care too much for this man named Egann, even though he seemed to dislike himself.

Foolishly perhaps, she found much to admire in him. Though he did not believe he would make a good king, she could see him as nothing but a great one. Mayhap with time he would realize it as well. He did not belong here, in the ordinary world. He belonged in that realm she was forbidden to enter, belonged in the world of glittering magic, of daffodil sunshine and birdsong—not her world of darkness and shadows.

Now that they had reached the village, he would move without her among the mortals while she hid from the daylight. Conceivably he would even find the amulet without her help. And after that, what would become of her?

Mentally, she shook herself. No good would come of such fears, and Egann would not leave her until he had made certain she was well protected. She had best think, plan for what she would do with her life once they had accomplished their task and recaptured the amulet.

But what would she do when she no longer had Egann?

Her thoughts remained troubled as she finally drifted off to sleep.

When she next woke, she knew instinctively that she could not rise. Though the crypts were below ground and thus windowless and dark, she felt in her body that the sun had not yet set. Waking before darkness had never before happened to her, and she puzzled at the reason it occurred now.

Mayhap the Amulet of Gwymyrr had something to do with it.

As if—she shook her head at the foolish notion—the mysterious amulet had a mind of its own.

She pondered for some time, and did not stir until she heard the scrape and grating of the granite door that led down to the crypts being moved away. Pushing herself to her feet, Deirdre met Egann halfway up the steps.

"I have news." The man took her arm, helping her climb the crumbling stairs. "I have spent the entire day roaming the village, and I have heard tales that lead me to believe that the amulet is not far from here."

The excitement in his voice made her smile. "Let us go into the fresh night air and find water. I am thirsty. Then I would hear what you have learned."

Keeping her hold on his arm, she let him lead the way up the stone steps. Once outside, she took deep, bracing gulps of the cool night air, careful to avoid looking at him. Foolish, she knew, but it seemed he might see in her eyes all the fears that had distressed her and kept her from a peaceful night's rest.

Apple trees, heavy with fruit, surrounded the weathered church in which she'd hid. The scent of their ripe fruit made her stomach growl.

Egann handed her the water-skin, then folded his arms across his chest. She drank deeply, relishing the cool water sliding down her parched throat. She could sense the impatience rolling off him in waves as he broke a length of crusty bread in half and shared it with her.

Too hungry to care about maidenly delicacy, Deirdre tore into the fresh loaf, accepting a chunk of yellow cheese with delight.

From the tree overhead, Egann plucked two apples, handing one to her. Biting into the crunchy fruit, she closed her eyes, savoring the sweet and tart taste of it.

"Deirdre." Egann's voice was a low hum, murmuring her name.

Still chewing, she raised her gaze to find him watching her. Swallowing, she saw his jaw tense visibly as the piece of fruit slid down her throat.

Again she closed her lips over the apple, never taking her eyes from his. The ripe fruit was juicy, and her fingers felt sticky. Feeling like a delightfully wicked cat, she let her tongue dart out and capture the juice, licking her fingers slowly for good measure.

For an instant, time seemed to stand still. Egann's gaze turned smoldering, warming her. The rapid pounding of her heart and his harsh intake of breath were the only sounds in the deserted orchard. Even the air seemed to shimmer, as she studied the Faerie prince's handsome, craggy face.

Her own face burning, she looked away, felt like a coward. Keeping her head down, she fixed her attention on the half-eaten apple, and she finished it quickly. Her skin still tingled, and every fiber of her was acutely aware of the seductive desire that flowed like warm honey between them.

She had to control this, for making love with Egann put her entire self, especially her vulnerable heart, at risk. If only she did not have to look at him, she might resist. One look, one touch would send her already aroused body out of control.

"Deirdre," he said again.

Girding herself, she raised her head, peering at him through downswept lashes. He reached out and took the partially eaten apple from her, tossing it behind him. Raising her hand to his lips, his dark gaze searing her, he took one finger into his mouth, suckling her.

The damp heat of his mouth turned her blood to molten lead. She wanted him violently, ur-

145

gently, with a passion that made her knees buckle.

Helpless, she swayed toward him, a shudder passing through her.

"Deirdre—" His arms encircled her, holding her upright as she buried her face against his neck and tried to breathe.

Perhaps his belief that the two of them had been enchanted was correct, for all she could do was writhe helpless against him, her body burning with a hunger she could not suppress.

Instantly, she felt him quicken, his need leaping to meet her desire. So in tune were they that no words passed between them; none were needed as their bodies spoke their own language. With quivering hands she stroked him, fondled him, caressing his arousal through the soft cloth of his braes. She was wet and hot and ready, the mindless need driving her so that she lost all sense of modesty.

"Woman," he groaned, as she pressed a hot kiss against his jaw, then tasted the sensitive lobe of his ear with light strokes of her tongue. "Have a care what you do to me, lest I take you where we stand."

"Take me," she heard herself whisper, her voice thick with desire. "Here in this apple-scented orchard, underneath the watchful light of a thousand stars. Oh please, Egann. Take me now."

"I cannot," he hissed through clenched teeth. "We must . . ." Head back, eyes closed, he stood stiffly while she touched and provoked him, the only signs of her effect on him his jutting manhood and raspy breathing.

With one hand, she untied the pouch that kept him from her. Sinking to her knees before him, she glanced up once before she took him in her mouth.

Again he made a sound, that of a wild beast in pain. With her mouth she caressed him, suckled him, loved him. How she knew to do such a thing, she could not have said. She only knew that it felt right, and it made her yearning so much sharper, more inevitable.

"Stop." He pulled her to her feet. "Ere I spill my seed wantonly, like a green and untried lad." He pushed her back against a tree, lifted her skirts.

She moaned as he slid into her, taking her standing, lifting her with his strong hands so that she straddled him at the same time as he straddled her. With swift, sure strokes he plunged into her, and she took him and melted and burned and the night sky seemed to explode.

Then he lifted her, cradling her in his arms as he lay with her on the soft, cool grass. Instinctively she arched against him, taking him more fully into her, thrilling as he entered her again and again and again.

Skin to skin, heart to heart, they were one.

As at last she gasped out her pleasure, quaking with the force of it, she felt him reach his own summit, felt the heartbeat and pulsing of him as he filled her with his essence.

Neither spoke as he held her close to him, still joined as they were. He pressed a gentle kiss to her forehead and she shivered. Unexpected tears stung her eyes. She wondered if he realized that more had passed between them than the mere slaking of passionate desire.

It took every bit of self-control she possessed to keep from leaning into his hand like an affectionate kitten. Instead she kept utterly still, swallowing, and raising her gaze to meet his.

Another shock ran through her, at the warmth she saw in his azure gaze.

"Your eyes are like the colors of the sky and sea," she blurted, foolishly, before she thought to guard her tongue.

Then, as she mentally kicked herself, he gave her one of his devastating smiles, and she felt herself drown.

"Yours are the color of fresh meadow grass," he told her. "Though the clouded moonlight makes them dark. Now come—we waste time, for I have news of an encampment of wanderers who lay claim to a potent charm. It could be that the Amulet of Gwymyrr is but a few hours' walk away."

Stunned, she could only gape at him while her riotous emotions threatened to overwhelm her. What would the finding of the amulet mean for their time together?

He rolled away and pushed himself to his feet, turning his back to her while he adjusted her clothing. Deirdre sat up and did the same, pushing away the trace of faint embarrassment that made her skin feel rosy. Would she never feel at ease with his lovemaking, with her own desires? This was Egann, after all, her companion, her friend. The man that she—

That she what? Mentally, she shied away from finishing the thought. Such thoughts were more than foolish, for true danger and heartache would follow were she to give her heart to one such as he. She didn't need magic to tell her that.

Raising her face, she found Egann watching her, his own expression shuttered.

"Let us go," she told him, making her voice carefree and untroubled. "If the amulet truly is kept within the camp you mentioned, then let us make all haste toward it. Perhaps the darkness will aid us this time, and we shall arrive with them sleeping and unaware."

Still he watched her, tilting his head to study her as though he found her words strange.

If he were to comment on what had just passed between them, she did not think she could bear it.

149

Not now, not knowing that if the amulet truly was obtainable this very eve, then their journey together would reach an immediate end.

How she would deal with this she could not say. Yet she had pledged to help him find his talisman, and a Shadow Dancer always kept her word.

"Come," she repeated, leaving the fragrant orchard and stepping out onto the rutted road blindly, hoping that she was headed in the right direction. "Let us go with all speed."

He did not correct her, so she kept walking, lengthening her stride so that he would not immediately catch her, so he could not see the foolish tears that streamed like rain down her cheeks.

Chapter Eight

Furious at both Deirdre and himself, Egann seethed as he strode toward the nomad camp where he had heard that his amulet might reside. That the mortal woman had seduced him so easily, then all but run from him in apparent revulsion, told him that she too suffered from the enchantment that ensnared him. Why else would she seem so eager to be with him, then so eager to flee?

When he found the one who had dared to cast such a spell . . .

As it had when the mysterious horse-beast—that thing which had looked so much like Weylyn—appeared in the village, the back of Egann's neck began to prickle. Pushing his anger away, he became became instantly alert. In a few short strides he caught up to Deirdre, placing his hand lightly on her shoulder.

She jumped, her pale skin coloring. "Sorry," she muttered, eyes downcast. "I was lost in thought. What is it?"

"I don't know. Something..." All his senses told him that they had no time. Something was about to happen.

Again the back of his neck prickled, more urgently. Faintly, he heard the approach of several galloping horses from past the rise behind them.

An instant later she heard it, too. Lifting her head and scenting the wind, Deirdre tensed. "What is that?"

"Riders." He grabbed her arm. "We must hide."

"Where? There is naught but open ground on both sides of us."

Cursing, he glanced around. Not even a thorny shrub graced the side of the dirt track. They were out in the open, exposed. They had no choice but to meet the riders, face to face, as soon as they crested the hill behind them. He pulled Deirdre close to him.

On the exposed road at the top of the hill, a cloud of dust moved, murky gray in the dim moonlight.

"I will protect you." Low-voiced, he gave her his oath.

"I know." With a seeming utter lack of fear, she smiled up at him. Complete trust shone from her emerald eyes.

Trust that he knew was greatly misplaced.

"I cannot use magic against them, but only to make us vanish." This was the truth of the Fae; never could they harm a human, even if the human sought to harm them first.

"Mayhap they mean to ride past. What would they want with two road-weary travelers?"

"They travel west, as we do. Perhaps they are for the nomad camp, or even from it. They may seek to keep us from retrieving the amulet."

"But how would they know who we are, what we want?" she asked.

It was a reasonable question. "The amulet may have enabled them to see," he told her simply.

As the hoofbeats grew louder and the riders drew near, Egann braced himself. Most likely these men, be they knights or bandits, would have weapons, swords made of metal, deadly to his kind. His best hope was that he could somehow find the right words that would convince them to move on without violence. Otherwise, if they were mortal and threatened him, he would have no choice but

153

to use his magic. He did not want to use it, for he sensed the amulet was near.

The dust cloud parted, the shadows inside forming blurred shapes. There were three riders, approaching at a full gallop.

The road seemed to waver, the air to darken. There came a sudden ripple in time, an instant burst of energy—had he not been attuned to such things he might have missed it. He saw a flash of light, bright and quick, like a streak of lightning—then it vanished.

The thunder of horses' hooves, the swirling dust—they too disappeared. One minute the earth trembled with the fury of their approach, the next: nothing. Not even the warning cry of a hawk broke the utter stillness of the night.

"*Magic.*"

"Did you do that?" Deirdre's stunned question let Egann know that he had breathed the word out loud.

"Nay." Disbelief mingled with his impotent anger, and he stared at the place where the riders had been.

"Then from where did this magic come?"

"I do not know." Slowly turning, he tested the immediate area with his mind, widening the net until he moved far into the distance, far enough to have reached the camp of the supposed nomad tribe. He found nothing. Not even a trace that any sentient being, mortal or Fae, had traveled hereabouts. Neither behind nor ahead of them. And he no longer sensed the amulet.

A ripple of apprehension skittered up his spine. One glance at Deirdre's worried face showed him that she shared the feeling.

She looked up. He did too. Clouds scuttled over the moon, diminishing its silver glow and dimming their surrounding to a solemn gloom.

"Perhaps it is time to summon Weylyn," he told her quietly, smoothing her silky hair with his hand. "Until we know exactly what we are up against, 'tis best that we give the appearance of normalcy. And the presence of a war horse, as well as our ability to ride him, will be useful should we find danger."

"Do you feel the peril is that great?" She lifted shadowed eyes toward him, and the alarm in her lowered voice bespoke her fear.

"Perhaps." He glanced around then, at the empty ribbon of road as it wound off into the murky distance. "I know not what manner of man has possession of our amulet."

Again she inclined her head in concurrence. So shaded was her face, he could not read her expression.

"No harm will come to you," he promised, though he had no right to promise her anything.

The moon above broke free of the cloudy sky, brightening their path once more. Egann could see the uncertainty in Deirdre's lovely eyes.

"What of the nomads' camp? Do we still travel there?"

"It lies ahead." Taking her arm, he urged her forward once more. He broke the news lightly: "Yet I fear they too have vanished."

Though she continued walking beside him, he felt her stiffen. "Vanished? Then . . . the nomads were not human?"

"Nay."

"And they were not Fae." It was more of a statement than a question, and quiet resignation sounded in her voice.

"No, they were not my people." He sighed, dreading relating his suspicions, for they were only guesses, unfounded until proven. Yet she, who had the most to lose, had a right to know whom he believed the riders to be.

She tilted her head up at him in inquiry, her gaze dark and intense. The moonlight kissed her upturned face, streaking her black hair with silver.

"I fear they were the Maccus." Reluctantly he said the words, knowing her quick mind would leap ahead to the obvious conclusion. She did not disappoint him.

"The Maccus are magical?" Stammering, she swallowed and then shook her head, as if to clear it. They walked on for a pace or two, him letting her think, while he kept alert for any differences in the bleak landscape around them.

"You do believe the Maccus have magic, then," she said, her tone flat and unhappy.

"I *know* they do." Though he did not want her to carry more fear on her slight shoulders, in order to protect herself she had to know the truth. "A Maccus I met in the forest, one who called himself Monk, could vanish at will, much like those riders."

He heard the quiet hiss of her breath as she processed his words. Glad he and she still moved forward, he increased the pace slightly.

"The nomad encampment was ahead, over that small hill. 'Twill be safe for you, as they have already abandoned it."

A quick lift of one shoulder was her only answer. She pondered the implications of his words; he knew she would have a hundred questions later.

They climbed the slight rise in the road, and Egann searched ahead, looking for some sign, however small, that anyone remained. He found nothing.

Indeed, once they reached the rock-strewn area that seemed to have been the nomad's brief stopping place, they found only the blackened ashes and glowing coals of a still-warm fire.

"Those accursed fools," he let himself rage. "If indeed these are the ones who have stolen my people's amulet, they demean it by their petty use. They don't even realize its power."

He paced the camp, seeking any hint, any trace that magic, foul or otherwise, had been used there that eve. Oddly enough, he found only emptiness. Which made him believe that cloaking spells of great strength had been used.

Wandering slowly behind him, Deirdre said nothing. A great sadness seemed to have come over her, from the slight rounding of her shoulders to the downcast turn of her head. Egann felt compelled to go to her, so he did—but he was careful not to touch her. After all, he had no idea whether the enchantment that followed them would grow more compelling here in this place where the most powerful magics had so recently been used. Magic was like that; it could grow when one least expected it.

Deirdre stopped, stiffened. Glancing at her, Egann saw that all her attention was fixed on a bundle of charred cloth that lay near the still-smoldering fire pit, partially covered with a handful of stones. She moved forward to inspect it. The bundle wiggled. She jerked away, looking back at Egann.

"It lives," she whispered. "Though I know not if it can be helped."

Though he sensed no threat, Egann held up his hand to stop her when she moved to reach for it.

The bag squirmed again, dislodging several rocks. This moved it a bit farther from the heat and danger of the live coals.

As Egann reached out to take it, the sack made a noise: a strange sort of sound, an odd mixture of a growl, a mewl and a moan.

Perplexed, Egann glanced at Deirdre again, raising one brow in question. She frowned, then her forehead cleared and she flashed him a smile.

"What is it?"

"It sounds like a kitten." Pushing past him, she scooped up the bundle of cloth and began to untie it. "I only hope whoever trapped the creature has not wounded it mortally."

As she unwrapped the bindings, a tiny head appeared, with diminutive pointed ears and glowing amber eyes. A kitten it was, though the strangest-looking kitten Egann had ever seen. Tufts of singed hair decorated its striped ears and the soot-covered whiskers of its face were curly and short rather than long and straight.

As Deirdre pulled the cloth away, the remainder of the small cat appeared. Equally odd-looking, its orange-colored fur was dotted with black stripes and swirls.

Holding the squirming kitten firmly, Deirdre lifted it in the air and inspected it as it began to mew.

"She is unharmed," she pronounced after a moment. "Though she does sound hungry."

How Deirdre knew this, Egann could only guess. Shrugging, he glanced around the deserted campsite. "Mayhap they meant to burn her. Who can understand the rituals of power, if indeed that was why this beast was to be slain? Let her go. She is large enough to hunt, and all cats are fine hunters. I am certain she will find both food and water with equal skill."

"Let her go?" Staring at him as though appalled, Deirdre brought the small creature close to her chest, wincing as it dug its claws into her left shoulder. "I cannot turn her loose. She is too young, and we are all she has now."

"All she has?" he repeated in confusion.

"To look after her."

Egann could only stare at her as she cuddled the small animal close. "We don't have time for this," he said.

She shifted from foot to foot, still stroking the now-still kitten in her arms with one hand. "Time? This small animal will not be any trouble."

The words he wanted to say, that he did not need one more thing to look after, to protect, died on his lips. He found himself watching as her delicate fingers threaded through the kitten's fur, caressing the beast so lovingly that it made his chest ache.

"Have you never had a pet before?" he found himself asking.

"Nay, I have not. The people of the cliffs believed such things would distract me from my purpose."

"Your purpose?"

"The rituals, the dance, the calling forth of blessings upon their crops. All these things I did for them and more."

She sounded so matter-of-fact, yet so forlorn, he knew in that instant he would have to let her keep her tiny cat. So little had she been allowed—how could he deny her this one small pleasure?

"Very well." He pulled from his pouch a bit of dried meat and handed it to her. "Give her this to ease her hunger. 'Twill make her less restless once her belly is full."

While Deirdre fed the kitten, Egann walked the perimeter of the deserted camp. Though he doubted his luck would be so good, he hoped to find tracks, a sign, some hint or clue as to the direction the nomads had gone.

161

As he had feared, he found nothing but a small stream, which Deirdre greeted with delight. He let her bathe, promising to guard her pet. Then he resolutely turned his back and tried to ignore the sensuous images that the sounds of her splashing conjured. When she finished, he took a turn, glad for the icy water. Striding back to camp, he found her waiting and alert.

"Listen," she said abruptly. "In the distance, that way." She pointed north.

Straining, holding his body perfectly still, Egann heard nothing. He sent his mind north, traveling with his powers and listening all the while. Still, he could not . . . Ah, now he heard it. Very low, very faint. The exquisite cry of the amulet, calling to him to follow.

Moving blindly, he started forward, his chest aching with unnamed sorrow. Shuddering, he took a breath, the cool night air filling his lungs. Through the roar in his head he knew dimly that Deirdre followed him, the young kitten cuddled in her arms.

"The Amulet of Gwymyrr," he heard himself say, then repeated it twice more, like a chant or a litany. Its song soared, keening like the wind, touching his ears and his heart and his soul.

Then, as abruptly as it had begun, it ended.

The utter lack of sound caused him to stagger, a sharp sense of loss twisting and turning inside of him. Blinking, it took several heartbeats to clear the fog from his eyes, a second more before he became aware of Deirdre, her beautiful face wearing a quiet expression of dismay.

" 'Tis gone," he said simply.

She nodded. "But at least we now know in which direction we must travel."

Her soothing voice was like a balm to him, and he wondered how much of his riotous emotion she had been able to discern. Carefully schooling his face into a mask of nonchalance, he lifted one shoulder in a casual shrug.

"We have much of the night ahead of us. Let us go with all haste."

Deirdre crossed the small space between them, lifting her free hand to brush back the hair from his cheek. Stunned at the tenderness of her action, he could only stand frozen, the slow pounding of his heart a steady thump in his chest.

"Thank you," she told him softly, a sweet smile curving her lips. "I will treasure this always."

Not trusting his voice, he inclined his head in a brusque motion, then started forward. He heard Deirdre sigh as she moved with him, the ridiculous kitten asleep in her arms.

Carrying her new companion proved easy, especially once the animal hooked its tiny claws in the folds of her gown and slept there, with Deirdre's arm underneath for support. Instead of thinking about the torment she'd seen on Egann's face, she focused on the softness of the kitten's fur, relishing the way it purred so loudly, the quiet vibrations pleasing and soothing against her chest.

Still, she could not help considering what had just happened. She too had felt the amulet's grief. She also knew its sense of loss, recognizing Egann's own sorrow in the amulet's cry, though he would not admit it.

Perhaps the amulet could only be worn by Rune's true king. And if that king was Egann, unless he accepted this fact, would the amulet ever cease to mourn?

She voiced none of her thoughts, knowing that Egann struggled enough with the choices he had made. Such a thing, were it to turn out to be true, would be something best learned on his own.

They would recover the amulet—of this she had little doubt. Whether or not Egann would decide to become ruler of his people, she was less certain.

And of her own future, she had no idea.

Why had the Fates decreed Egann enter her world? For years she had longed for something more than her simple life among the people of the cliffs. More than anything she had wanted to feel the warm kiss of sunlight upon her pale skin. Her yearnings had been foolish and impossible; craving sunlight was to those of her kind the same as wishing for death. Yet desire this she had, and, truth be told, still did on some very deep level. In Egann's golden brightness, she tasted a hint of the yellow luster of day, a heady suggestion of what could be, were she able to reach out and live as normal humans did, as did others of her tribe.

Perhaps Egann's magic, or that of his mysterious amulet, might somehow be able to make it so. She dared, just for a moment, to dream of such a thing, then put the thought firmly away.

"Hold." Egann's low-voiced command brought her from her reverie. "I sense . . ."

She felt time slipping; a stirring in the air filled her senses, telling her that some sort of magic occurred. Egann grasped her hand, pulling her closer.

A blur of white circled them. There came the cry of an owl. Then Fiallan stood on the path in front of them, his white robe glowing.

Chapter Nine

"I have heard the cry of the Lady." Fiallan's voice was harsh, accusatory. "I have heard this in the sorrowful voice of the Amulet of Gwymyrr."

Instantly Egann remembered the old fable, of a Queen named Gwymyrr, of her terrible grief and lamentation.

"So it was this song," he asked slowly, conscious of Deirdre's slender fingers gripping his, "that we heard just now when the amulet called out?"

Fiallan's cobalt gaze seemed to pierce him, and Egann wanted to cross his arms in self-defense. Only Deirdre's hand prevented him.

"Do you not recognize it?"

Egann felt a flash of annoyance. "How could I, when I have never before heard its sound?"

With a nod, Fiallan conceded the point. "True. It does call your name, though."

"This I knew." It was Deirdre who spoke, fiercely clutching Egann's fingers but facing the Wise One of Rune bravely just the same. "Even when I heard the lament in my dreams, I sensed that the amulet called to Egann."

"In *your* dreams?" Fiallan stepped forward, focusing on her with a predatory glare.

Egann tensed, not certain why. Fiallan would do nothing rash.

"Yes." Deirdre's soft voice sounded sad rather than afraid. "I have dreamed of this talisman more than once. Always it has seemed to me that it calls to Egann."

"Do you know where it is?"

Deirdre did not answer. Glancing down at her, Egann saw that she worried her bottom lip with her teeth.

"Do you know where it is?" Fiallan repeated, his harsh voice ringing out in the stillness of the night.

"I have seen it," Deirdre went on, her voice cautious, yet undaunted. "Amid great crowds of people in a place of darkness and magic, fire and sea."

"These people," Egann asked, wondering why she had not told him of this, not liking the doubts that crept back to him at learning she had secrets of her own, "were they human or Fae?"

Fiallan too seemed to wait anxiously for her reply.

"Human, I think," she said at last. "For not all of them were fair of face, as I have heard the people of Rune to be." She shot Egann a quick look as she said this, making him wonder if she would find his countenance more attractive than those of others of his people.

Fiallan laughed. "I am very ancient, child. It has been decades since anyone called my visage beautiful."

Slipping her hand from Egann's, Deirdre stepped forward. "Ah, but you are, old one. The gray in your beard and hair remind me of the first frost of winter, when ice kisses the silver sea."

Though Fiallan did not reply, Egann could tell by his faint smile that Deirdre's words had pleased him.

"Did you see the face of the one who wears it?" he asked her, vaguely jealous of the old man.

"Nay, though I beheld the heavy chain and the bright sparkle of its colorful gems. But the face of he who wears it has been hidden from me." She turned to Fiallan. "Perhaps it is because all is as Egann believes: this evildoer is Maccus."

"Maccus?" The Wise One of Rune said the word slowly, his snowy brows raised in question as he turned to look at Egann. "So . . . you have news then?"

"We believe that the one who has the amulet has begun to use it." From years of past experience with Fiallan's omniscience, Egann suspected he did not say anything the Wise One did not already know. Quickly he relayed the events of the last few hours, telling of the mysterious riders who had vanished and of the disappearing camp.

"And you think they were Maccus?"

Egann nodded. "Though I know not why the Maccus would want our amulet."

Fiallan did not respond at first, appeared deep in thought. When he finally lifted his head, he focused his attention on Deirdre. "The Maccus," he said, "are tied to the Shadow Dancers. Though you refused my earlier offer to tell you, would you now like to hear the tale of the curse?"

"Which curse?" Deirdre's voice sounded bitter. "The one I have lived under since birth, or the one that Egann believes shadows the two of us even now?"

Stunned at the rancor in her voice, Egann took a step toward her. Then, realizing that touching her at this point might be ill advised, he froze. "I have never called it a *curse*."

She glanced quickly at Fiallan and spoke. "Egann believes some outside force compels and controls us. What would you call that?"

Fiallan's chuckle told Egann that he found this exchange amusing.

Egann shook his head, frustration making him clench his fists. "Enchantment, perhaps. Or—"

"Children," Fiallan interrupted, no longer laughing. "What I have to say is important. It concerns the Amulet of Gwymyrr, the Maccus, and both of you."

Still glaring at Egann, Deirdre bobbed her head in response. "I would like to hear your tale."

Egann simply waited, the dim light of the moon competing with his own glowing presence.

"I will listen too," Egann said.

After a moment, Fiallan began to speak. "Though I have not yet been able to gain entrance into the Hall of Legends to verify this, I believe that long ago the Maccus lived in Rune."

Deirdre gasped. "You say that these evil ones who hunt my kind like animals are Fae?"

"I do not believe it," Egann said.

"Did you not see proof of their magic?"

"The Amulet of Gwymyrr aided them."

"Be that as it may," the old one argued. "So long ago that neither race remembers it, the Maccus were part of our people and lived in harmony with us."

Narrowing his eyes, Egann watched Fiallan, searching for some hint in the older man's face that this was somehow not the truth, that the old man was twisting his words. He saw nothing, no suggestion of any guile that might make him think Fiallan did not believe in the veracity of what he said.

"There was a battle," Fiallan continued, his voice sonorous and heavy.

"There are always battles."

"This was worse than most, for Rune was split asunder by the horror of it."

Egann had heard this tale before, or some variation of it. Always had Fiallan loved telling epic stories, and Egann had loved to listen.

"One group used magic to compel mortals."

Now *this* Egann had not heard of. "But to do such a thing is forbidden," he said, his voice hoarse.

"Aye, it is. Yet enchantments were made, spells were woven, and many mortals were made to fight against the Fae."

"With no magic to aid them." The flat statement came from the depths of Egann's soul, for he had not known of this shameful act on the part of his ancestors.

"With no magic," Fiallan concurred. "And so they attacked and they died, and still they came in waves. Hordes of them, before the Fae realized what some of their number had done. By then it was too late. Most of the mortals had been slaughtered."

Deirdre made a slight sound, but Egann could not look at her.

"When our queen learned of this, she organized a group of her most powerful advisors to weed out those who had done wrong, who had inspired the mortals to throw themselves suicidally against us. The Maccus. 'Tis said that the spell they cast against these once-Fae caused the sun itself to disappear for several hours. Well-intentioned it was, but so against their bright natures that something went wrong."

"What do you mean?" Deirdre asked, a bleak and sorrowful shimmer in her shadowy eyes.

"The Fae are forbidden to do harm," Fiallan explained. "As this spell was forbidden the magic became twisted. It affected more than was intended, and differently."

"But the Maccus were banished from Rune." Egann clenched his jaw, wondering why he had not been told of this before.

"Aye, the Maccus were sent far away, into the world of men. Their supposed punishment was—and is—to make amends for the damage that they caused to mankind. Against this they rebelled."

A flash of confusion passed across Deirdre's pale face. "What has this to do with me? Why cannot Shadow Dancers go into the light of day without dying?"

Egann wanted to know as well.

The tense lines on Fiallan's face deepened. "The curse of the Shadow Dancers was meant for the Maccus. You, Deirdre of the Cliffs, are descended from the very humans the Maccus enchanted. The ones who attacked Rune. The curse struck your tribe instead."

Eyes widening, Deirdre seemed to tremble as she took all this in. Egann fought the urge to go to her, to hold her close as she digested the truth of her life.

"You mean the curse I live under," Deirdre swallowed, glowering at Fiallan, "is merely a spell gone awry? An error in judgment meant as punishment for the ones who seek to kill those of my kind?"

Slowly, with great dignity, Fiallan nodded.

Such pain, such sorrow did Egann hear in Deirdre's soft voice, he saw no choice but to go to her. Moving toward her, he froze when she, peering up at him through lowered lashes, flinched and took a step back.

"Your people did this to mine."

Egann hesitated, attempting to measure the depths of her emotions. "My ancestors," he clarified. "So long ago that it has nearly been forgotten."

Fiallan placed his gnarled hand on Deirdre's shoulder. This time, she did not flinch; instead she lifted her chin and tilted her head.

"If this curse were made in error, is there not a way to remove it?" This question was directed at Fiallan, her firm voice full of entreaty.

"I do not know." The old man sighed. "No one knows. Perhaps the secret lies in our Hall of Legends—but as I said, the stone door will not open and I cannot enter. I only just learned of this curse and do not know everything about it yet."

Deirdre turned her gaze on Egann, the brilliant emerald of her eyes sparkling with hope. "What of you? Think you that your amulet could do it? Remove the spell that would allow me—and all my kind—to live safely in the bright light of day?"

Though he would have given much to be able to answer her in the affirmative, Egann shook his head. "I know little of the powers of the amulet. And the use of it belongs only to the rightful king of Rune."

Deirdre's eyes narrowed as she looked from Egann to Fiallan, then back again. "Will you not help me?"

Fiallan coughed. He too seemed to be watching Egann, waiting for a response.

"You look to the wrong man for an answer," Egann said, letting his irritation show. " 'Tis Fiallan who must find my replacement, for he is known as the Wise One."

Giving Egann a black look, Fiallan held up his hand. "Enough of this. Child"—he smiled down at

Deirdre, squeezing her shoulder once before releasing it—"if there is a way to remove your curse, I will endeavor to find it. But for now we must worry about the Amulet of Gwymyrr, and the fact that the potential of its power lies in evil hands."

When Deirdre gave a slow nod, Fiallan clapped. Once, twice, then a third time. Again the fabric of time shifted, again the air seemed to shimmer, the veil to part.

Egann blinked, wondering what tricks the wise one was up to now. In a moment, he had his answer. When the world righted itself again, Weylyn pawed the path in front of them and nickered.

"Welcome back, old friend," he said. Laying a hand on the stallion's silky coat, Egann shot Fiallan a look of gratitude, then turned his attention back to the great beast. "I am sorry that you had to cut short your hunt. I can but hope that it was a good one."

With a snort, the animal seemed to indicate that it had.

"He balked at first at wearing again the form of a horse," Fiallan noted. "But I thought you might have need of him, since it appears you must now travel northeast up the rocky coast."

Had the old one been following them? Listening while cloaked in invisibility to every word they spoke? About to ask, Egann took one look at Deirdre's stricken expression and realized that she wondered the same.

Did Fiallan know that Egann and Deirdre had made love? Not once, but two times, that each time they touched or kissed, their passion flared more intensely than before?

"How do you know where we must travel?" he asked instead.

Fiallan's face creased into smile. "I have heard the amulet sing, remember? And I have heard it before. Methinks it comes from Barras Head."

Egann cocked his head, considering. Barras Head had no human settlement that he knew of. "I thought we would travel inland, to Suttin Montis or Cadbury."

Fiallan did not immediately reply; rather he stroked his long beard and appeared deep in thought.

"Are there caves in these places?" Deirdre asked. "For I have seen such in my dreams.

As Egann opened his mouth to answer, Fiallan lifted one hand in warning. Egann held his silence.

"Describe this cave," the Wise One ordered. "Tell me what you saw."

Nodding once, Deirdre closed her eyes. When she spoke, her voice was flat, no inflection or emotion coloring it. "I saw jagged cliffs, much taller and more forbidding than my home at Carn Vellan. The dark mouth of the cave blended with the rock, making it hard to see. The wind blew, great gusts of sand swirling across rock. I felt a sense of mystery and danger there."

She opened her eyes, and even in the dim light of the moon Egann could see an excited light burning in the vivid green of them.

"Go on," Fiallan urged.

"I heard the amulet's sweet song calling me from within."

"And inside?"

"In my dream I was not allowed to enter." She lifted her shoulder in a delicate shrug. "Though I longed to do so."

Egann frowned. He knew this place. Myrddin's Cave. 'Twas a place he had no desire to again set foot.

Stomping his massive hooves and snorting, Weylyn let them know he was impatient to be off. Deirdre's kitten let out a loud yowl, and both Weylyn's and Fiallan's gaze swung in her direction.

She blinked then, with a delighted laugh, and Deirdre held the furry cat in front of her and slowly approached the horse.

"Here, noble beast, is a creature you must meet," she said. "Cinnie, meet Weylyn. He is the most powerful steed in all of Britain."

That she had named the ugly little cat a word which meant *beauty* did not surprise Egann. Generous in spirit, only his Deirdre would find loveliness in such a bedraggled creature.

Fiallan raised his brows again. "From whence did that small animal come?"

"We found her," Egann answered, watching as Weylyn extended his massive neck, nostrils flaring as he breathed the kitten's scent. "In the deserted camp of the Maccus, trapped in a sack and left to die by the coals of a fire."

Weylyn nickered in approval, causing both men to subconsciously smile.

"It is of *his* kind—Fae creature." Fiallan shrugged, and his smile faded. "Now, enough about your pet. Go where you must, but take care. I sense that whoever has the amulet is learning to use it. If he fully harnesses its power, he will be a formidable opponent indeed."

Then, with those cryptic words of warning, the wise man vanished.

At Deirdre's questioning look, Egann grimaced. "Some say that if the wrong man wears the talisman and tries to use it, madness will overtake him. I do not know if it is true. Come." He gestured toward the endless ribbon of road before them. "Let me help you onto Weylyn's back. I want to ride as fast as we can before the sky begins to lighten."

"Yes," she agreed, tucking her kitten back in the folds of her skirt. "I am ready."

As soon as they were mounted, Weylyn needed no second urging. Tossing his head, he launched into a smooth lope.

Deirdre made a sound, a small squeak of protest at the pace. Amused, Egann wrapped his arms around her to keep her from becoming unseated during the ride. It took but a moment for him to realize that it might have been a huge mistake.

The movement of her small bottom—seated as Deirdre was in front of him, against him—created a torturous friction, compounded by the her clean, fresh scent.

What *was* it about this woman? Though he had complained that the intense attraction she caused in him was an enchantment, some sort of spell cast on them by Goddess knew who, he was beginning to disbelieve that. Nay, if there were an enchantment, it was in Deirdre herself; something about her called to him on an elemental level.

Clenching his jaw, he tried to control his unruly body, knowing she must feel him hardening against her. They rode through trees, blocking the dim light of the setting moon and making the darkness more complete. Lucky he was that his mount still saw with the eyes of a lion.

Knowing Weylyn would watch the road ahead, Egann concentrated on trying to determine why this small mortal woman had such an effect on him.

She was beautiful true, but he had known many exquisite women—and the females of his species were known to be far above mortals for their attractiveness.

Her body was well formed—he stopped this line of thought, knowing if he dwelled on her soft curves and lush body, his own would become unmanageable.

She was kind, he thought, desperately trying to focus on some other path than the one his aroused body wanted him to take. Kind, yes, and generous, and giving. Goddess, take him, this endless fixation on Deirdre would help him not.

Best he try to think on some other thing, such as the mysterious Amulet of Gwymyrr.

They broke free from the canopy of the trees, and Egann could see once more. The road stretched ahead of them, as Weylyn's stride ate up the miles.

"Fare you well?" Deirdre's voice, concerned and gentle, broke into his thoughts. She half-turned, the additional movement of her sweet little backside causing him to grit his teeth.

Not trusting himself to answer, he gave her a brusque nod.

"Tell me the rest of the story," she requested, the amused breathlessness of her tone indicating she was well aware of his arousal. But then, how could she not be, when he felt as huge and hard as that of a stallion in rut?

It took a moment for her words to register. Then, realizing she waited for his response, he could not fathom her meaning.

"The story?" Was she talking about the story of his people, of her people, of the Maccus?

"Yes." She gave him a patient smile over her shoulder. "Though it sounded as if he meant to tell me, Fiallan never finished telling of how this amulet of yours got its name. I'd like to know now. Who was Gwymyrr and why did she weep?"

Chapter Ten

In seeking a means to distract him, Deirdre wondered if she'd asked the right question. Egann's handsome face had gone dark, his expression shuttered.

Her hair blew, dancing from her braid in unruly disarray, getting in her eyes. The breeze had picked up, and seemed to carry the scent of rain.

"Gwymyrr lived long after the time Fiallan spoke about," he said. "She had nothing to do with the Maccus or your people."

Patience, she told herself, suppressing her desire. The urge to wiggle against his swollen manhood burned like a live coal against her backside. For the first time in her life, she understood desires of the flesh and the power such needs held over her body.

How she could want Egann again was beyond her, for she had felt completely sated after their lovemaking in the fragrant orchard. Yet want him she did, and the yearning to turn until she faced him and take him deep inside her was undeniable.

From the harshness of his breathing, she could tell Egann thought much the same way.

Yet if they kept on in this fashion, mating at every opportunity, she would end up with child—and then where would she be once he left? Alone to raise a child of both darkness and light, cursed to not provide it everything it needed—both a sun and a moon, a mother and a father.

Because she was determined that such a thing never happen, she shook her head to clear her thoughts.

"Tell me the tale," she insisted, her voice a smoky invitation even to her own ears. Clearing her throat, she tried again, staring straight ahead at the expansive fields that moved past. "Mayhap if I know more about the talisman's past, I will dream true when next I sleep and we will be better able to find it."

With a single word, Egann slowed Weylyn's pace to a brisk walk. Unable to resist, Deirdre glanced at him over her shoulder. For a moment he only stared at her, the harsh planes of his face achingly beautiful, softened by the silver light from the moon. The wind, which now had grown chilly, whipped his golden hair about his head and made Deirdre shiver.

"I have no cloak," he said. He'd obviously noted her discomfort.

"Please, tell me the story," she insisted, refusing to be distracted.

" 'Tis a long tale," he hedged, still sounding reluctant.

"The moon still rides in the sky," she persisted, crossing her arms over her chest in the vague hope of warming herself. "She is but halfway through her nightly journey. Weylyn carries us closer to the amulet. There is enough time for you to tell this tale to me."

After she spoke she turned her face away, taking great care not to move against him. She tucked her wayward hair under her collar, for the wind teased and tugged at it, and would cause tangles and snarls that would take hours to comb. Facing straight ahead, focusing on a point of the road directly between Weylyn's powerful ears, she adopted an attitude of intense listening, hoping he would see it and believe her pretense of indifference. If she could convince him that she remained unaffected by his arousal, perhaps his own desire would go away.

"Very well." He gave an exasperated sigh. "Long ago, even before the Romans first came to your land, in Rune there lived a queen named Gwymyrr. She did not wish to be queen and had in fact fought before being forced to accept the throne."

The sound of the Weylyn's hooves thudding against the hard-packed dirt of the road echoed the beat of Deirdre's heart, and the hiss of the wind seemed ominous. No wonder Egann had not wanted to speak of this queen, for much of her situation mirrored his own.

When he did not continue, Deirdre ventured a quick look back at him. Stony-faced, he stared straight ahead, as though in his mind he saw the ancient Faerie Queen of whom he spoke.

"How was she forced?" Deirdre asked. "Magic? And did she not have her own magic, her own powers?"

"Aye, she did." Reluctance seemed to color Egann's voice. "But she also loved deeply a mortal man. When he lay injured and dying from a wound of war, she knew only Fae magic could heal him. But it would take more than her magic alone, for in bringing him back from the brink of human death, he would then become Fae himself. She needed the help of her Council.

185

"With this, they had something to bargain: the life of her lover for her acceptance of the throne."

Deirdre found herself holding her breath. "So she became queen. And her beloved, did he live?"

"Nay." Egann's answer was sad, his tone reflective. "He did not. She waited too long to make her decision. By the time the healers reached him, the man's wounds had become fatal. It was because he did not live that Gwymyrr became queen."

Was there a warning in this tale? And did it make any sense? Still watching Egann, Deirdre worried her bottom lip with her teeth. "There is no reason in your tale. Why would she accept the throne she had not wanted if she had no cause to do so?"

He lifted his shoulder in a half-hearted shrug. " 'Tis the tale I know. So long ago did Gwymyrr live, much of her life has been lost in the mists of time. I only know that become queen she did. She ruled Rune wisely and justly for an extensive time, though she never ceased to mourn."

"What happened to her?" Deirdre whispered, her throat tight, her heart aching in sympathy for this queen of ancient times. As if in answer, the wind blew a sudden gust, so strong that Deirdre clutched at Weylyn's mane to steady herself. Still, she had to know. "Since Faeries do not die, where did she go?"

Egann's short bark of laughter startled her. "I forgot. That is another myth you mortals believe. Our lives are long, yes. Especially in comparison with those of mankind. But we do all eventually die, some of us sooner than we might wish."

From the bleakness of his tone, she knew he thought of his brother.

"But the amulet?" Doggedly, she persisted, still trying to fit together the jagged pieces of Gwymyrr's tale in her mind. "How came this magical talisman to be?"

"It is believed that over the centuries, the talisman has grown in strength. There are those who think it absorbs power from the ones who have worn it, and others whisper tales of the intensity growing on its own. As to how the amulet was made, no one knows for certain." He lifted one shoulder in a quick shrug.

"Some say Gwymyrr forged it from the deadly metal of the sword that killed her human lover, changing its substance with a powerful spell so the touch of it was no longer deadly."

Chest aching, Deirdre shook her head. "How sad."

"And the gemstones," he continued, "are supposed to have been created from her tears. The legends say the lament of mourning is Gwymyrr's own; the amulet cries eternally for the one she loved and lost."

"No. I don't think so." Pushing her hair from her eyes, Deirdre spoke without thinking—but immediately wished she could call back the words. Behind her she could feel Egann's body stiffen in surprise.

"So . . . you think you know more about this than my own people, little mortal?" he asked. He sounded vaguely offended.

Deirdre took a deep breath, tasting the wind. The scent of rain seemed stronger now, and she shivered in earnest. "The amulet mourns, this is true," she said quietly, yet loud enough to be heard over the wind. "But it mourns because it does not have a queen or a king. Perhaps the grieving first began when Gwymyrr died; I cannot know. But *this* I do understand: The talisman will weep until a ruler comes forward, a rightful monarch who will accept the empty throne of Rune."

She did not say that this sovereign should be him; she did not have to. Either Egann would realize that himself, or another would have to be found to take his place.

"You would have me be like Gwymyrr?" The bitter incredulity she heard in his voice made her grimace.

"Of course not. I only say what I hear in the amulet's song."

"I see."

Chancing a glance back at him, she could tell by the set of his jaw and rigid profile that Egann did not find her words to his liking. Ah well, she had only spoken truth. 'Twas not her place to convince or coerce this proud man; she would leave that to wise Fae like Fiallan. What cared she for the doings of the Fae anyway? Those bright beings' lives and hers would never mesh. She would never see Rune, never walk in bright sun- or moonlight among the exquisite beauty of its landscape.

Sometimes the injustice of her curse made her want to weep; other times she wanted to raise her fist and rail against the capriciousness of fate. Now that she had learned of the reason for her exile into darkness, she did not understand why she— or any of the other Shadow Dancers who surely existed throughout the world—should have to pay for the mistakes made by the Maccus and by Egann's ancestors.

That was the worst of it, that it all had been a blunder, an error in judgment. The knowledge sat like a lump in her stomach, heavy and sour.

Though, Deirdre reflected resentfully, she now had more reason to help Egann find the missing amulet. If in doing so, she could retrieve a powerful magic that could help him lift an age-old curse, any situation she found herself in would be well worth the danger.

And what of her? Could the small magic she created when she shadow danced be of any use? Somehow Deirdre doubted it. The people of the cliffs had used it to bless their crops and promise a fruitful harvest, nothing more. Truly, she had little magic, not like the Fae. Egann had told her as much, before. She was mortal, after all. What magic she was able to create with her dance was not going to add anything Egann could not already do. She had only her dreams and her visions of the amulet, and the powerful attraction between her body and Egann's. Those things would have to be enough, for now.

It would be enough . . . as long as she could avoid the Maccus, with the killing fires they made as they sacrificed to their red and angry god. Now that she knew more of why they sought to kill Shadow Dancers and that they had their own sort of magic, they were a most formidable threat indeed.

She peered at the winding road ahead, trying to see where they were going. As if the weather mocked her, clouds scudded across the face of the moon, plunging them into darkness.

She knew a moment's disorientation, then the solid feel of Egann on the horse behind her gave her ease.

"If the Maccus have the amulet, strengthening their magic," she began, speaking her fears aloud,

190

"what protection will I, or others who dance in the shadows, ever have from them?"

"If I knew *why* they hunt only Shadow Dancers"—his voice sounded as cool as the ice that sometimes crusted the winter sea—"I could better answer that. For now I will try to ensure that you remain hidden, especially when I locate the one who has the amulet."

This so irked Deirdre that she found herself speechless.

But only for a moment. Incredulous, she shot him a glance and a stiff smile. "Have you not heard a single word I have said? Have my dreams and the visions I have seen had no influence on your thoughts?"

"You would risk your life?" He sounded incredulous, as well as weary.

"I have no choice," she answered, meaning to explain. But before she could finish, he shook his head.

"Nay. Once before I lost someone to recklessness, while I stood by and did nothing to stop him. I will not allow you—"

"Allow me?" Though she knew he spoke of Banan, how could he think that her actions were his to dictate? "I make my own choices."

He reined the horse to a sudden halt. "Then we had best part now. I will not have one more needless death upon my hands."

191

The pain that his words brought her stabbed her like the sharp edge of a knife.

"I will not leave you."

"Then you will do as I ask?" His dark eyes seemed to bore into her.

Throat aching, she slowly nodded. *For now*, she answered silently. *For now, I will do as you want.*

"Little time remains before dawn. I have no wish to quarrel with you."

No sooner had the words left his mouth then the wind began to howl. Above them, the clouds chose that moment to loose their contents. Icy needles of rain stabbed Deirdre, as the wind continued its vicious assault. She began to shiver in earnest, unable to control the tremors that shook her.

Egann spurred Weylyn on.

"We must find shelter," he shouted. "I like not how the air seems to crackle with energy."

Deirdre felt it too: the sense of lurking danger, like lightning waiting to strike them—not from the sky above, but from the ground below. Even the little kitten, snuggled within the folds of her robe, seemed to sense something. Poking her tiny head up, she yowled at Deirdre, fur bristling.

Weylyn began to run, though the night was dark and the slashing rain made it impossible to see more than a few feet ahead.

Egann pushed Deirdre down with a hand on her shoulder, crouching her low over the horse's powerful neck. Egann bent over, too, protecting her. Yet while he blocked some of the rain, she could not control her violent shivering.

They charged north into the inky darkness, while the storm did its best to discourage them.

Deirdre began to wonder if, when morning came, they would even know it. Never had she been so endanaged by the advent of day, until she met this prince of Rune. She'd always been safely ensconced in a cave at dawn before him.

"We will find you shelter before daylight," Egann promised, making her wonder whether he had somehow read her thoughts.

"I know," she told him. She took a deep breath, glad that he could not see her expression. "I worry more that Weylyn will stumble and hurt himself."

"Don't worry. He has better eyes then almost anything."

The explanation begged many questions, but Deirdre liked not the increasing feel of the strange current that still flowed and swirled around them; it took her mind off Weylyn.

"It grows stronger," she said, knowing Egann would understand her words.

"Aye, it does. This storm . . ." Though Egann shouted, the screech of the wind carried much of his voice away. " 'Tis not natural," he repeated. "Something else—"

Five riders, wind whipping their dark cloaks around them, materialized in the gloomy darkness nearby.

Sliding to a bone-jarring halt, Weylyn tossed his head and let out a warning sound. Two of the riders moved to block on the path behind them; three others barred their way in front. There were five cloaked and hooded riders total, and she doubted this time they meant to disappear.

Maccus. Deirdre knew it before Egann spoke the word in her ear. Her stomach clenched. Was this then how she would meet her end? Not by stepping into the hot light of the sun, but destroyed by these evil beings? Which was better?

The tale Fiallan had told of them came to mind.

"Egann," Deirdre leaned back, half-shouting at his face.

"If Fiallan spoke true, then these Maccus will carry no swords."

The savage smile Egann flashed her showed that he agreed with her conclusion. If the Maccus were originally of the same race as he, the metal of a sword would be deadly to them as well. None could carry them, for to do so would be to run the risk of becoming violently ill just by one touch of their poisonous steel.

As abruptly as it had begun, the storm died.

"Is your magic so powerful that you can control the weather?" Egann's question was cold, spoken in the tone of a righteous king chastising his enemy.

One of the three riders before them, the one in the middle, rode forward. His dark cloak hid him, for he did not remove the hood so they might see his face.

"We seek the secret of the gemstones." His voice, nasal and deep, sounded flat and somehow deadly.

Incredulous, Deirdre dared not look back at Egann. She was shocked that the riders were so bold, making no secret that they were the thieves who had taken Rune's amulet. It was also some relief that these Maccus did not seem to want her. Apparently they had no idea that a Shadow Dancer rode with Egann, or they did not care.

"Fools." Egann's hawklike profile exuded authority and, as she had many times before, Deirdre knew in her heart that none but he could rightfully rule Rune. "You admit then that you have the amulet?"

They remained motionless, and by their very silence they gave him an answer.

Egann's voice rang out. "You have stolen that which rightfully belongs to me. I would have you return it. Now."

To Deirdre's surprise the Maccus muttered uneasily among themselves, except for the one who had ridden forward. He remained motionless, his face shadowed by his hood and revealing nothing.

This one, Deirdre sensed, was the most dangerous. The others were merely henchmen.

The hooded man spoke. "I have nothing to return. I am not the one who wears the talisman. I was sent only to retrieve an answer."

"Sent by whom?"

Slowly, the Maccus shook his head. Still the hood did not fall away; still his features remained hidden from view. When he next spoke, his words seemed to come with great reluctance. "The one who wears the amulet has sent us. He would know the truth about this trinket he treasures."

"Trinket?" Egann snarled. He urged Weylyn forward, fists clenched on the reins. "That amulet is treasured greatly by my people."

Though he remained motionless, Deirdre sensed in the hooded man a flinching—perhaps in fear of Egann, perhaps in dread of the reprisal he would suffer were he to fail in his appointed task.

"I must return with an answer," the Maccus said finally, echoing Deirdre's thoughts.

"Why would you think that I know the amulet's secrets?" With his words and his tone, Egann mocked the Maccus. "But even more importantly, if I do know, why would you even believe that I might tell you?"

As though it felt its rider's impatience, the lead Maccus's mount pawed the dirt in front of him.

"Dawn will come soon." This time when the leader spoke, his raspy voice held a challenge. "I see no shelter where your Shadow Dancer might hide from the sun's burning rays. We will keep you here, keep her here, trapped in the open while you watch her slowly die!"

Incredulous, Deirdre watched the Maccus backup their horses so that three formed a solid line. The other two remained motionless on the road behind them.

"Fools," Egann said, his voice cold and hard. "Think you that your power is greater than mine?"

"We have been permitted to touch the amulet. Our power has increased. And with each Shadow Dancer we sacrifice, our strength grows tenfold."

Nonsense. Egann straightened.

"You forget who and what I am." His extraordinary eyes blazed and glowed. He spoke again, nonsensical arcane words that meant nothing and everything. Deirdre felt the now-familiar swooping pull of magic at her insides, the disorientation as the landscape shifted. Before the Maccus could do more than mutter among themselves, Egann had made himself, Deirdre, and Weylyn vanish.

Chapter Eleven

This time, since Egann did not attempt to take Deirdre into Rune, they both arrived on Weylyn's back at the same place, a fishing village many miles up the northern coast near Dunster.

They stood on a rocky bluff, in sand and stones and tall grass that waved in the wind, high above the dark sea.

'Twas still night, and clouds even here shrouded the waxing moon. The air smelled of salt, and the sound of the waves crashing against the rocks below reminded Egann of the cliffs where he had first seen Deirdre dance.

Here near the sea, more than any other place, the veil that separated earth and Rune was the thinnest. He felt the presence of magic, the tingle of awareness it brought, even in the energy that rolled up from the water.

From the cry of appreciation Deirdre gave and the joyous lift of her chin as she sniffed the air, he could tell she too felt something.

"The Maccus are gone," he said, unnecessarily.

Turning in the saddle, she flashed him a smile of such wondrous joy that he couldn't help but chuckle.

"You brought me home."

Though he meant to touch her as little as possible, he could not seem to stop himself from cupping her chin with one hand and dipping his head to give her a kiss.

"Nay, not home," he murmured, wondering why the very taste of her made him hunger for more. "We have traveled north, up the coast. My instincts and Fiallan's tell me that the amulet will be found here."

Deirdre's lovely eyes widened. Violet now, they glowed with the color of some rare flower. Fascinated, Egann felt he could easily drown in their depths if he were not careful.

Deliberately, he looked away.

"Your eyes have changed color again." He kept his tone flat, feigning disinterest.

She shrugged, the slight movement causing his body to stir. "It does not surprise me if they have.

I have never understood what makes them change, or why."

"Most likely it is some residual magic inside you, left over from your dancing or your race, which manifests itself thusly when affected by mine." Fixing his gaze on the dark horizon, Egann nudged Weylyn into a brisk walk. To his relief, Deirdre turned around to face front again.

"Odd," she mused. "Though we have ridden many hours, and this night has been long, I do not sense the arrival of morning on the breeze from the sea. How can that be?"

"Time passes differently when one travels between worlds."

"Is that what we did?"

He detected a faint hint of confusion in her husky voice. No wonder, for what mortal could possibly understand the intricate workings of magical travel?

Lowering his gaze to the back of her head, he found himself breaking into a wry grin, knowing he would have to try to explain.

"We did not go to Rune," she continued when he did not immediately answer. "So tell me how it is that we have traveled 'between worlds.'"

With a mock sigh, he shifted in the saddle, knowing she would no doubt feel the slight movement in much the same way he'd felt her shrug.

"There are many worlds that make up the fabric of time. Many existences, many levels. I cannot take you to Rune, but I can take you to other places—and it is through those that I brought us here. But such travel, while it occurs in a split second for us, removes us from this world for longer."

As though agreeing, Weylyn nickered.

"So, it is another night here? We might yet have many hours until morning." Though her voice was somewhat weary, Egann could hear an undercurrent of excitement.

He fought the urge to bend and place a kiss on the soft skin at the curve of her jaw. "Aye." He sounded gruff he knew, but there was no help for it. "You may yet have hours before you must find a place to sleep."

Weylyn snorted a loud warning.

Immediately, Egann tensed. Though a previous quick search of the area revealed nothing, he trusted the horse implicitly.

"We must go," Egann said. Weylyn needed no second urging. Wheeling from the bluffs, he broke into a brisk trot.

Deirdre let out a soft cry as she bounced hard against Egann.

"I'm sorry," she said, half-turning. Her words became a gasp as the jolt of the horse's gait brushed her full breasts against his arm.

201

Egann clenched his jaw and stifled his groan. Never before had he known a woman's innocent motions to cause him such torment. Even the practiced wiles of the most beautiful women of Fae had not aroused him so easily. And, strangest of all, Deirdre did not even seem to realize what effect she had on him.

Or did she?

Through narrowed eyes he watched her, so caught up in trying to determine the depth of her attraction for him that her next question startled him.

"Egann?" She was still half-facing him, and her expression seemed troubled. "To where do we ride with such speed?"

It took him a moment to drag his attention away from her lush lips. "I believe the Maccus make camp nearby. If we make haste, I shall have the advantage of surprise."

"What of me?" she asked. He could hear a tinge of bitterness in her voice. "Do you still intend to hide me while you do as you will?"

"Until I can judge the level of danger, yes."

She shifted restlessly against him, causing her captive kitten to squirm. "I would prefer to aid you."

Smoothing down her silky black hair, this time he did place a kiss on the top of her head. "I know you do. And if these thieves were anything but Maccus, I would welcome your help. But I have given you my vow that I shall protect you. . . ."

He let the words trail off, knowing Deirdre would understand how utterly important keeping her safe had become because of his promise.

The Shadow Dancer had come to mean something to him. Had this feeling always existed, buried deep inside him, since the moment he'd first beheld her lovely face? Or had this feeling been steadily growing, quickening with each soft touch of her hand, until it now held a firm foothold in his heart?

He could not say. Indeed, the why and how of it did not matter, not really. Not now.

Yet he could not help wondering—would his feelings matter when the time came to leave her?

As though she sensed his riotous thoughts, Deirdre began murmuring to her tiny pet in a soothing voice. Egann listened as she sang a low-voiced lullaby, finding himself aroused and amused at the same time.

"What of my kitten?" Finishing her quiet song, Deirdre whispered hoarsely. "What will become of her while I sleep?"

"You worry about the kitten? Still stunned by the impact her husky voice had on him, he shook his head.

203

"Yes." She answered in a firm tone.

Egann stared for a moment, his chest unaccountably tight. Softness, stubbornness—both resided in this mortal woman in equal measure. She cared not that she might look foolish, nay. Rather she worried about her small pet, and he knew what she wanted.

What could he do but agree? He opened his mouth to allay her fears, but Weylyn again snorted a loud warning. This time, it was a cross between the roar of a lion and the cry of a warhorse charging into battle. Without any urging from Egann, the steel broke into an all-out gallop.

The back of Egann's neck began to tingle a warning.

All around them, the night seemed still and silent except for the pounding of Weylyn's hooves. Shrouded in darkness, the ghostly shapes of dwarfed trees whipped past. Away from the sea they raced, from the cliffs and the rocks, inland . . . to where danger awaited. Where was Weylyn headed?

Egann saw no safe way to deposit Deirdre. Furious with himself, he cursed out loud.

"What is it?" Deirdre gasped.

"I know not." Grim-voiced he spoke, knowing that they would find out soon enough. "But if we ever become separated, speak my name three times, and I will find you."

Rounding a curve in the road, ahead they saw the glow of several small fires. Cries and shouts echoed out over the darkened plains, and the shadows of many cloaked and hooded men could be dimly seen. Several of them surrounded a woman, seemingly trying to drag her to a fiery death in the largest of the fires.

Maccus!

With a savage curse, Egann reined Weylyn to a sliding stop. He had no time. He could not safely leave Deirdre, but he had to rescue the woman . . .

"Let's go," Deirdre urged, understanding the reason for his hesitation. "Or the Maccus will kill her."

"I will not take you among Maccus in a sacrificial fren—"

"We have no choice!"

Another quick look around showed Egann the truth of her words. And, as he'd seen before, the undulating landscape of fields contained no safe haven for Deirdre; if he kept her with him, he would have a better chance of protecting her.

The captive woman screamed.

Egann touched his heels to Weylyn's side. Pawing the ground, the enormous beast snorted. Then, tossing his massive head, he reared up and leaped forward.

Into the midst of Maccus they charged.

The men scattered.

Only the crackle and hiss of the nearby flames broke the shocked silence that greeted them. Those Maccus who held the woman captive did not release her, but she had ceased her struggles to stare in awe and wonder at her would-be saviors.

"Release her," Egann ordered. Although he carried no sword, his tone held no room for argument.

Yet not one of the Maccus moved.

Finally, their captive, an elderly woman with a mane of silver hair, spoke: "Help me," she said, her voice quavering yet strong. She did not shout or beg, and an odd sort of resigned dignity seemed to cling to her. Shaking off her captors' hands, the gray-haired woman took a step forward. Something about her reminded Egann of Deirdre.

"She is a Shadow Dancer," one of the Maccus said, his defiant voice echoing through the night. "Of darkness and evil. We take her to be sacrificed. It is our right to purge the earth of ones such as she."

Deirdre stiffened, clutching a handful of Weylyn's mane. With a light touch to her shoulder, Egann forestalled her. He did not want her to draw the Maccus's attention.

Instead, he raised his voice in challenge. "Who gives you such a right? You would stoop so low as to murder an elderly woman who cannot fight you or defend herself?"

But instead of shaming them, Egann's words seemed to make them stand taller.

"Our god gives us the right. 'Tis our divine purpose, our reason for being. Have you not heard of the Shadow Dancers, and the curse they carry?"

Since Egann could not lie, he did not answer directly. Instead, he cocked his head. "I would hear this tale," he said.

The utter stillness of Deirdre in front of him told Egann that she too wanted to hear the Maccus's version of the story.

The elderly Shadow Dancer, however, had other ideas. While the two Maccus who flanked her focused their attention on Egann, she used the opportunity to run. Whirling with the speed of one who had many fewer years upon her, the aged one spun free and moved to stand near Weylyn's shoulder.

To Egann's amazement, the Maccus fell back rather than following their escaped captive. Weylyn nickered a welcome to her.

When one of the Maccus shook off his daze and made a move toward them, Egann held up his hand. "Come no closer. This woman is under my protection now."

"And who are you?" The tallest of the Maccus,

hidden in the dark folds of his black cloak, moved forward boldly. "Think you that you can overcome six of us?"

Piercing each man with a look that left no doubt as to his belief that indeed he could easily prevail, Egann spoke quietly, knowing his next words would be answer enough. "I am Egann of Rune."

To his immense satisfaction the Maccus fell back. All except one—the tall, bold man who had first issued the challenge.

"This is a matter between Maccus and mortal. We but prepare to sacrifice to our god. You of Rune have neither reason nor right to interfere."

The back of Egann's neck began to tingle yet again. This Maccus, whoever he might be, knew enough of the lore of Rune to be dangerous. But how?

"Show yourself," he ordered. "Cease this hiding, and remove your hood."

Evincing no fear, the Maccus stepped forward until he stopped a mere ten paces from them. Behind him, the bonfire's angry orange glow made his hooded form into an ominous silhouette.

Though Deirdre did not overtly move, Egann could feel her shrinking away from the evil this man emanated. To his surprise, the older woman laid a gnarled hand on Deirdre's leg, as if in comfort.

The man on the ground reached up and slowly lowered his hood.

"So we meet again," he said, grinning slyly.

'Twas the Maccus Egann had met before in the forest, the one who called himself Monk and who might even be he who led the Maccus. Yet he did not carry the Amulet of Gwymyrr, for Egann would have sensed its presence.

Weylyn tossed his massive head and pawed the ground.

Monk's grin widened. "Your mount wishes to hunt."

Egann studied the other man. This one, even though he had been banished from Rune, still knew how to use his eyes to see beyond appearances. Evidently he was able to discern, where mere humans could not, Weylyn's true form.

"Have a care," Egann warned, "lest he decide to hunt you."

For some reason Monk seemed to find this amusing. His mad chortles had even his own followers muttering among themselves.

Then, abruptly, Monk went quiet. Looking up at Egann, he gave a fierce shake of his head. "Now is not the time, Prince of Rune. We are not ready, not yet. But we will be, and soon."

Before Egann could dispute his cryptic words, the air began to shimmer. The bonfires roared, the flames leaping higher, sparks shooting into the night sky. Then, with a flash like lightning, Monk and his men vanished.

Magic. Again.

Stunned, Egann stared at the empty place where the Maccus had stood only moments before.

With a fierce shake of his head, Weylyn uttered a futile challenge, a trumpet of sound that blared into the night. Deirdre's kitten, startled by the noise, poked her head up from the folds of Deirdre's skirt and yowled.

"I am called Ula, and I would go with you."

The gray-haired Shadow Dancer spoke, reminding Egann of her presence. He bit back his refusal when Deirdre glanced over her shoulder at him, a blatant look of entreaty in her exotic violet eyes.

"Of course you will," he said instead. "But we will need another mount. Though Weylyn's back is strong, even he would balk at carrying three."

The horse nickered, rolling his eyes so that the whites showed. Egann couldn't help laughing.

Deirdre's Cinnie mewed again.

"You would make a fine steed, little one," Egann said.

Deirdre made a sound of protest.

"Think on it, little dancer. What better way to protect this small cat than to make her into a fine steed like Weylyn?"

Weylyn snorted in agreement.

"See?" Egann grinned at Deirdre, knowing he was right. "Weylyn will protect and teach her."

With a wordless nod, Deirdre handed him the kitten. Unafraid, the small beast tilted its head and looked up at Egann with what he could have sworn was eager anticipation.

"Place her on the ground," he told the other Shadow Dancer, who took Cinnie from him and did as she was asked.

Weylyn nickered again.

The spell was a simple one, ancient and familiar. Quickly Egann spoke the words, using a simple gesture and a minimum of power. One moment, a kitten sat beneath Weylyn's hooves, licking her small paw and purring.

The next, a spotted palfrey, coat gleaming with health, touched noses with Weylyn.

Deirdre laughed out loud with delight and amazement.

The other Shadow Dancer took a step back. "Much thanks to you," she murmured. With a spryness at odds with her advanced age, she went to the smaller horse, grasped the long mane, and pulled herself up onto Cinnie's back.

Once she was settled, they started forward.

"How are you named?" Deirdre asked, sounding lightly cautious.

"I am called Ula," the older woman said. "As the Maccus claimed, I am one of those who dances in the shadows."

Egann watched Deirdre's averted profile for a re-action, but found none. Instead, she merely dipped her head politely. "My name is Deirdre. For what tribe did you dance?"

Ula sighed. "Long have I danced in the shadows, and for many tribes. But now, thanks to the Maccus and their evil god, I have no home."

Egann thought of the fires in the cliff caves and his and Deirdre's furious ride to escape. In front of him, Deirdre shuddered, and he knew that she re-membered as well.

"The Maccus burned my home too." Deirdre's quiet voice held sadness. "But Prince Egann has promised to find me another home, after we find that which he seeks." Staring straight ahead, she did not look back at him.

That she used his title and such a formal tone gave Egann momentary pause, as did the fact that Deirdre did not name the object of their quest, the amulet, to the other woman.

"I have heard of one who seeks a talisman." Ula said slowly. "All the northern tribes have begun speaking of it."

Egann felt a momentary sharpening, a drawing together of his intellect, spirit, and body. "Do any say," he asked, keeping his tone level, "where one might find this talisman?"

"Nay." The older woman replied at once. "Though it is rumored that the Maccus have recently acquired a magical amulet. That is what makes them so bold."

Deirdre half-turned, glancing at Ula riding beside them. "How were you captured?"

Though Egann heard nothing but polite curiosity in her voice, he sensed an undercurrent of suspicion as well.

"They came upon my people by stealth and set fire to our village. I tried to run." Ula made a rueful *tsk*ing sound. "But these old legs of mine are not so swift anymore. They caught me easily, and I did not have the strength to fight them."

The same would have happened to Deirdre, if Egann had not been there to protect her. The knowledge infuriated him, as well as causing him unexpected pain. The thought of a being so loving, so exquisite as Deirdre having her existence snuffed out by one as callous and cruel as the madman called Monk made him wish for only the second time in his life that he could touch iron and arm himself with a sword.

"The Maccus must be stopped." This declaration he uttered with contempt. "No matter the cost, I will stop them so that no more Shadow Dancers will die."

Deirdre lifted her face to his, violet eyes glowing. "You would do this," she whispered, "for me and my kind?"

"Have a care what you promise," the old woman admonished. She didn't seem taken aback by Deirdre's confession of being a Shadow Dancer, but she *was* astonished by Egann's words. "Though I am certain you already know to make such an oath becomes binding."

This he knew well, for he had always honored his word. Except once, the most important time of all, when he had promised to protect Banan and failed.

He would not do that ever again.

Though now his vows had become numerous, he would keep each and every one. He would find and return the Amulet of Gwymyrr to his people, keep Deirdre safe, and find a way to remove the curse that haunted her and her kind. Dipping his head, he touched his lips to Deirdre's, sealing his latest promise.

Bizarre. He, who once had wanted no responsibilities at all, had just willingly taken on another.

Chapter Twelve

As they rode swiftly in the darkness, Deirdre shot covert looks at the older woman named Ula. Never having met one of her own kind, Deirdre did not know what to make of her. Something about the woman's mannerisms seemed familiar, in the way that dreams sometimes brought false memories of strange places.

Occasionally the breeze carried the sharp scent of the sea, and Deirdre fancied she could hear a gull screech in the distance. They rode north, she knew, and the dirt path did not stray too far from the cliffs.

Clouds still blanketed the night sky, and when

occasionally the moon revealed herself, she seemed to be nearly half full.

Soon, too soon she saw, 'twould again be time for her dance.

Again she looked at Ula, wondering what it would be like to watch the shadow dance of another. To her knowledge, such a thing had never been done.

Shadow Dancers were, according to legend, few in number. Now, thanks to Fiallan, she knew why; they were the beleaguered survivors of one small group of wrongly cursed people, scattered like chaff on the wind among the various tribes of this land—and hunted eternally by the relentless Maccus.

"Where did you dance, child?" Ula asked, making Deirdre wonder if perhaps the older woman had read her mind.

"I lived south of here, by the sea and among the cliff people." Though she tried, Deirdre could not keep her sorrow from resonating in her voice. "I danced the harvest until the Maccus came with their evil and their sacrificial fires. Egann—the prince—helped me to escape. I do not know how many of my people did not."

"The Maccus only wanted you," Egann pointed out from behind her, tightening his arms around her, his deep voice a soothing rumble. "When they did not find you—"

"Think you that they massacred my people?" *There*. Deirdre closed her eyes, reliving the anguish. She'd finally spoken her greatest fear out loud, the guilty worry that had haunted her since she'd fled her home.

"I know not," Egann said. "What think you, Ula?"

'Twas a reasonable question, and Deirdre waited to see what the older dancer would have to say.

The woman remained silent, though, the slight breeze ruffling her moon-colored hair. The clop of the horses' hooves was the only sound for a while, as Deirdre stared blindly at the tall grasses that lined both sides of the dirt path they traveled. Finally, she could bear the silence no longer.

"Tell me, old one, if you know! What happened to your people when the Maccus came?"

"The Maccus may have harmed all your people," Ula said with a lift of her brows, "but there is no way to know for sure. Though the Maccus hunt us and not regular mortals, sometimes they hurt others who get in their way. Sometimes they kill them. But do not blame yourself. There is nothing you can do to change that. Our kind never asked to become so hated and hunted."

"There is much I did not ask for." Deirdre shook her head, trying to clear from her mind the unwanted images of fire and screams and her people

217

dying. "But still I would know all I can. Tell me what became of your tribe."

"I do not know." Reluctance colored Ula's tone. "When the Maccus captured me I was beaten and rendered senseless. When I regained my mind, I was far from home and my people."

"I am sorry." Deirdre bowed her head. This senseless hatred had to stop. The Maccus, instead of atoning for their crimes of long ago, were simply trying to eradicate the very ones they'd abused. Never would they stop. They had misplaced their anger, and were now violently acting out retribution. Their god demanded the fiery sacrifices of her people so nay, never would they change.

Unless one such as Egann were able turn them from their evil ways.

To end an age-old enmity, to right the wrongs done by a mistaken curse, to bring unity and joy to two separate races—this would be a task for a great warrior-king indeed!

Stunned, Deirdre stared unseeingly ahead, compelled by a vision of such magnitude and beauty that she wanted to weep. Was this then the path Fiallan had spoke of, the walk of greatness Egann might take were he so inclined?

Humbled, yet thankful she might live to see this with her own eyes, Deirdre muttered a quick prayer to the Goddess. The rocking of Weylyn's gait seemed soothing now, and she drifted into a light sleep, her head pillowed on Egann's broad chest.

"We near a village," Egann rumbled. As he spoke, he slowed Weylyn to a brisk walk. "And, though the moon remains high, I would like soon to find a place where you both can hide."

Beside them, Ula pointed ahead. "There is an abandoned barn in the southern fields outside the village."

Sleepily, Deirdre peered at the older woman. "How do you come by this knowledge?"

" 'Tis where the Maccus kept me while they searched for you."

"Is it dark enough to provide shelter?"

"Yes."

Surprised, Deirdre tilted her head. "They found you a safe place, even though they meant to kill you?"

Ula's smoky chuckle was interrupted by coughing. When she spoke again, she sounded weak. "I was but bait, a lure put out by the Maccus to trap you and your man. That their plan failed I can only marvel."

Egann laughed. "I do not think they know the true extent of my power, though they had to know that I am Fae."

Deirdre added silently, *And I bet they did not realize that you are the rightful king of Rune.*

"This I do not doubt," Ula agreed. "Though I truly believe they want above all to know the secret of this amulet they have found. They sense its magic and this frustrates them, because they don't know how to use it. Mayhap they think you can teach them its secrets."

Deirdre's suspicions grew. "How came you with such intimate knowledge, Ula? Did you see the one who has the talisman?"

"Nay, though the Maccus I traveled with could talk of nothing else. I listened well, and merely relay to you what I heard them say."

The older woman's voice contained a hint of resentment. That, and an awful, aching weariness that Deirdre sensed as sharply as if it were her own. She knew this feeling, knew it well. It was the prelude to the utter exhaustion that always claimed her as she reached the end of her dance.

"I have lived many years, child," Ula spoke softly, so Deirdre had to strain to hear her. "I am old and tired." Her words once again made Deirdre wonder how Ula seemed able to read her thoughts.

"I have seen numerous deeds, both good and evil," the older dancer continued. "Long have the Maccus hunted us, though never as successfully as they do now with the aid of this magical amulet."

"Another reason we must track them with all haste." Egann sounded grim, and Deirdre knew he believed the loss of the amulet was yet another great failure on his part, like that which had caused his brother's end, though this failure could result in the loss of more than one life.

Before she thought better of it, Deirdre turned her head and rubbed her face against his broad chest. She listened to the steady thump of his heart, finding the sound comforting. "We will find it," she said. "Do not doubt that."

He did not answer, just stared down at her up-turned face with a predatory look, reminding Deirdre again of a hunting falcon. What fools these Maccus were, she thought with a shiver, to think that they could best someone as formidable as Egann!

"That dim shape across the field," Ula spoke up, interrupting Deirdre's wandering thoughts. "That is the farmhouse of which I spoke."

Though the sky remained dark for now, Deirdre did not doubt that soon it would lighten. Soon it would show the tell-tale streaks of color that presaged the fiery rise of the sun. How many times had she watched in secret with an aching heart, waiting until the last possible moment to take necessary shelter in the cool darkness? She had prayed for sleep to come quickly then, for only in slumber could she submerge her fierce longing to feel the warm kiss of the sun on her pale skin.

221

Yet she had also dreamed of such a day, so sleep was no surcease. She wondered if one as ancient as Ula had ever shared such a desire, had ever longed to walk in the day but not be destroyed by it.

At Egann's command, Weylyn left the rutted road, traveling instead over the grass field. The scent was different here—of grass and grain and dark, rich earth, making Deirdre think of the fragrant orchard where she and Egann had made love.

That, she thought with mixed amusement and unhappiness, *would not happen again soon*. Not with Ula to act as chaperone. She supposed she should feel gratitude, though, to be protected from her wanton desires.

Wanton. She—Deirdre the Untouchable. So had the men of the cliffs named her when she'd rebuffed all of their advances.

As they drew nearer to it, the shape of the farmhouse became better defined. Deirdre could see that, although the building appeared sound and whole, none lived within its stone walls.

"Where did the people go?" Egann mused aloud, echoing Deirdre's unspoken question.

"This place has not been empty that long," Ula told him. "Perhaps the people ran off with the coming of the Maccus."

222

"Or were murdered by them." Egann's tone was dark. "I sense death in this abandoned place."

"More blood on their hands." Staring hard at him, Ula inclined her head. "There is also magic here, though I know not enough about it to tell you why."

With a swift motion, Egann dismounted, then lifted Deirdre down as well. His hands were warm where they touched her waist, and 'twas with only the greatest of efforts that she kept herself from pressing into him.

Swallowing, she concentrated instead on the older woman's words. "Was magic used for evil here?"

'Twas Egann who answered, his voice hard. "Using magic to kill is forbidden. If the Maccus did so, then by their own hands they are thrice damned."

If she did not look away from him, Deirdre would drown in the smoldering heat of his eyes. Turning, she pretended to study the abandoned cottage.

It occurred to her that she could see much better now; the weathered stone exterior of the farmhouse was cracked in places. A quick glance at the sky confirmed her fear; it *had* begun to lighten, though she could not see the faint glow of the sun on the horizon as of yet. Still, dawn would not be far behind.

"It is time we take shelter," Ula said. "I find even a hint of sunrise painful, and I wish to rest without soreness."

Deirdre hurried to take Ula's arm. She glanced back at Egann, noting his fierce scowl. It struck her then that perhaps he did not want her to go. How she longed to go to him, to smooth the lines from his face, to kiss into softness the rigid set of his mouth.

Instead, she looked away, commanding her foolish heart to stop pounding. "Cinnie will be fine," she said, pretending to study the small cat-horse with interest.

"Aye," Egann answered, his voice sounding flat. "Weylyn will watch over her."

Avoiding his intent gaze, Deirdre nodded. "Come, Ula. Let us go inside. You can show me the best place for us to sleep."

But before she left, Deirdre could not help but chance another quick look at him. He stood, legs planted apart in the rich earth, a fierce warrior outlined by the lightening sky. It was right that they leave him now, allowing him time to piece together his thoughts, to formulate a plan.

Ula went with Deirdre without protest. Once inside the dark confines of the abandoned farmhouse, they switched places, Deirdre following where the silver-haired one led. The air inside carried a damp chill and the faded, elusive scents of those who had stayed there before.

Unerringly, Ula guided her down a short hallway to a room that had appeared to have been built into the back of the small house. Down three wooden steps, it seemed this room was part cellar, used for storing vegetables and meats. Though windowless, Deirdre could see enough in the stale air to tell that the bed Ula showed her was made of straw, covered with an old, musty blanket.

Holding the older woman's arm, Deirdre helped her settle comfortably. Then, missing Egann with a terrible ache, she climbed over to lie down beside the old one. The straw scratched and the blanket stank of unwashed flesh, but she felt herself drifting off to sleep almost as soon as she closed her eyes.

Egann liked this not. Pacing outside in the gathering dawn, he eyed the rustic farmhouse with unease. The place carried echoes of dark deeds, both past and present, and lives violently lost. With a quiet oath, he scooped up a handful of damp earth, sifting its fertile darkness between his fingers and letting it fall to the ground.

Humans had fought for this land, died for this land. Now the place was empty—but he found the abandonment too convenient. Yet who would set a trap in a place where the prey could see for miles in every direction? Approach by stealth would not be possible, and the Maccus did not need to surprise their enemies if magic were to be attempted.

It could not be a trap. Still, he could not rid himself of the niggling sense of unease that prickled the back of his neck.

Nay, he did not truly believe that Ula would knowingly endanger them. She and Deirdre were kindred spirits, two of the same race, and from the wary curiosity he had seen in her vibrant violet gaze, the younger Shadow Dancer could learn from the elder. How could he begrudge her that?

No, his annoyance was perhaps of a different kind. He could not help but miss the way Deirdre had, before the arrival of Ula, freely touched him with unabashed pleasure. He longed again for the simple honesty of her kiss, for the lush sensuality of her body as it welcomed his.

By the Goddess, could he not even think of Deirdre without growing aroused? It appeared not, for again he was hard and swollen, as though her soft tongue had stroked him to life.

If Deirdre slept alone inside the cottage, he knew he would go to her now, go to her and sate his lust.

He muttered a curse. His involvement with the lovely Shadow Dancer had become more than mere lust, more than a simple diversion. He could not allow himself—by thought or by deed—to become so completely consumed by a mortal woman. Bad enough that he had given his oath to protect her and to try and lift her curse.

He must find the amulet, find a way to be done with all his oaths.

Turning, he forced himself to concentrate on the rapid lightening of the sky. As he waited for the sun to make its daily appearance on the horizon, he found himself wondering what it would be like, never to have greeted the arrival of day. In the squat, leafy trees around him, birds began to sing, welcoming the morning. The night insects, unwilling to be stilled just yet, continued their songs as well, blending into a cacophonic chorus. Streaks of rose and orange colored the sky, and the air grew still, expectant.

As the bright golden disc rose in the east, Egann lifted his face, feeling the renewing of spirit the arrival of day always brought.

How he wished Deirdre could stand at his side, her hand tucked firmly in his, and greet the sunrise with him.

Thinking this, he remembered again his oath and his debt. Once he found the amulet, his task would only be half done. He could not simply retrieve the powerful talisman and return it to Fiallan's waiting hands. Nay, for if there were a way to use it to remove the curse that Deirdre and her kind carried, he must find that as well.

Only when Deirdre was truly free could Egann seek his own freedom. The revelation annoyed him. He had not wanted to tie his own destiny so closely with another's. Therein waited nothing but grief and sorrow.

Weylyn nickered, echoed by Cinnie, reminding Egann that the valiant beasts were surrounded by fertile fields yet still wore bridles. They needed to be freed to graze.

Once he had accomplished that task, and the horses were roaming happily, Egann lowered himself to a grassy area in the front of the farmhouse. Though he would have liked to search the nearest village for clues to the whereabouts of the Maccus, he could not leave Deirdre and Ula unprotected. Careful to keep the stone wall at his back, he decided to simply wait in the sunlight and keep watch.

Still, he could not shake the sense of impending danger.

A profound silence seemed to come over the day as the sun continued its brassy rise in the sapphire sky. The air grew warm and humid, but except for the drone of an occasional insect, he detected no obvious threat. As the perfect spring morning waned into afternoon, he ate one of the apples he'd taken from the orchard with a bit of bread and cheese. He took water to Weylyn and Cinnie, and then continued his restless vigil. No longer could he sit; instead he found himself pacing the exterior of the squat stone building, alert for signs of danger.

Despite his nervousness, nothing disturbed the peace of the abandoned farm. He saw no wildlife, not even a sparrow. Though he found that odd, he was grateful, as magic could give danger many forms. Still, he had lived long enough to trust his instincts, and every nerve ending screamed silently that he'd better beware. He would remain alert.

At last, as the amber orb of the sun dipped below the darkening horizon, and the crickets began to chirp again, he allowed himself to relax. With dusk, he ventured inside the shadowy confines of the farmhouse.

His purpose was simple, yet so profound that his mind skittered away from acknowledging it. He wanted to be at Deirdre's side when she awoke.

From one room to another he went, finding each successively empty. The third room, one that had been added to the back of the farmhouse at a later date, had a tattered curtain hanging in the entrance. This makeshift door separated the room from the others and kept any light from penetrating its murky depths, which lay a few feet below the rest of the house.

This place then was surely where Deirdre and Ula slept.

The back of his neck, which had tingled before, now began to prickle painfully.

Taking a deep breath, Egann pushed aside the torn curtain. With a rising sense of urgency, he went in. It took his eyes a moment to adjust to the darkness, but soon he could make out the shape of a crude straw mattress, saw too the dark cloak that perhaps had covered Ula and Deirdre while they slept.

But that was all. No sign remained of the two Shadow Dancers. 'Twas as if they'd disappeared into thin air.

For a moment Egann could not breathe. He could hear the loud thump of his heart, the blood roaring in his ears. His vision blurred as rage filled him, rage and an awful, certain fear.

They were gone. But how?

Chest tight, Egann searched the closed room, shoving against the walls with his hands, seeking a hidden doorway, a window, even some sort of storage room large enough to hide two women.

He found nothing. How had they gone? They had not left by normal means. He had not abandoned his post; not even once had he relaxed his vigil beside the only door to the cottage.

How? He slammed his fist against the wood that framed the doorway, feeling it splinter beneath his knuckles, welcoming the pain. Once again, the elusive thief of fate had stolen something precious from him. Once more, he had failed.

Magic? It had to be. Though he had not sensed the tell-tale ripple in the air that always before had warned him of its presence, the fact remained: Deirdre and Ula were missing. And if—as there seemed to be few other explanations—the Maccus had taken them, their lives were in grave danger.

Chapter Thirteen

Awakening from a sound slumber, Deirdre sensed immediately the wrongness in the air. She rubbed her eyes and looked around, her head beginning to ache. The straw mattress in the cramped little room had vanished, the abandoned farmhouse as well. The place in which she now awoke was dark, as it should be. But, scrabbling to her feet, she realized she stood on rough rock that had a slippery feel, and around her she saw naught but stone walls. Indeed, it appeared that she'd been transported by ethereal means, to a dank place that had no sky.

She could see little except the distant glow of a fire. The air smelled of sulphur and smoke, of stale air stirred by no breeze. Once when she had been only a small girl, a Christian friar had traveled to her village and told vivid stories of demons and their home. This place reminded her of that; deep within the bowels of the earth, in the pits of the Christian Hell they seemed to be.

"Take my hand," Ula appeared before her and commanded, her voice no longer sounding quite so weak or so old.

Deirdre did not move. Instead, she regarded the older woman thoughtfully, tamping down her anger. Such orders could wait, at least until she had some answers.

"Where are we?"

The other Shadow Dancer gave a mocking laugh. "In a place where neither the moon or the sun, nor the whims of others can affect us. Come with me and I will show you a place the likes of which you could only have dreamed.

"No." Keeping her voice flat and unemotional, Deirdre stood her ground. "I want to go back to the farmhouse. Egann will be looking for us there."

"The Prince of Fae?" Ula's expression soured. "What do you want with him? He is the opposite of all our kind."

"I value him, as he does me."

"You delude yourself, child." The older woman spun in a slow circle, her silver hair fanning behind her. "His kind belong to the light and the sun. Once he finds that which he seeks, you will never see him again."

"You cannot know this."

"Ah, you need to think on it, young one. What would one such as he want with a woman like you, beautiful or no? You are mortal and can only move about in the darkness, while he must have the bright light of day to survive."

That Egann had promised to remove the curse, Deirdre dared not say. The hope of a cure, however remote, would be far too cruel of a thing to dangle without assurance of its validity. And Deirdre did not know Ula, or Egann's possible cure, well enough to provide such assurances.

"Let me go back," she stubbornly said.

The other woman's smile turned sly. Eyes glowing in the dim light, she moved closer. "Do you wish to help this Egann of yours?"

Deirdre stiffened, but she held her tongue.

"I know where his talisman is hidden." Ula held out a hand, her voice wheedling. "Come with me and I will show it to you. How wonderful would be your welcome, were you to return to your Egann with the amulet he seeks?"

Though she knew giving in might be foolish, such a powerful lure she could not resist. Ignoring the other woman's outstretched hand, Deirdre did incline her head briefly in acquiescence.

"I will go with you," she said, conveying some of the icy anger she felt in her tone. "But Goddess help you if you have spoken falsely." She did not trust this woman, even if Ula was of her own kind.

Still, if there was even a chance, however slight, that Deirdre could help Egann in his quest for the amulet, she would have to take it.

"Take my hand. We cannot go down the path unless we are together."

Deirdre did as the older woman asked, noticing immediately that the hand she took was no longer gnarled and coarse, but was soft and smooth, the hand of a much younger woman.

Magic.

She wished the light were better, so that she could see what the silver-haired woman looked like now.

"Was it you who brought us here?" Low-voiced, Deirdre squinted around into the all-encompassing darkness, trying to make out the features of things they passed. She might need to remember them if escape were necessary. Unfortunately, lit by flickering torches, all she saw were dark stone walls, rough with the passage of time and wet from some unknown source.

"Nay, not I." With a tug on Deirdre's hand, Ula pulled her forward, moving through the darkness as if by memory. "You know as well as I do that our kind does not have that kind of magic."

"If not you, then who?"

The other woman ignored her and simply increased her pace.

Deirdre dug in her heels, trying futilely to yank her hand free of the Ula's surprisingly strong grip. When she finally succeeded, stumbling backward, she folded her arms across her chest. "I would have answers."

"And you will get them." Frustration sounded in the older woman's tone. "But you must come with me to get them."

"No. I will not follow you blindly."

"Even if doing so means you will get Prince Egann's amulet?"

Ah, again the lure, again the tone of utter insincerity. Still, Deirdre could not help but think of Egann and how pleased he would be if she were able to retrieve his lost talisman.

"How can I be certain that the amulet is even here?"

Ula spread her hands, palm up. "How else do you think we were brought here? 'Twas only with the power of that object to aid him that he had the strength to work such a spell."

"Him?"

"He who wears the amulet."

"Who is that?"

Her question brought only silence; then the older dancer smiled, an expression of utter serenity on her pale face.

"I have given you my real name, and the truth of what I am. You and I are the same, Shadow Dancer. Have you spent much time with others of our kind?"

Reluctantly, Deirdre shook her head. "You are the only other I have met."

"Many of us have assembled here to follow one who would unite our people."

Deirdre narrowed her eyes. "Who is this man?"

"No man, not even mortal. He who wears the amulet awaits us. Come with me to meet him and see for yourself."

Now Deirdre began to see. "He would be king?"

"Enough of this." Fingers like claws, Ula grabbed Deirdre's arm. "Come with me now and meet him. You will have your answers soon enough."

Truly curious, this time Deirdre went, allowing the other woman to lead at a brisk pace. She would not call Egann's name yet, not until she learned if she could retrieve the amulet without him.

It appeared they walked along a stone path, for that which sounded beneath her feet had the feel of the cliff ledges of her former home. After a moment, they rounded a corner and Deirdre could see that they indeed walked along a mountainous pass of some sort. Steep walls of smooth stone rose on either side. Below lay utter blackness, a deep pit. Ahead the ginger glow from the fires grew brighter, the air heavier with smoke.

Fire. Always would leaping flames remind her of the Maccus, monsters who killed for their murderous deity.

She tamped down her rising panic. Ula had mentioned other Shadow Dancers. Surely no Maccus would have been allowed to infiltrate the home of those they sought to destroy.

As they approached, the dancing fires provided more light. Now Deirdre could better see. The woman who pulled her along looked both the same and yet different than the elderly Shadow Dancer Egann had rescued. Her hair was still the color of milk, startling in this dim light because it seemed to glow. Many lines remained and deepened the skin around her mouth and eyes, proud symbols of her advanced age.

But the way she carried herself had changed. Where once she had walked with stooped shoulders and a bowed back, she now moved with her head held high and her shoulders straight. Her stride no longer seemed little more than a painful shuffle; rather she walked with the determined gait of a much younger woman. A woman with a purpose.

She was a woman who served the man with Egann's amulet. The servant of another who would be king. 'Twould be well of Deirdre to remember that.

Egann spun on his heel, ready to go outside and summon Weylyn, when a tiny mewing came from the bed. Deirdre's kitten poked its head up, bits of straw clinging to her tufted ears.

This gave him pause. When had the animal changed back from horse to cat? And how? Studying the small furry beast, he saw no answer. With a frustrated sigh, he reached down and scooped up the creature. Of course he must take it—he had no choice, not really. Deirdre would never forgive him if he left her pet.

Outside, Weylyn waited, as though he'd heard an unspoken summons. Rested, the sleek beast exuded power and strength.

Leaping on his steed's back, Egann retreated into his senses. To find the two Shadow Dancers would require even more skill than searching for his amulet. Which reminded him: the amulet had gone silent. He sighed.

Cinnie yowled, her sharp claws digging into his shoulder. With a shake of his head, Egann shifted the small cat so that she might rest on him more comfortably. 'Twould all be much easier were he to simply use his magic to travel, and so he would, once he had determined the direction they must go.

He sent out his mind to seek Deirdre. Surely it would not be so difficult to locate a tendril of her essence, a hint of her being? He could only hope she remembered to call his name so he could find her.

It took but a moment to find that which he sought. A faint flash of vision: cliffs, the sea, then darkness. Deirdre—one moment he sensed her, the next she vanished. Puzzling it was, but he would have answers soon enough.

He paused before working the spell, indulging in a moment of misery. It seemed he was forever doomed to fail those who trusted him. Even now, Deirdre's life was in danger because he had failed to protect her.

He thought of calling to Fiallan. The wise man had been like a father to him, his closest friend and greatest confidant. Yet how could he bear to see the look of disappointment that would surely come into the older man's eyes once he learned that Egann had failed someone yet again?

Twice now had Egann let his mentor and his people down. And Deirdre! Forever would he see the absolute trust shining in her ever-changing eyes as she gazed at him, forever would her words of confidence haunt him. She had become more important to him than he would have believed possible.

He turned Weylyn west, toward the coast, and began to speak the words of a spell to transport them there. He and Weylyn and Cinnie would go to the ocean, to the northern cliffs and caves so like Deirdre's home in the south. He hoped not too much mortal time would elapse while he was between worlds. He'd never tried to control time before, but to save his Shadow Dancer he must.

He *would* rescue her. In this, there was no room for failure. His life was bound up in the vows he'd made, and thus his life was bound to Deirdre's.

In the instant before he made the air begin to shift, Egann glanced at the sky. The moon, no longer merely a crescent, was half full. If he succeeded in controlling time, soon Deirdre would soon dance. He vowed to be with her when she did, and sent himself through time and space.

As usual, it took only a moment of his time, but he and Weylyn appeared on the coast with the sunrise. Shimmering into the sharp air of morning, Egann dismounted, freeing his faithful companion of bridle and saddle with a twist of his hands. Immediately, the great beast dropped on his side and rolled in the fragrant sea grass that grew along the tops of the rocky cliffs.

With a yowl, Deirdre's kitten leaped from Weylyn's discarded saddle, scampering over to join the other beast in the grass.

Watching them frolic, Egann pushed off his exhaustion. Though the Fae needed less rest than humans, the use of magic was taxing, and his body was weary. Yet he knew he could not afford to stop until he had found Deirdre and knew she was safe.

Here, with the air smelling of salt, and with the gulls wheeling overhead, the sense of her felt stronger. And, because she and Ula had to rest during the day, now would be the best time to seek her.

Crossing to the edge of the cliff, Egann saw that a rough path had been cut into its side. After glancing once more at Weylyn and the kitten, who still played in the tall grass, Egann took a deep breath and began his slow decent to the caves below.

"Maccus!" Recoiling in horror, Deirdre yanked her hand free from Ula's.

"Nay, child." The woman's long fingers clutched at Deirdre's arm. "Not Maccus. You must not allow terror to rule you."

"But . . ." Deirdre pointed, caring not that the other woman could see the violent trembling of her fingers. The acrid smell of smoke clogged her nostrils. Ahead burned a huge bonfire, flames leaping and blazing into the inky darkness. Hooded figures, wearing the telltale black cloaks of the Maccus circled the fire.

" 'Tis how the Maccus worship their god."

"Aye, but these men are not Maccus. They wear their hoods for warmth. And the bonfire brings warmth and light, nothing more," Ula soothed, still gripping Deirdre's arm. "There will be no sacrifices here. Come with me. You have much to learn."

Deirdre balked. "I do not think that I—"

"I have told you that you will have to make a choice. You will be allowed to choose. How can you do so if you do not know all?"

Deirdre's eyes stung in the smoky haze. Dizzy, she coughed, then shook her head, trying to clear it. She felt drugged. Something in the smoke . . . in the air . . .

"Let us go," Ula said.

This time, Deirdre allowed herself to be led forward, muzzily feeling her way on the uneven stone floor. As they drew closer to the bonfire, she saw a large gathering of people, both men and women. Some of them unquestionably wore the black robes of the Maccus.

Or did they? She looked again. She couldn't think—her mouth felt dry and her eyes unfocused.

243

"See, child." Ula's voice seemed to come from a great distance. "It is as I promised. You have nothing to fear."

Ula led her with unerring purpose through the throngs of people who parted for them as if they were royalty. Here, so close to the fires, the smoke took on a sickly sweet odor. Some sort of potent herb burned, some sort of drug that fouled the air. Most likely it was this that so clouded Deirdre's mind.

As she and Ula moved through the crowd, Deirdre took note of the people for, except in her dreams, never had she seen so many gathered in one place. Unlike her dreams, however, the colors these people wore—apart from their black cloaks— were muted, various shades of white, milk and cream, and moonstone.

They milled about, talking in voices too soft for her to hear their words, small clusters of them and the occasional couple. Some appeared to be arguing fiercely, heads bent low, arms around each others' shoulders in a secretive circle. Others stared dreamily into the fire, their vacant grins attesting to the potency of the burning drug.

Most glanced up as they passed. A few offered a slow smile of welcome; there came a nod of this one's head, a wave of that one's hand. All around were Shadow Dancers with hair as dark as midnight, hair like Deirdre's, or the brilliant silver that denoted great age like Ula.

Suddenly, Deirdre longed for Egann. What must he have thought when he went to wake her and found her gone?

A terrible ache filled her. She knew all too well what the proud Fae warrior would think. He would somehow believe her disappearance was due to some failing of his.

Would he search for her? Or would he be glad to be rid of her, free of the burden of keeping her safe from the sun?

Her heart hurt. Her chest hurt as well, from the smoke, and she found it increasingly difficult to inhale air into her sore lungs. Blinking rapidly, Deirdre took shallow breaths, hoping the air would be less tainted the farther they traveled away from the fire.

She was right. Once they'd left the fire and cavern behind, they traveled a narrow passage similar to the one they'd used to enter. Again lit on both sides by torches that flickered and cast dancing shadows on granite walls, it seemed to travel ever downward, into the very bowels of the earth. Here Ula stopped, releasing Deirdre's hand and turning her roughly so they faced each other.

"How much do you know of the heritage of our people?" Ula asked.

"I have learned of the curse and how it was misdirected on our people." Choosing her words carefully, Deirdre hesitated, waiting to hear how the other woman would respond.

"Truly?" Ula's white brows arched, indicating her surprise. "How came you to be so educated?"

For some reason, Deirdre felt reluctant to tell her of her association with Fiallan, Wise One of the Fae. Never having doubted her instincts before, she saw no reason to doubt them now. A bit of caution could not hurt, especially until she found out what Ula was up to. Instead of answering, Deirdre shrugged her shoulders, hoping her gesture indicated nothing more than confusion.

Ula's eyes narrowed in suspicion. "No matter," she said finally, her voice brusque. " 'Tis only recently that one of the Maccus came to us with a plan to regain our heritage."

"Maccus!" Recoiling, Deirdre took a step back. "Have you gone mad? The Maccus exist only to kill our kind."

"Not this one." The older dancer made no move to come after her, only watching with a serene smile on her lined face. "He has tired of the evil perpetuated by his kind and wishes only to return things to the way they should be."

Neither woman spoke, each eyeing the other. Deirdre tried to hide her distrust and fear. Beside them, the torches danced their wild dance, flames leaping in response to some unseen breeze.

"Come with me," Ula coaxed. "You have my word that you will not be harmed."

Deirdre lifted her chin, facing the other woman bravely. "Your word means little to me. I was not brought here of my own free will."

This time it was Ula who shrugged, though her tight-lipped smile belied her casual air. "You cannot go back, or the others will know you have not listened. The one you thought would protect you cannot find you here, for his magic cannot penetrate beneath the earth. Always has it been so. You are alone, though you do not have to be. Come with me to meet Hearne and hear his words."

Deirdre gasped. "Hearne? 'Tis the ancient name of the hunter god."

Ula nodded. "So? He is Maccus. Where once he hunted our kind, now he pursues only the truth."

"No!" The word slipped out before Deirdre could stop it. Ula was a fool if she believed that any of the Maccus wanted to help Shadow Dancers. For too many centuries they had pursued her kind, killing in a ritual sacrifice of fire and blood, paying homage to their red and angry god.

The flickering flames ceased dancing; the air was still and stifling. Glancing behind her, Deirdre tamped down her rising panic, wondering if she would ever again breathe the fresh air of spring.

"Then there is the amulet." Ula's tone was coaxing. "Hearne has the precious talisman."

The amulet. In her terror and drugged confusion, she had nearly forgotten. Now, with the air much clearer, she could think again.

"I will go with you," she said, deciding. "If you can give me your promise that I will be released if I determine that I want no part of this."

"If you do not wish to join us, that is your right." Ula smiled sadly. "But there are other Maccus who have not yet joined us. They still seek to kill all Shadow Dancers, and we cannot protect you from them."

Deirdre's heart sank. "By chance do these other Maccus wait here, for disbelievers to sacrifice?"

The older woman laughed. "Nay, worry not. We do not allow those killers to know of our secret home. Once you meet Hearne, you shall see and seeing, believe. I am confident of this.

Deirdre found it difficult to believe that this Hearne, a Maccus, had a sudden change of heart and no longer wanted his people to hunt Shadow Dancers—not when doing so was so deeply ingrained in every fiber, every being of the Maccus. 'Twas the reason for their existence.

"There are many Shadow Dancers here who have joined our cause," Ula said, her tone still cajoling.

"How many?"

"Hundreds."

Deirdre began to guess what this Hearne meant to do. Gather all Shadow Dancers with false promises and honeyed lies. Then, when he had them all assembled in their hundreds or thousands, he would call down his Maccus warriors and kill them all in one fell swoop. If he believed power could be garnered thus . . .

"Come now." Without waiting to see if Deirdre would follow, Ula moved away, down the stone corridor.

Yet . . . did this Hearne truly have the Amulet of Gwymyrr? Because she had to know, and because of those other Shadow Dancers she had seen, kept drugged and in a stupor by the potent herb in the smoke would be like lambs for a slaughter, Deirdre reluctantly followed.

The sun rose with a fiery presence, warming Egann's back as he made his way down the jagged rocks, finally reaching a small, sturdy ledge just above where the waves crashed over the stones below.

A few feet away he saw the cave mouth, a yawning black hole in the cliff face that surely filled with the rising of the tide. He stepped inside, taking a moment to let his eyes adjust to the dim light. There were two passageways. They were side by side with no markings to aid him in making a choice.

Closing his eyes for a moment, he went utterly still, his mind reaching, searching for the same hint of Deirdre's essence he had detected on the cliffs. It had been faint, an elusive trace carried on the salty breeze, but here he could find nothing.

Cinnie made a sound, a cross between a purr and a growl. Weaving between his legs, she went ahead, down the stone passageway to the right. At the first curve, the small kitten hesitated, looking back over her shoulder at Egann and mewing three times before disappearing.

Somehow, Deirdre's pet knew where to go. This way then, he would follow.

Though the sun now burned bright in the sky, once he had gone a few paces into the bowels of the cliff, it ceased to matter. The deeper he traveled, the less light he had to guide his way. Perpetual night reigned here. He stopped and used his magic to make a torch. It took three attempts to do so—strange in one as skilled as he, who could ordinarily do such minor magic with only a snap of his fingers. Most likely the arduous journey and days without rest had finally taken their toll.

Maneuvering the uneven passage became easier with the torch to light his way. Following the kitten, he made quick progress, noting the increasing chill and the faint smell of sulphur that tainted the air.

He sensed no other life, not even the small, furtive creatures that normally thrived in such caves. But Deirdre and Ula had passed this way, so their assailant must have taken them, for whatever reason, to some awful lair underneath the earth itself.

The silence became oppressive, and the stench of sulphur in the air most foul. Yet trusting Cinnie and that inner sense he believed implicitly told him his course was accurate.

He heard a faint sound, sharp, then gone so quickly that he might have imagined it. Rocking forward on the balls of his feet, he continued to move with the silent stealth of a hunter, though he dared not extinguish his torch and blind himself.

Then, again he heard it, a weak cry and the low murmur of many people talking all at once. Though Cinnie had led the way thus far, she came back to him and sat at his feet, tilting her furry head and appearing to listen.

Whatever created the sound, it lay farther down the passage, deeper in the earth.

He pressed on, Deirdre's small cat now trailing behind.

Rounding yet another sharp turn in the passage, he was surprised; though each step carried him deeper into the earth, he saw that the darkness here grew less absolute. Yet he could not determine the source of light.

It increased his sense of urgency. Yet, try as he might, he could not find Deirdre's essence. Mayhap magic did not work well underneath the earth's surface.

But, then, what created the light?

Placing his torch against the rock wall to burn harmlessly, he went ten paces ahead without it, around yet another twist and turn, and found he could see quite well. This was good, as his bright flare would have given away his presence if sentries or guards were posted by whatever manner of being lived in such a dark place as this. He continued on without his torch.

With each downward step the air seemed to grow more heavy, more foul. He smelled a faint sickly sweet scent—incense or an herb of some kind—and more bitter, acrid smoke. Then in the distance he saw the ominous glow of a huge fire, and his heart seemed to stop in his chest. Always now he equated the blaze of flames with the dark deeds of the Maccus and their blind devotion to their god of destruction. Fire had come to mean one thing: sacrifice and death for Shadow Dancers.

Deirdre!

Had it been Maccus who had somehow transported Deirdre here? Had they been able to increase their magical talent by so great a leap? Mayhap the amulet had aided them in this respect.

No matter how they had done it, if the Maccus had been the ones to bring the Shadow Dancers here, then Deirdre and Ula were in the greatest possible danger.

Chapter Fourteen

"Here," Ula hissed, her bony fingers digging into Deirdre's arm. "You will meet the one who has the power to change your life." Her intense gaze seemed to bore into Deirdre, as if by the force of a look alone she could compel belief.

The effects of the smoke-drug had by now totally worn off. Deirdre blinked and swallowed, her mouth dry. Fanaticism. Only once before had she witnessed such a thing. A woman in the village on the cliffs had once become obsessed with Shadow Dancing and the limited magic the dance created. This woman, not living under the curse that Deirdre did, had gathered a group together to try and force Deirdre into the sun. Luckily, she had not prevailed.

The power to change her life? This man Ula followed—this Maccus?—it seemed unlikely he would change her life in any way except to end it. And he gathered Shadow Dancers to him like moths to a dancing candle flame?

She could only think of one reason, one method of such wholesale seduction, and it chilled her blood.

A man stepped from the shadows, a sparkling pendant hanging heavy around his neck.

The Amulet of Gwymyrr!

Hand over her mouth, Deirdre stifled a cry of recognition.

Egann's missing talisman. Worn by a clever and ruthless wizard. Thief of dreams, evil murderer. *Maccus.*

She stared at the amulet. Even in the smoky light underground, its brilliant gemstones gleamed with radiant life. Its heavy silver chain lay flat against his broad chest, and his arms were easily twice the size of Deirdre's own. Hands clasped behind his back, he stood in a fighter's stance, legs spread apart and planted firmly on the hard ground. His golden hair was the same color as Egann's, yet duller. 'Twould appear that this Maccus was not only a warrior but Fae also.

Even where he was in the shadows, Deirdre could see that the man's eyes gleamed with lust—though not the ordinary sort a man had for a woman. Nay, this man thirsted for one thing: the power of the magic that the amulet had awakened in him.

'Twas this man who stood in the way of Egann's happiness. For a moment Deirdre saw the thunderous battle between the two of them, and knew fear for Egann and his people. Her stomach clenched.

"I would be king," he said softly, as though he responded to Deirdre's thoughts. "I am Hearne, and I wear without harm that which proves me rightful monarch of Rune."

"And of Earth." Stepping forward, Ula's expression seemed full of worship and awe. "Never before has one lived who could lead us to such glory and happiness."

Hearne acknowledged her comment with a regal nod, but watched Deirdre closely. "Know you the legend of how the Shadow Dancers came to be?"

Lifting her chin, Deirdre met his eyes calmly. "Yes, I do. And I also know how the Maccus arrived at their fate."

His expression darkened, but only for a moment. "Then you know it will take one man to right the grievous wrong done by our ancestors."

"You seek to remove the curse that has haunted the Shadow Dancers over centuries?" Disbelieving, Deirdre held herself utterly still. She would reveal as little of her thoughts to this man as she could.

"And to the Maccus." His arrogant tone rang in the stone-enclosed place. "Never forget how the Fae mistreated the Maccus."

Knew he not the true heritage of his own people? They were Fae themselves, only banished from their home that was Rune.

This time, Deirdre knew it would be wise to hold her tongue. This Hearne would not take kindly to the knowledge that she understood the truth behind his words. He sought only to restore the Maccus to the place of power they had once sought, so long ago when they had first brought battle against their brothers.

Ula spoke then, after a quick bow of her head in deference to Hearne. "It is because of the Fae that you are condemned to a life of darkness," she said, watching Deirdre with eyes that gleamed in the darkness. "So explain why you, knowing this, traveled with one of them, and he a prince of them besides."

"Egann is a good man." Quickly, Deirdre sought to turn the talk from words of fault. Though in a way, the older dancer was correct—it *had* been the

Fae who cast the misdirected spell. "Though I once blamed Egann for this as well, now I know Egann is blameless and the rightful king of Rune." There, she had spoken his name three times. He should have no difficulty finding her.

The smile Ula gave her seemed smug and full of self-importance. "Be that as it may, there are those who would see your prince fail." She darted a quick glance at Hearne, who nodded.

"Fail?" This Deirdre could not comprehend. "Fail at what? I do not understand."

"Enough," Hearne commanded. "Understand this, little dancer. Only here, under the earth, can you truly be free from the sway of the moon. Only here can you dictate when and why you dance, or even if you dance at all."

Nodding in agreement, Ula seemed to vibrate with excitement.

Control. So this was the bait they used to entice the Shadow Dancers to join the Maccus. It might seem tempting to some, for complete control of one's actions was the most basic sort of freedom, one that was denied to those who danced in the shadows.

But to never again have the faintest hope of one day seeing the sky? To never again see the night, stars winking like rare gemstones? What of the wind, the rain, and the tantalizing scent of fresh-mown hay?

"There is little difference," Hearne said, smiling matter-of-factly, as though her hidden thoughts had been spoken out loud, "from the life of darkness you must all live now, dancing at the bidding of others and the moon."

Deirdre tried a different question. She was curious to see how Hearne would answer. Part of her did not expect to hear him speak a word of truth, only a strange misshapen version of it. But there was one fact he had left out, something she wanted Ula to know. "Tell me this, then: Why do the Maccus hunt and kill Shadow Dancers?" With bated breath she wanted for his answer, for if he spoke true, Ula would know she and all the others were to die.

To her shock, Hearne seemed to find her comment amusing. "I thought you said you knew the truth of how Shadow Dancers came to be."

Striving to be calm, she spread her hands before her, indicating she did not know what to say. 'Twas the way of fanatics to twist what was real and shape their own truth, one that better served their own purpose, but she could not imagine what justification he would give.

"I would hear your account," she said, letting him know that she knew another version: the one that Fiallan had told her, the one that she believed.

With a dry chuckle, Hearne moved closer. He opened his mouth to speak, but Deirdre did not hear his words. The amulet had begun to sing. It was not a lament or a dirge this time, but an ecstatic call, full of excited welcome, the kind of joyous cry a wife might give when her husband has just returned from years away at war, and it completely drowned out the Maccus's speech.

The notes rang out, sharp and clear. They echoed off the stone walls, barely fading before the next one sounded. Ula made a shrill noise, a keening cry, and dropped to her knees, covering her ears.

Hearne's expression grew hard, his gaze full of fury.

Deirdre, whose heart had seemed so heavy, felt all her fear and worry lift. She recognized Egann's name in the cry of the amulet. The talisman sought to reach out, to find Egann, the rightful king and the only one truly meant to wear the silver chain and glowing gemstones.

She knew Hearne perceived this too.

Such a song could only mean one thing: Egann was near. Her heart leapt. He had found her. She closed her eyes and muttered a quick prayer of thanks to the Goddess.

Running with Egann, the small cat was something of a nuisance. She darted in front of him, tangling herself in his legs and causing him to slow his run to a walk. As he drew close to the roaring fire, Egann realized that he heard no screams of terror, saw no struggling between the people who gathered around the leaping flames. He slowed his pace and, still unnoticed, kept to the flickering shadows, one eye on the crowd.

Though some wore the black-hooded robes of the Maccus, none appeared to be currently worshipping or holding any arcane ceremony in honor of their red and angry god. Indeed, and Egann squinted at this through the smoky haze, Shadow Dancers mingled freely with Maccus. Small groups of them clustered in conversation; others appeared intent on the leaping flames, taking great gulps of the heavy smoke.

Something felt . . . wrong, though none of those gathered in the cavern seemed to notice or care. Perhaps he alone suffered. Perhaps it was the sensation of the weight of the entire earth, pressing heavy above and around him, that made him feel so uneasy. Surely none of these others felt, as he did, how unnatural it was to travel so deeply within the bowels of the world.

Then he heard it—the cry of the Amulet of Gwymyrr. At once the gathering throng went silent, their voices stilled by the eerie notes of the talisman's song.

261

He felt a tug of recognition. In the joyful call of welcome, he quite plainly heard his name.

Heedless of the watching crowd, he moved forward. Never so greatly had he wished he might wield a sword, or any iron weapon for that matter, the way a human warrior could. But he had his magic to protect him and, if indeed he faced the Maccus here, his opponents would be under the same constraints as he.

The amulet's song increased in volume and strength, causing many of the people he passed to drop to their knees, faces contorted in agony. He found it odd that such an exquisite sound could cause them pain, when to him it was a haunting song of overwhelming beauty.

The crowd fell back as he moved among it, unerringly following the musical notes. Deeper into the earth he went, leaving behind both bonfire and people. Flickering torches burned to light the path, but there were no guards to bar his way.

Now he felt the pulse of the amulet, the same throbbing beat he had felt before. Its voice seemed to urge him along, though he did not detect any warning of danger in the splendor of that echoing cry.

The amulet! Finally, 'twould seem the precious talisman was within reach!

Gradually, he became conscious of his surroundings. The slippery path he trod now became a stone bridge, linking the cavern he had left with another. Over a deep precipice he strode, Cinnie a few paces ahead on the narrow ledge. He took great care with his steps, glancing down only once and seeing nothing but a bottomless darkness.

The amulet fell silent. The quiet seemed absolute, except for the muted sound of Egann's careful footfalls. Finally stepping off the bridge onto the other side, he rounded a jagged corner and saw—Deirdre! She met his gaze, and he saw joy and fear and sorrow in her magnificent eyes.

She was not alone. Next to her stood Ula and another man, a massive warrior who, his golden hair swirling around his shoulders, wore the stolen Amulet of Gwymyrr around his thick neck.

At last. Everything he sought, all in one place!

Deirdre made a sound—a choked laugh or cry, he wasn't sure which. Though the sparkling amulet seemed to beckon him, Egann went to Deirdre first, letting his gaze roam over her until he was satisfied that she had come to no harm.

"My name is Hearne." The other man stepped forward, placing himself in the path between Egann and Ula. "I am the savior of these people."

Her gaze never leaving Egann's, Deirdre gave a slow shake of her head. "He claims that he gathers Shadow Dancers here, in the darkest bowels of the earth, to give them a chance at a new life." Her tone showed exactly how little she believed the man's boast.

"You do not gather them here to destroy them, as has always been the way of the Maccus?" Egann stared at Hearne, willing him to tell the truth.

The other man acquired a smug smile as he fingered the glittering amulet. "Now what would be the point of that?" he asked. "And, besides, are you just trying to scare them? Your people have certainly done nothing to help either the Shadow Dancers or the Maccus, these peoples you have cursed and banished. Thus, 'tis none of your concern, *Fae*." He made the word sound like a curse.

Egann shook his head. "We have failed in the past, but this *is* my concern. And you wear that which is mine by right." His low tone was, to those who knew him, deadly.

Hearne looked uncomfortable and tried to change the subject. "I would know how you found us."

There was a silence, then Cinnie mewed, drawing their attention. Giving a soft cry, Deirdre scooped up the kitten and cuddled it.

" 'Twas the cat who led this man to us," Ula hissed, stepping out from behind her leader. "It could not have been any other magic."

Egann did not comment. Instead, now that he knew Deirdre was in no immediate danger, he focused on the amulet. "Give me back the amulet, that which belongs to me by right of my birth," he ordered. He would allow this Hearne a choice, to surrender it peacefully or suffer the consequences. He did not want to continue unnecessary bloodshed, though it seemed as if all would end as it had been for ages, with Maccus against Fae.

Hearne's smile grew broader. "Your magic will not work down here. None does. I do not know the reason. Only the power of this talisman"—he lifted the heavy pendant as if to examine it, then let it drop back onto his chest, as though taunting Egann with his casual handling—"will allow one to use spells in this place."

Clenching his hands into fists, Egann took a step forward. "The Amulet of Gwymyrr is mine. It is my birthright."

Hearne laughed, a scornful sound, and continued to twirl the pendant so the gemstones shimmered in the dim light.

"If you have the amulet, why do you need the Shadow Dancers?" Egann exchanged a glance with Deirdre, who stood proud and unafraid. At the look of fierce resolve in her eyes, he knew an instant of sharp terror that she might do something reckless, something that would endanger her and cause her to lose her life.

"Why do I need the Dancers?" Hearne's voice rang out strong and certain. "With the sacrifice of one, the supplicant's power increases a hundred-fold. By sacrificing many, I shall be unbeatable."

At his words Ula let out a cry of bewilderment.

"You have been misled," Deirdre told her. "He means to kill you and all the others he has gathered in this place."

Ula looked from Deirdre to Egann, then once more to Hearne.

"Your words . . ." Her voice trembled. "Are they spoken with truth?"

Again Hearne laughed.

With a cry of rage Ula launched herself at him. Seeing his opportunity, Egann leapt forward. If he could hit Hearne at the same time as Ula, he could grab the amulet as Hearne fell to the ground.

But some invisible wall stopped him when he was yet inches from the other man.

A low growl, like the rumble of faraway thunder, came from Hearne. He moved his hands, the motions quick, and muttered words too low for Egann to hear.

A spell. And without his own magic, Egann did not know what kind, which words he might speak to counteract it.

The torches nearby sputtered, then flared bright. Deirdre screamed. Cinnie leaped from her arms with a frightened yowl. The fabric of the air around them shifted, whirled. Egann stepped forward.

But Deirdre no longer stood beside him. Instead, she dangled from the edge of the bridge, her hands clawing for purchase on the crumbling stone, her legs swinging over the bottomless chasm.

"She will die if she falls," Hearne said softly, almost conversationally, once again lifting the Amulet of Gwymyrr and admiring its sparkle. Then he removed the heavy chain from around his neck, holding the sparking pendant before him like a lure. "If you had to choose, Prince of Rune, which would it be—the amulet or the woman?"

Egann's heart began to pound. He spoke a spell of his own, a summoning spell that should have raised Deirdre up from the rock edge to safety, but nothing happened. No movement, no shimmering. Nothing. Hearne's warning had been correct.

One of Deirdre's hands lost its hold, the unstable rock of the bridge giving way. Immediately she clutched at another stone, scrabbling to get a grip. A low moan sounded from deep within her throat as her terror-filled gaze met Egann's.

He gave nothing else any thought. In three strides he reached her, taking hold of her wrist and pulling her to safety. She collapsed against him, her shuddering breath coming in gasps. Wrapping his arms around her, Egann held her tightly, ignoring all possible danger and relieved by the solid, soft feel of her body.

Again the air altered, parted. Egann did not need to turn to know that the other man had fled, and with him had gone the Amulet of Gwymyrr. But turn he did, keeping Deirdre close to him, simply to see who and what remained. Only Ula stood where before there had been two.

"Rodan's teeth," Egann swore. So close he could almost reach out and touch it, the amulet had once again been snatched from his clutches.

"I should have grabbed it." Deirdre moved restlessly against him, lifting her head to give him a sorrowful look.

"We will find it again." Egann dipped his head and kissed her. As always, she went soft and pliant at his touch. "You are safe. That matters most."

Her eyes widened in surprise, and he saw that they had changed color again. In their rich, dark mahogany, he saw an absolute trust mingled with desire. And he wondered at his own words.

But he wanted to drink her in, absorb her, inhale her. His concentration should have been on the missing amulet, but he wanted only to think of her.

"Are you all right?" he asked.

"I think so." With a hesitant smile, she looked beyond him to the place where Ula waited alone and silent, looking somehow beaten. "And you?"

He felt his shame retake him. "The amulet was within my reach." In his voice he heard the bitterness mingled with rage. "Once again, I have let it slip away."

"This Hearne has discovered how to use it."

Deirdre's words, half questions, only increased his unhappiness. "Apparently so," he said. "And he has drawn upon its power to keep him hidden by magical means. I cannot follow him or find him from here, for it seems my magic deserts me in this dark place."

"I am sorry." She stepped away from him, slipping free of his arms and making him feel a momentary sense of loss. Then she blamed herself: " 'Twas my fault that you lost the talisman yet again."

"Do not take this burden upon yourself." The fierceness of his tone surprised even him. "Instead, tell me what you know of this one called Hearne."

"Wait." Ula moved forward, fierce resolve showing in her lined face. "You must know that Hearne would never have hurt you," she said to Deirdre, her gaze bright and full of ardent belief. "He would not hurt any of us. It was merely a test."

"A test." The grim set of Deirdre's mouth matched her clipped, hard words. "Believe what you must. But tell me this, Ula, since you seem to love this Hearne and know him well. Why did he not stay and fight? Where did he go?"

With a lift of her shoulders, the older woman held out her hands, palms up, to indicate that she did not know. "He travels where he pleases, out into the bright light of day where I cannot go."

Egann sensed Deirdre's mounting anger. "We must leave this place, too." He took a deep breath, trying to ignore the acrid scent of burning herbs in the foul air. "I like it not. Come, Deirdre. Let us find another path from here up to the world above."

Immediately she moved to his side and took his hand. "We have already stayed here overlong," she agreed.

Ula let out a screech. "You fool," she spat. "You would leave the one place where you can be normal!"

"Normal?" Deirdre looked around, and Egann knew she was indicating the flickering torches, the slick dampness of the stone walls, and the rank, stale air they breathed. "How can you say *this* is normal? You cannot ever see the velvet night of the sky, or smell the seasons on the breeze. You are trapped worse here than the moon ever trapped us."

If she heard the logic in Deirdre's words, Ula gave no sign. Just as she seemed inclined to disbelieve that which she'd heard with her own ears—Hearne's plans to massacre her own people—she could not see the wrongness in this place.

"Go then." Scorn rang in Ula's voice. "You alone will remain condemned to walk in darkness, while we who believe shall be allowed to move freely in the bright light of day."

Shaking his head, Egann motioned to Deirdre that they must leave. It was obvious the other woman remained under the sway of whatever spell Hearne had placed upon her.

"We can do nothing if she does not wish our help," he said.

Cinnie hissed, drawing their attention. The kitten took a few steps down another passage, then sat and waited.

"Your pet has found the way out," Egann said to Deirdre. " 'Twas she who led me when I could not find you. Gladly will I follow her." Together, Egann and Deirdre moved past Ula and away.

They saw none of the others in the new passage that led up. No one stepped forward to challenge them. Climbing steadily, they soon reached the original passage that connected to the large cave inside the cliff where Egann had first made entrance. The salty scent of the sea became stronger, seeming to refresh Deirdre, who had begun to droop with fatigue. Cinnie wound herself around their legs, purring softly as Deirdre reached down to scratch her.

"Tell me," Deirdre asked. "Why did Cinnie change into a kitten again? I thought she would stay a horse with Weylyn."

Egann found himself grinning. "Your small pet has been a blessing—but I know not why or how she changed her shape without my help."

Deirdre nodded, swaying on her feet. When she turned her mahogany gaze on him, he saw that she was troubled.

"What of the others?" she asked. "Never have I met more of my own kind. Seeing so many gathered below the earth, following this Hearne so blindly, worries me. It pains me to think that this man might cause them all death."

"They have chosen their own path," Egann said. "We must remember that we can only take responsibility for own well-being. However, if there is a way to save them, I will do it."

As he spoke, he realized it was yet another promise, another oath. Another burden for the man who once had been unwilling to commit to anything. Egann passed his hand over his eyes, considering. The crippling fear of failure that had so haunted him since Banan's death seemed curiously faded now, with Deirdre gazing up at him with such unshakable confidence.

"Wait." Realizing that he still held her hand, he released it and pointed to a large boulder she could use as a seat. "Let me go up first and determine if the sun rules the sky or the moon."

"Nay," she protested, grabbing for his hand again. "I do not wish to be parted from you again."

He placed a quick kiss on the top of her head. "I will not be long. 'Tis only that I do not wish to endanger you. When I entered this place it was day."

She lifted her chin with that stubborn resolve he had begun to recognize. "I will go with you."

"Deirdre—"

"I will not remain here without you. Not when I can travel a little farther without danger."

Shaking his head, Egann gave in. "I see I have no choice. Very well, we will go together. But if sunshine lights the interior of the cave, we shall find you a place in these passages to rest."

A look of surprise crossed her delicate features. "I have not rested since I came here," she said with wonder.

Reaching out, he brushed back her hair from her cheek. "Then you must be exceedingly weary."

She pursed her lips, making him want to kiss her. "Weary? Nay, I cannot say that I am tired."

She lied, and Egann wasn't sure why. Was she trying to be strong for him? Did she simply want to be free of this place?

"Time does not pass so quickly down there," she added.

"This I can believe," he said. He kept his face expressionless with difficulty. She was brave, this woman, and he would not dishonor her by forcing her to rest.

"Tell me," she said as she moved closer. "Does the moon wax now or wane?"

Reluctantly, he told her. "The last time I looked at the sky, the moon was half full and on her way to ripeness."

She nodded, her face set.

They began to walk again, she at his side, and he tried to match his much-longer stride to hers. With each turn they rounded, he expected to see sunshine, but still it seemed dark, as though the sun had set long ago.

At last they stood in the big rock cavern where Egann had first gained entrance to the underground world.

"I do not feel the painful sting in my eyes that tells me the day has dawned," Deirdre said, her voice breathless with exertion.

"It was sunrise when I arrived here," he repeated, wondering how it could be that he had remained underneath the earth for so long without realizing. "But this is good, for if you are not too weary, let us go to the top of the cliff. I must summon Fiallan. There is much I need to discuss with him."

Together they climbed the cliff, Egann keeping below Deirdre so that if she lost her grip and fell, he might catch her. When they reached the top, Deirdre stood a few paces apart from him, her face to the sea, breathing deeply of the salt-tinged air, the moonlight streaking silver on her hair.

Egann too breathed deeply, sought to clear his mind of thoughts of her lush body, silhouetted by moonlight. He felt his magic, returned in full strength and surging through his blood, and he did not wish to cloud it with his desire. The amulet—he focused on it, emptying his mind of all else.

Still, there were questions he must ask, answers he needed to know. He had to summon Fiallan, and as he spoke the first words of the spell to do so, he felt the ripple and swirl of the power within him.

In a shimmer of lights, Fiallan appeared. His white robe seeming to glow, he stood between Deirdre and Egann. He did not speak, unusual for him, but rather folded his arms across his chest and watched Egann with all the ferocity of a hawk about to swoop down on an unsuspecting hare.

Before Egann could speak, he and Deirdre heard the pounding of hooves, and Weylyn appeared at the top of the bluff, moving gracefully toward them. Still in the form of a small kitten, Cinnie rode upon the larger beast's shoulder, yowling in greeting. Neither he nor Deirdre had noticed that Cinnie had left them.

Weylyn slid to a stop in a cloud of dust and nickered.

"Thank you, my friend," Deirdre said, "for taking care of any small pet." After softly stroking

Weylyn's head, Deirdre reached up and took Cinnie, gathering the cat close to her chest.

"You have called for me?" No surprise sounded in Fiallan's voice, but rather a kind of caution.

"I have need of your wisdom." Egann swallowed, conscious of the enormity of the question he wanted to ask. " 'Tis time for you to tell me the truth. What fate would befall our people were I to fail to retrieve the Amulet of Gwymyrr?"

Chapter Fifteen

Deirdre stood frozen in shock, hardly daring to believe her ears. "Not retrieve the amulet?" she echoed. "But we—"

Egann scowled, his expression fierce as he met her gaze. "We are no closer than we were when this began. Hearne could lead us on an eternal chase, for it already looks as if he has learned to channel some of the amulet's magic."

Slowly, she raised her gaze to meet his. "Truly, would you leave a Maccus in control of such a powerful talisman? One who wants only to destroy my people?"

"Of course not." He glared at Fiallan over Deirdre's head. "I am well aware that such a thing must not be done. However, the Wise One agreed to seek another to become King of Rune. I ask now, has this new king been found?"

Fiallan said nothing, only stood with the proud, stiff posture of a very old dignitary, the expression in his faded eyes unreadable.

"I would have an answer, my old friend." Folding his massive arms in front of him, Egann faced the sage.

"I too would hear this answer," Deirdre said, coming forward so she stood at Egann's side. If her instincts were correct, Egann would not find the Wise One of Rune's reply palatable.

"I think you already know what I will say." An eternity of sorrow lay in Fiallan's quiet voice. "When you traveled under the earth, you'd lost your greatest ally, then your greatest strength. But because you are strong, you managed to regain both of them. You are our chosen champion and our rightful king. 'Tis impossible for me to believe that you would walk away from the need of your people."

Egann recoiled, taking a step back as if the old man had slapped him. "This is not the same," he said, passion making his ardent tone ferocious. "If another has been found, I ask that he step forward to take up the quest. Hearne and his kind threaten Deirdre and her people. I have given her my oath to protect her. How can I do both? If I continue on this quest, she is put in direct danger. She could be hurt or killed. And I do not want another life to be lost because of my actions."

An awful ache bloomed in Deirdre's chest. "This is because of me?" she whispered. "You would abandon your search for this reason?"

Egann ignored her, continuing to watch the older man, who remained stubbornly silent.

Fiallan looked at Egann, then spoke. "Your Shadow Dancer has a role to play. She must accompany you in this quest. That is how it must be."

Deirdre closed her mouth and bowed her head. Because of her dreams, she'd suspected this. And, truth be told, she was glad; she was not yet ready to let her prince go.

"Tell me the truth—exactly how strong is the amulet?" Egann demanded, frustration plain upon his chiseled features. "It seems to me that if this Hearne has learned to use its powers, he would be able to wreak more havoc. Perhaps the amulet is not as powerful as you think." He stared at Fiallan then grew quiet. "If Hearne and his kind master its magic, what will become of Rune?"

"What do you think?" Fiallan roared, his slight frame shaking with emotion. "We would have another war on our hands, Maccus against Fae. Even the humans would be dragged into it again. Is that what you want?"

Egann narrowed his eyes. Deirdre could almost feel the irritation rolling off him.

"All I know of the amulet is from legends and stories you have told me." His mouth curved in a bitter smile. "Never have I asked for much, other than the right to live my life in a way that hurts no one. Yet you insist on placing the weight of the world upon my shoulders. Have a care, old one. I will only allow myself to be encumbered for so long—especially when I know your wishes in this."

At Egann's statement, Deirdre looked from one man to the other, not in confusion, but with dawning awareness. "Is this all a game to you?" she asked the older man. Then she allowed her gaze to rake over the prince as well, including both men in her fierce question. "I begin to think Egann and I are both but pawns in some master plan of yours, moving about at your whim."

To her surprise, Fiallan gave a slow smile. "Don't you realize what is at stake?"

The knowledge did not come to her in a bright flash of blinding revelation, the way she might have expected, had she any expectations at all; the realization came slowly, as she saw the pain-tinged pride in Fiallan's golden eyes, as he waited for

Egann, the man he plainly regarded as a son, to accept his destiny.

Judging from the quiet fury in his clenched jaw, Egann had no immediate plans to accept any such thing.

Stepping forward, Deirdre placed a hand on Fiallan's pristine white sleeve. "If this task truly is so important, can you not aid us somehow, more than you have?"

The Wise One shook his head before she even finished speaking. "A king is forged by his choices," he said, giving her a long look. "And I was never one to interfere. However, I will tell you this." He fixed Egann with a piercing stare. "You have less than a fortnight to find the amulet. Before the full moon disappears from the sky, you must bring the Amulet of Gwymyrr home."

"But—" Before Deirdre could ask anything further, Fiallan disappeared, leaving her clutching at empty air.

"By the balls of Ronan," Egann swore, his eyes full of anger. She wanted to go to him, to somehow comfort him, but before she could move he cursed again and strode away, leaving her with the sound of the sea and the wind, and the familiar night sky, empty except for the stars winking like snowflakes overhead.

* * *

He had spoken truth to Fiallan: never had he asked for this. Indeed, by leaving Rune he'd sought to avoid the crushing responsibility that was the role of king. But now . . . now . . . He clenched his fists, wishing he could laugh but knowing if he did he just might go mad.

According to Fiallan, the fate of Egann's entire race rested on whether he could retrieve the amulet—not to mention Deirdre's precious life and the ever-present threat to all Shadow Dancers of death at the hands of the Maccus. And he had the dancer's terrible curse, that of forbidden sunlight, to deal with as well.

Yet, even as the weight of such duty threatened to devastate him, he knew that despite his attachment to Fiallan or Deirdre, he still had a choice. He could still walk away, let them find some other man to become their defender.

He could . . . but, of course, he would not. Always had this been his greatest fault and, truth be told, the true reason he had declined the throne. He cared too much. Thus, the possibility of failure, acceptable in others, would devastate him. As it had when his beloved brother had perished.

His people should have chosen a better champion.

Dragging his hand through his hair, Egann stared at the silver moon above. It seemed his refusal to assume the throne of Rune had set into motion a series of events that conspired to keep him exactly where he didn't want to be.

"I am sorry." Deirdre's soft voice behind him made him turn. She came to him, wrapping her arms tightly around his middle, resting her head over his heart.

As he held her, he realized that by allowing himself to wallow in self-pity and doubt, he wasted time and energy. Both would be better spent finding the blasted amulet and putting an end to this Hearne and the man's evil plans.

Smoothing her hair back with his hand, he released his breath in a great sigh. "I have promised you that no matter the cost, I shall stop the Maccus, so that no more Shadow Dancers will die at their hands."

"Yes," she whispered, her voice muffled against his chest. "But now the amulet helps them hunt us, though Hearne must not have mastered all of its power, or he would have fought us rather than flee."

Shame filled him then, shame that he had momentarily allowed his uncertainty to rule him, to make him weak. He would not do so again.

"Deirdre." He spoke her name with hesitation, wondering how it could be that she still believed in him.

She lifted her head, meeting his questioning look with one of pure trust, the dove-gray of her eyes glowing with it.

"Your eyes are . . ." he began.

"Another color?" She smiled up at him. "Yes, I know."

The sweet curve of her mouth distracted him, and he became conscious of the way the soft arch of her body pressed against him. He felt his own flesh stir, and by the darkening of her pupils he knew she felt it as well.

"Not yet," he cautioned, when she made to rub against him, much like her small kitten would. "There is much I must say to you."

Still smiling, she made a small sound and stood on her toes to touch her lips to his. "No, there is not," she whispered against his mouth, before giving him another sweet kiss. "Words are only that—mere words. I do not need to hear you speak them. I trust you," she said.

His chest swelling with unfamiliar emotion, he captured her lips, his blood thickening with desire. She moved seductively against him, and he felt his manhood swell and harden.

From the tall grass, Weylyn nickered a reminder. Cinnie echoed it, telling them that she had once again changed form. Neither of them paused to wonder how. Reluctantly, Egann pulled away. Placing one last kiss on Deirdre's soft mouth, he took her hand. "We *must* move on while the darkness still holds. The sooner we find Hearne and

the amulet, the better advantage we will have—
the less likely he is to have discovered more how
to use it."

With a soft sigh, she nodded. "How will we find
him, when he has the talisman's magic to hide him
and can travel about at will?"

"Like attracts like." Lifting his hand, Egann
called Weylyn to him with a gesture. The huge
beast ambled over, Cinnie following. He laid a
hand on the horse's thick neck. " 'Tis time to send
you home to Rune, my friend. Cinnie, do you wish
to travel with him? You will likely regain your true
form once you arrive."

Deirdre made a sound of protest, and Cinnie the
horse went to her, butting her gently with a shaggy
head. Wrapping her arms around Cinnie's furry
neck, Deirdre gave a fierce and quick hug. "You
have my leave," she said. "If this is what you want,
go."

Both horses nickered.

Egann muttered the words to begin the spell of
sending. The telltale shift in the atmosphere lasted
but a moment; then Weylyn and Cinnie shimmered and vanished.

Deirdre turned away, but not before Egann saw
the sadness in her expression.

"Your changeling will be fine," he said, knowing
he must not attempt to comfort her, not as long

as the fierce desire for her still simmered in him, barely under control. "Weylyn will take her to roam the plains of Morthar, and together they shall hunt."

"I know. I believe you that she will be fine." When she turned back to face him, she wore a determined smile on her lovely face. "What now?"

"We go forward. The moon is past her first quarter." He pointed to the silver crescent, which still hung above them in the middle of the sky. "It will be less than eight days before she swells with fullness."

The look Deirdre gave him was bleak. "That means soon I will begin to hear her call."

"Aye."

She shivered, maybe because the night air had become cool. "How will we travel?"

Taking a deep breath, Egann gathered himself, centering the energy that hummed inside of him. "By magic, of course. The elements of secrecy and surprise no longer matter. Hearne expects us to follow, and I believe he is the only one we need consider."

He held out his hand for her. "Come, we must return to Tintagel. There is a place of magic along its rocky coast. There, I believe, we shall find Hearne and the Amulet of Gwymyrr."

Deirdre was pleased they would remain along

the sea coast; after all, it was a place where she felt at home and thus safer than anywhere else in Britain. Still, she had always trusted her dreams and felt it her duty now to remind Egann of them.

"Do not forget the cave I saw when I slept," she said quietly. "Though after going underground I cannot bear the thought of it, that cave is where I dreamed I saw the amulet."

"Hearne." The tensing of his jaw revealed Egann's animosity toward the other man. "I believe I know the cave of which you speak—it lies up the coast near Tintagel. Long has it been a place of great power. Perhaps Hearne has traveled there. Certainly from this cave, I believe he has stayed deep under the earth."

The mere thought made Deirdre shudder. "Under the earth," she repeated.

Egann shrugged. " 'Tis possible. We shall go and find out." She took his hand, sliding her fingers into the warmth of his much larger grip.

Then, with the now familiar disorientation and shifting of gravity, he invoked his magic, and they went.

As always, the journey took but a second; Deirdre closed her eyes and let the sweep and swell of the magic claim her, her one connection to reality the comfort of Egann's big hand. When she opened her eyes and took a deep breath, her first thought was that the air smelled the same, heavy with moisture, and that the same salt-scented wind blew. But then she heard a hum, resonating from the rocky earth beneath her feet, and she realized that Egann had spoken true. They were in a new place. Magic resided here indeed, and if the presence of it was great enough for one such as she, a mere mortal, to discern, then most likely Hearne had detected it as well.

The sharp screech of a gull drew her from her thoughts, and she became conscious of Egann watching her.

"Are you prepared?" he asked.

At first the question seemed strange, and she opened her mouth to tell him so. But then she thought of the enormity of the task before them and contented herself with a tiny nod of agreement. "I am ready," she told him, letting her gaze travel the stark planes that made up his beloved face. "But one thing remains that I would like to know."

He raised one golden brow as he waited for her question.

"I know he has the amulet and that he covets its magic. And I realize he wants to lead an army of Maccus into Rune, to overcome the banishment. But what does Hearne truly want with the Shadow Dancers? Surely he does not believe their deaths will feed his power."

" 'Tis my belief that he simply seeks the most efficient method by which to end the lives of all of that race." His blunt answer only confirmed her own suspicions. "He gathers them in one place, a place where they believe they are safe, so that they will be easy to kill. He will destroy you all in one fell swoop."

"But why?" Stubbornly she persisted. "I would know the truth. Why does he want to kill my people all at once? Hearne has said that by doing so, his power will increase, but I don't believe it. What do the Maccus truly gain by sacrificing an entire race to their red and angry god?"

"Power." Egann's clipped tone told her he found the notion repellent. "For Hearne and his kind believe what he told you—when a Shadow Dancer dies this way, the one who offers the sacrifice will absorb that soul's magical power."

"Is it true?"

He met her gaze unblinking. "It is possible. No one of Fae knows for sure, as we do not kill. Until Hearne began to control the Maccus, there has never been one so evil to try."

Horrified, Deirdre could only stare. "So Hearne thinks by exterminating so many all at once, he will—" The thought was so awful she could not finish, and she found herself blinking back tears.

"We must stop him," she said.

Egann's fierce smile told her he meant to do just that.

With her hand still gripped tightly in his, Egann led her down the rocky path. The area appeared deserted, the savage spray of the surf pounding the jagged rocks below. With a quick glance up, she noted the slow descent of the moon in the still-dark sky.

"Worry not, little dancer." Egann's voice was meant to soothe. "Once we enter the cave, you will be well protected from the sunrise."

She squeezed his hand in answer.

Not until they arrived at the mouth of the cave did she hesitate, remembering the acrid smoke and stale air underground, and the terror and blackness.

" 'Tis of here that I dreamed," she told him. "Yet because of the other place, I fear to enter."

"Worry not, for this cave will not be like the other," Egann promised. "This is a place of great magic, but also of truth. Long have the men of my people traveled here when the need to be alone become overwhelming. This cave is for meditation, the inward seeking of insight. You will find naught of the other place here, the only unease will be the minor disturbance caused by Hearne on his passage through."

"You do not think he remains?" Though she tried to keep the fear from her voice, she heard its uncertain quaver and sighed.

"Nay, not here in the entrance." Egann sounded certain, calm and sure and fierce. "One such as he, with so much evil inside him, would not like the way this cave encourages one to look within oneself. He will have moved on, gone deeper into the dragon's lair, seeking the answers to his questions about the amulet."

Deirdre heard only one word. "Dragon?"

Egann laughed, the sound half-swallowed by the roar of the sea. "A dragon of ancient times. It no longer exists, at least not here in this world. That particular dragon was hunted by men and killed over one hundred years ago. But this cave is the entrance to his old home—a deeper, more mystical place farther below. 'Tis there I believe we will find Hearne."

"But magic is suspended so far beneath the ground."

"Aye." Egann's voice was grim. "And Hearne has the amulet."

When they reached the uneven sand of the short beach they stopped, facing the towering cliff. Because the moon was not full and provided limited light, she could not make out the shape of the cave in the dark face of the rocky wall.

"It is there," Egann assured her, seeming again to have read her mind. "Worry not. We will find it, for already I sense the amulet's presence."

Deirdre listened, hoping to hear again the sweet sound of the amulet's song of welcome. She heard nothing but the crash of the waves, the screech of the gulls, and the empty howl of the wind as it battered the sea.

"Will the amulet sing again?" she asked, pushing away the odd flash of wild sorrow that stabbed her.

"Perhaps." He sounded doubtful. "While the residue of its magic lingers, something is missing. Somehow the amulet does not seem as strong as before."

"How is such a thing possible?"

He hesitated, his gaze distant as he stared up the hulking shadow of the cliff. "Perhaps the cave has had a negative effect on the amulet's magic."

Watching him, Deirdre worried her bottom lip between her teeth. "Tell me more of this cave."

Egann made a sound, a short bark of laughter or some other, more feral noise. " 'Tis known in both our worlds, yours and mine. Many say this place belongs to Myrddin."

"I have heard the name," she admitted. "Once, a bard traveled to my home and sang of this wizard."

"Aye." Egann's face might have been carved from the same black stone as the cliffs, so grim did his countenance appear. "The magic that he made here remains so powerful, that—"

An otherworldly shriek, rising and falling rapidly in pitch, issued forth from the dark mouth of the cave. 'Twas both human and inhuman, terrible and terrifying. It rose with the wind, an awful howl that quickly, as abruptly as it had begun, fell silent.

"What was that?" Deirdre gasped.

"Come." Egann grabbed her hand, pulling her at a cautious run toward the cave. "Something bad has happened to the amulet, as well as to the one who wrongly wears it. We can only hope we are not too late."

At the base of the cliff Egann pulled her to a stop. Cupping her chin in his hand, he kissed her mouth hard. "As I started to tell you earlier, my people have made it law that only males of our people may enter the Cave of Myrddin."

"Why?" She cocked her head inquisitively while she tried to catch her breath and waited for him to finish.

He met her gaze, his own expression grim and unreadable.

"The cave gives truth and some cannot bear it. It must be worse for Fae women too. Only a few times can I remember when one was unwise enough to attempt to enter."

"What happened to them?"

"They went mad," he said, his tone flat. "Each and every one."

Chapter Sixteen

"But you are mortal," Egann continued. "And mortals do not have magic shimmering in their blood. So you will be safe."

He had just wanted to warn her, not to scare her, so he was gratified when Deirdre simply nodded, lifted her chin and asked a simple question.

"Why? What made the women go insane and not the men?"

He glanced up to the yawning mouth of the dark cave. No more sounds issued forth; rather an ominous silence had fallen.

"I do not know," he admitted. "Though men find truth and wisdom inside, 'tis said the cave speaks differently to women. Some say it is the unbroken darkness, the sense that the walls narrow and close in. Others mention the voices of the past that are said to echo in eternal whispers from within the stone itself. No one knows for certain, as the poor victims were never coherent enough to tell. It is something to do with magic and what is feminine. I just wanted you to be prepared, aware, so that you can protect yourself if need be."

Still watching him, she shrugged. "Worry not. I do not think this can be worse than that foul place under the earth where Ula took me." Bravado and confidence sounded in her husky voice, and again Egann found himself full of pride. She had an uncommonly brave spirit, this mortal woman of his, and he longed to kiss her yet again. He did not, though. Kissing Deirdre made him forget everything else.

He felt himself harden. Her own quick intake of breath told him that she felt his arousal pressing against her. Her nipple pebbled beneath his hand, begging for his touch. Mindless with desire, he cupped her full breast with one hand, stroking, kneading.

She moaned into his mouth and writhed against him. As he considered making love to her, plunging himself into her, standing there in the sand at the base of the cave, another shriek, sudden and sharp, issued forth from the cave entrance above.

He jerked himself away, stumbled backwards in the shifting sand.

"Come. Hold fast to my hand," he instructed. "No matter what you see or hear, do not let go."

Pulling on her hand, they made their way carefully up the slippery steps carved in stone and wet with ocean spray. Once again the air had gone silent, and Egann felt once more the overpowering pull of the Amulet of Gwymyrr.

"But the cry of the amulet grows faint," he mused out loud.

They stood on a small, smooth ledge of rock, mere feet from the entrance to the cave.

"I do not hear the song, neither its lament nor cry."

He shook his head. "Neither do I. But I sense something, a slight residue of magic." Glancing once more at Deirdre, he squeezed her hand. "Are you ready to go within?"

She gave a wordless nod, her perfect pale face a study in determination, the ever-present moonlight giving her an alabaster glow.

Egann forced himself to concentrate on the task in front of them. "Remember what I have told you. No matter what you see or hear, do not let go of my hand."

A sudden gust of wind brought ocean spray, gently misting her face. "The tide comes in," she said, licking her lips. "What if it rises so much that we are trapped within this terrible cave?"

"It will not." He spoke with more confidence than he felt. For an instant he wished that things could have the simplicity of childhood games, or of a story book. How much easier life would be if he could simply say the words to a magical spell and draw the amulet to him.

"I see," she said. He saw her swallow hard; then she set her jaw in that stubborn line he had come to know so well. The expression, despite the possible danger that lay ahead, made him smile.

Into the ringing silence they stepped, their footsteps echoing on rock. Just inside the small stone opening, the darkness was not yet immediately absolute; 'twas similar to the other cave in that. Egann could see well enough to determine that there was only one passage leading forward, this one most likely borrowing even deeper into the bowels of the earth.

He could feel the ancient vibration of magic, the thrum of deep-rooted power. So strong was it that he felt off-balance, uneasy and uncertain, for he could not tell if this energy came from good or from evil. But he could tell that it was to this place Hearne had brought the Amulet of Gwymyrr.

With Deirdre holding fast to his hand, they began their descent. The chill in the air grew more pronounced before they had even gone a few feet, and around the first turn. The light vanished, enveloping them in darkness. 'Twould be slow going in the total dark, but the sloped path was smooth and even. There was only one direction they could go, so finding their way seemed a simple enough task.

"I cannot even see my hand in front of my face." Deirdre sounded peevish. "I like this not."

"Soon it will be better," Egann soothed, though he knew not if he spoke truth. " 'Tis not so bad really, and the faint pull of the amulet tells me we travel in the right direction."

Deirdre sighed but said nothing more, only clutched his hand and kept pace with his cautious stride.

Naught appeared out of the ordinary; indeed, Egann found he enjoyed a quiet that was broken only by the soft sound of their footfalls. He might have even relaxed the slightest bit, had he not heard Deirdre's startled gasp and felt her hand tremble.

Madness comes to all Fae women foolish enough to enter the Cave of Myrddin. The knowledge began to worry him. But that only applied to women of his kind. Deirdre was mortal, and therefore would have naught to worry about on that score.

"What is it?" His whisper sounded loud.

She did not answer at first, though her breathing had become harsh and rapid. He pulled her closer, wishing he had a torch or some other kind of light so that he might see her face.

"What *is* this thing?" She moved, giving him the impression that she swatted at the air with her other hand. "Why does it swirl around me, insubstantial as mist, yet solid enough for the faintest of teasing touches?"

"I do not feel it," he said. Her remark troubled him further.

"It tortures me, touches me," she said, her voice bleak. "I would give much to be able to see it."

Egann began to be afraid for her. What had he done, bringing her down here? He increased their pace, not sure if they could simply outrun this wraith or spirit that apparently sought to drive Deirdre mad, but knowing he had to try. She kept pace with him, the harsh gasps of her breathing sounding to his ears both sexual and frightening at the same time—which disturbed him even more.

Deep within the earth they traveled. Unlike the other caves, this stone passage did not widen into cavernous chambers. Rather, it seemed to continue in an unerring line ever downward, its blackness absolute.

Deirdre moaned, and Egann felt a different form of alarm. Was this what had driven those Fae women mad? The sounds Deirdre made spoke of some kind of strange suffering, though she continued to move with him, keeping pace at his side. Her hand, while occasionally twitching, was still firmly within his grip.

"Egann, make it stop." Her request came a harsh whisper, pleasure and pain mingled as one in her smoky voice.

"What is it that you wish me to stop?" he asked. Should he scoop her up in his arms and simply carry her? Perhaps that would afford her some protection from her ethereal tormenter.

Panting now, she moaned again, her soft cry reminding him of the sweet sounds she made when he'd pleasured her body.

"I feel a touch," she gasped, her breathless whisper ending on a sigh. "Sensual like yours. It strokes me, enflames me, and brings me to the edge of the peak over and over, without consummation! Stop it, or finish it, I can no longer say which, but can bear the torment no longer! I need to feel you inside of me!"

Vivid images danced before him in the darkness: Deirdre, nipples swollen and pouty, her body aroused and sensual and beautiful, begging for his touch.

"I sense nothing!" he protested, his body swelling and throbbing as erotic thoughts filled him.

"Then whose caress is this?" She staggered; only his firm grip on her hand kept her from falling. "I can take this sweet torment no more."

"Morthar's blood," he cursed, ignoring his own fierce arousal. He gathered her up in his arms in one motion, lifting her so that he might carry her the rest of the way. "I will hold you."

"Nay," she protested, even as her feet left the ground. To his disbelief she began to struggle, fighting his touch with the mindless fury of a wounded animal. To his shock he heard her clothing tear. Her breasts brushed against his chest, her nipples pebbled and full, causing his engorged body further arousal.

He clenched his teeth, remembering the curse of the cave and tried to tell himself he would somehow help Deirdre get through this and remain sane. Yet, he could not do so and hold her; with the way she fought he would be lucky to keep his own feet firmly planted on the smooth slope of the stone path. Releasing her with great care, he tried to lessen the impact, should she fall, by cradling one arm under her breasts.

Her frantic movements ceased as she felt his hold on her slacken. She slid down the front of him, another soft cry escaping her. Grabbing for his hand, she moved it between her legs, sliding it against her. By the Goddess! He felt the honey of

Karen Whiddon

her desire, even as she pressed herself against him, leaving no doubt that she was fully aroused.

His own body, already hard beyond belief, responded. Though he tried to warn himself against the treacherous cave, he struggled to control his lust. It raged through him, consumed him, and urged him to do one thing, one thing only: to plunge his swollen staff deep within Deidre's ready body. Over and over and over until they were both mindless with pleasure.

"Nay," he shouted in defiance, hearing the faint echo down the passage. "I will not be overcome so easily."

"Give me what I need and end this torture," Deirdre's voice was a breathless purr.

The utter darkness meant he could not see her, but that only served to enhance his other senses. She caressed him, her touch both soft and forceful, capturing his nipple between her fingernails and gently pinching, then skittering her hand down the expanse of his chest, inside his braes to capture his swollen rod in her fist.

He felt himself surge at her touch, helplessly pump as she caressed and squeezed him.

"Stop," he gritted out. "We must continue on to find the—"

She sank to her knees and her mouth, warm and wet, closed over his swollen length. He could not

302

speak. Could not think, could only moan as desire had its way with him.

Somehow, even though he shook with the force of his need, he found the strength to bring his hands up to Deirdre's shoulders and hold her off.

"Deirdre—"

"I *want* you." Her words were a soft sigh, a breath against his swollen flesh. Then abruptly, she let him go, aching and throbbing. She rose and embraced him with her slender arms. Of his own accord, he felt his arms go around her and hold her.

Then she arched her back, placing herself in such a way that her woman's center touched the swollen tip of him. His manhood seemed to surge of its own volition and, with a shattered groan, he pushed himself into her. He told himself it would be only a little, just a sample, just enough to feel— oh, by the Breath of Morthar, he could not resist such sweet temptation. He drove into her; she met him in kind, and still standing, he held her while he gave himself over to the exquisite pleasure of her body.

"Egann," she moaned. He felt her honeyed flesh clench tightly around him as she shuddered, finding a release in waves that seemed to go on forever. It was his undoing; he could hold himself back no longer, and with one final thrust he shattered.

While their heartbeats slowed he held her, still standing, unable to believe that he had lost control so thoroughly, yet reveling in the sense of utter completion that filled him now.

"I thought you said magic was suspended under the earth," Deirdre said, her breath soft against his chest. "How then—"

"Enchantment lurks in this ancient cave," he told her. "Though I know not why or how it works. I do not know why it chose you. . . ."

In his arms she went very still. "What of you?" she asked softly. "Was it not enchantment that drove you to this mindless need?"

He did not give himself time to ponder the answer. "No spell moved me," he admitted, giving her the truth at last. "Simply my own reaction to your desire. I would feel the same no matter where we might be."

"Truly?" Stretching against him, Deirdre sighed. She seemed pleased. "I have felt the same for many days now."

"I might search the world over—" he admitted, encouraged by her words. Placing a gentle kiss on the soft curve of her neck, he continued "—and never find one so precious to me as you."

She went utterly still, no longer murmuring wordless endearments against his chest, and tried to back away out of his embrace.

"For some reason my words have displeased you?" Refusing to let her go completely, Egann kept hold of her arm.

"Yes." Her voice sounded sad. She did not resist when he drew her back to him, embracing her again, pushing her long hair away from her face. To his stunned disbelief, he felt the wetness of tears on her cheek.

"Why do you weep?" he asked, wishing he could see her, but knowing she was probably glad now of the darkness.

"No reason." Her answer sounded curt. Then, softening her tone she added, "Or at least there is no explanation that I can say to you."

He could hear the rustle as she sought to adjust her torn gown. Without the benefit of light, she would have no way of knowing how she looked. Nor, he reflected with a wry smile, did he.

"Come, little dancer," he said, suddenly feeling sure she would tell him her feelings when she was ready. Deliberately making his tone light, he took her hand. "We have an amulet to find."

Love. At last she could put a name to the feeling that Egann evoked in her. And, though she knew he did not mean to do so, his words had made her hunger for the promise of a future together. Their lovemaking in the utter darkness had been a sensual experience, yet full of emotion as well. And, while she did not fully understand the ghostly touch that had so aroused her, Deirdre somehow suspected it had been but a manifestation of Egann's magic. It had been his desire that had seduced her on this dark tunnel, not the evil that had destroyed those Fae women.

Was it possible Egann loved her?

Truly, now that she thought on it, she knew not how to take his words. He had already made certain that she knew, once his tasks had been completed, he meant to go roam the mortal world alone. To be rootless, completely without ties— such was his fervent desire. Only then did he believe he could experience the dubious joy of freedom. Would he ever understand that true freedom came from within?

Since she had only just arrived at this conclusion herself, she knew it was not something that she could simply tell him. No, Egann would have to learn the truth himself, in his own way and time.

Yet knowing that did nothing to ease her aching heart. She loved Egann, and she knew she would forever. Such a thing came but once to the life of a Shadow Dancer. 'Twas more the pity she had given her heart to this man who existed in sunlight, this man who was not mortal, this man who would leave.

The dry taste of ashes in her mouth, Deirdre curled her fingers around Egann's, ready to let him lead her forward.

"Odd, but I sense the amulet no longer," he said.

"Ah, the amulet." She shook her head, wondering if the magical talisman would *ever* reveal itself fully to them. "Think you the amulet is gone?"

No answer. Suddenly, his hand no longer held hers.

"Egann?" Nothing. She felt the blackness closing in on her. She found it hard to draw breath.

"Egann?" Her voice wobbled, trembled, hinting at the rising terror that she would not acknowledge.

No response. She would not panic, could not afford such foolishness, not now.

Raising her voice, called again. "Egann!" She had spoken his name three times. Surely he could now find her.

Knowing he would not willingly leave her did not help allay her rising terror. Remembering his warning tale of madness, she took a deep breath and tried to collect her thoughts.

Yet the situation remained. Egann was gone. She was alone.

Utterly, totally alone.

She had a choice to make. She could turn back, make her way up the steep path, until she emerged into the mouth of the cave. Beyond that, the sea and what passed for the ordinary world awaited her. But to return would be true madness. She nearly laughed out loud.

Of course she would not flee. Not with Egann down here somewhere. Truly, she had no choice, no other option. She would continue down into the earth, alone for now, to try and find her love so they could face whatever fate awaited them. Together.

Resolved, she took a tentative step forward. Then another. How she wished she had enough magic to be able to create a torch so she could see.

Her stomach clenched. Even Egann, who truly had magic, had told her that his magic vanished when under the earth.

"Except for the magic of this enchanted cave itself."

Deirdre spun, hating her utter lack of sight. The voice had come from nowhere, yet seemed to echo everywhere. Was this perhaps the shadowy spirit who had stroked and aroused her earlier?

"Even the amulet is powerless here," the voice said.

Mayhap this was the madness Egann had spoken of. Never before had she heard disembodied voices, even in her dreams when the visions came to her.

Yet she would not let such a thing sway her. Determined, she continued to move forward and downward, always downward.

"*Your power has grown.*" The insidious whisper continued, volume rising to an echoing hiss. "*You are a child of the darkness and should be truly at home in this place.*"

At that Deirdre faltered, though she quickly recovered her stride. She would not dignify the speaker by responding to it, especially when it baited her with half-truths and lies.

"*Your power truly has grown, mortal woman. Perhaps your Prince Egann will have need of you after all.*"

This gave her pause. After all, Egann *had* said the cave was known for revealing truths. What if—

She shook her head, setting her jaw. How easily she had nearly been seduced by the mere temptation of power. As if a cave-spirit could bestow such a thing, merely by speaking it.

"*Especially now.*" The whisper had turned malicious, and it was so loud it carried a faint echo.

When it did not finish, Deirdre knew the thing waited for her to ask the question, but she would not. Her footsteps sure and steady, she continued her progress and pretended she did not hear.

"*Especially now!*" The whisper became a roar, and Deirdre fancied she actually felt the earth tremble. How powerful was this spirit, that its voice could make the ground shake?

If the walls collapsed she would be trapped here,

buried alive beneath tons of dirt and stone, with no hope of ever seeing the sunlight, or of touching Egann's beloved face again. Her stomach clenched. No! 'Twas another trick. She would not allow the fear to claim her or sway her from her path.

"*Do you not want to know what I mean?*" Once again the voice sounded soothing, sly. Though she did want to know, quite badly in fact, Deirdre clamped her lips together and held her breath, waiting silently.

"*His seed grows within you, Deirdre of the Shadows. You carry a child of light and of darkness, both of Rune and of earth. You carry Prince Egann's child.*"

Chapter Seventeen

Of all that the voice might have said, this was the one phrase guaranteed to stop Deirdre in her tracks.

Truth or falsehood? Was this reality or the beginning of a slow slide into madness? She knew not which. And truly, what did it matter? Whether she actually carried her and Egann's child or not, she would always feel bound to the prince, for she loved him.

She stumbled through the darkness as if pursued by some malicious spirit, but she thought only of him. His golden presence would be her light, guiding her out of all evil. She would find him, whether he needed her or wanted her or not.

This time, she believed, he *would* regain the amulet. That, more than anything else, was what really mattered.

Giving herself a mental shake, she took one step, then another.

"Deirdre, what is it? What is wrong with you?"

It was Egann's voice, full of concern. And it was right beside her, so close that his breath tickled her ear. She became conscious that in truth, her hand still rested in his larger one.

Had he never truly vanished?

"I—" Relief flooded her, closing her throat and rendering her unable to speak.

"Are you all right?"

She managed a nod and then, realizing that he could not see her in the inky blackness, squeezed his hand. "I think so, now. Some enchantment took me, and I thought you had gone."

"Left you? Not likely." He muttered something else, too low for her to hear.

"It seemed as though I were alone. And something spoke to me. . . ." Letting her words trail off, she knew she could not tell Egann what the voice had said. He had enough weight on his shoulders, broad though they were. She would not add another burden without first ascertaining the truth of it.

"You went somewhere"—he sounded grim as he explained—"and left only the shell of your body here with me. You would not move or acknowledge my touch, and though I called your name many times, you would not answer."

She shuddered. "I know not what happened, but it seemed to me that I searched for you, walking alone in the darkness and calling out for you as well."

"I never let go of your hand."

The air around them stirred, though no wind from outside could enter the narrow passage.

"You have my thanks for that," she said after a moment. "I believe it was your touch that kept the restless spirit that haunts this place from succeeding in driving me mad."

"What happened to you?"

About to answer, she was interrupted by a sharp cry. It sounded much like the dying wail of a wounded beast, and it came from the depths below them.

"We'd best hurry." Glad that this distraction would prevent Egann from wanting an answer, she tugged at his hand. "I have a feeling the amulet is very close."

He allowed himself to be led for only a few paces. Then he moved ahead, squeezing her hand. "I have that sense as well," he told her. "Though I know not why we cannot hear its voice."

As they rounded a sharp curve, the darkness seemed to lessen. Gradually, as they walked along the passage, the blackness began to lift until Deirdre could plainly see the chiseled features of Egann's beloved face. Her heart swelled with emotion, causing her throat to close and her eyes to tear. Since she could not share all the feelings the sight of his face evoked in her—longing, joy, love, and even regret—she swallowed. To distract herself, she concentrated on the rosy quality of the cavern's growing illumination.

"This glowing light is like the faint awakening of the day, before the sun has fully risen, is it not?"

She knew she sounded wistful, yet could not summon the strength to mask the sentiment. She could not focus on anything else. If the spirit had spoken true, she carried a child. She would have to tell Egann. But now was not the time, and this was not the place; she would do so on the surface of the earth, with the summer breeze blowing her hair, under a hundred stars in the ordinary night sky—not here, where the light surely was not natural, and where magic was not necessarily their friend.

She would tell him, that is, if he did not leave her first. Once he found the amulet, he would be free. The choice would be up to him, then. . . .

"Like the sunrise? Aye, so it is." Egann's tone was preoccupied. "But I sense the working of something more than the mere lifting of the darkness.

We will proceed with caution and remember: No matter what you see on this journey, do not let go of my hand." His fingers tightened on hers for emphasis.

They walked, and the hollow sound of their footsteps seemed to echo. Again the cry from below sounded, fainter this time, though with equal urgency and fear.

"From what nature of beast does that sound come?" Deirdre asked.

"I know not," Egann replied. There was a warning implicit in his low voice. "But the cause of such a noise cannot bode well for its maker."

"Think you that it is Hearne?"

Egann shrugged and did not answer.

"I do not smell smoke," Deirdre said, nervously sniffing the air. "Nor do I hear the sound of a large gathering, as there was before in that other place under the earth."

"Listen." Halting, Egann motioned her to silence.

Muffled sounds came from below.

"Weeping?" Deirdre whispered.

Egann frowned. "Or laughter."

Together they listened. Deirdre wondered if he felt as hesitant as she to continue.

"We must find the amulet."

"True."

Expelling his breath harshly, Egann cupped Deirdre's chin with his free hand. "I know not why Fiallan insisted that you must be with me in this journey." His magnificent eyes glowed. "But know this, little Shadow Dancer, I would not willingly take you into such danger were it not necessary."

This time she could not prevent her emotions from showing—not with him so close, looking at her in such a way. Hand trembling, she reached up and brushed a lock of his golden hair from his brow.

"I know," she told him. "But there is no other place that I would rather be than here with you."

His reaction was swift. He lowered his head and kissed her, fiercely, with a possessive violence that shook her all the way to her soul.

When he let her go, holding only her hand, she swayed, unable to take her gaze from his face.

"I will protect you, Deirdre." He spoke his vow in a harsh voice.

"This I know." Striving to lighten the mood, she summoned a wavering smile. "And because I believe in you, I have little fear." This was not entirely a falsehood, for truly she did not fear for her own safety. But she worried for Egann and what this Hearne might do if he had found a way to unleash the amulet's power.

She said none of these things, however. Instead, she swallowed hard, lifted her chin, and deliberately tore herself away from Egann's intent gaze, focusing on the deep cleft in his chin.

"Shall we go?"

After a moment's hesitation, he inclined his head slightly. "I am ready." Together they rounded the next corner.

Now that they could actually see the sharp slope of the stone path, Deirdre found the unrelenting downward spiral slightly less intimidating than traversing it in total darkness. As they continued, the turns came closer together, sharper and more abrupt.

"We near the end," Egann said.

Indeed, after several final, dizzying turns the path ended, leaving them standing on a large, flat stone floor in a room with only three visible sides. There had to be a fourth wall, yet they could not see it in the shadows ahead.

"A huge cavern," Egann said, running his free hand over the uneven surface of the rock wall they went past. "And so much light."

"There are no torches." Deirdre answered his musing. "Yet we can see as if there were a hundred lit candles. From what source comes the light?"

His reply was brief and to the point. "Magic. 'Twould seem this place makes its own rules."

They continued forward, yet Egann's steps slowed. Though she shared his hesitation, Deirdre wondered at his reason for it.

317

Karen Whiddon

"Know you something of what lies ahead?"

He shot her a grim look, and what she saw in his expression made her catch her breath. There was a lethal readiness in his dark gaze, the intent ferocity of a warrior, and for the first time she understood how some could fear him.

He was after all, a prince of Rune. And, were he to ever admit and accept the past, the true king of the Fae.

"Whatever awaits us—Hearne or something else—cannot be good," he warned. "And if I must fight, I cannot keep my hold upon your hand."

"I understand." Worrying her lower lip between her teeth, she wished Fiallan would put in an appearance. There were many question she wished to ask the wise man, and there was one she knew she must ask Egann even now.

"What of your magic?"

"What of it?"

Matter-of-factly she reminded him of his own words spoken earlier. "You have told me that your magic deserts you while under the earth—yet this place seems full of enchantment and spells."

His face was full of strength and an assurance that instantly buoyed her spirits. "I have no doubt that the amulet will assist me. You have heard the talisman welcome me with great joy. I do not believe that Hearne will be able to keep it from coming to my aid when I call."

318

Stunned, she tilted her head. "Truly, you think it will be so simple?"

"Simple?" Flashing her a confident smile, he gave an eloquent shrug. "Not simple. But doable. And I will not know until I try."

Egann saw from her expression that she wanted to believe him. Disbelief and hope warred with each other, but in the end he knew that she would have no choice but to accept his words and hope for the best.

As he himself did.

In truth, he had no idea whether the amulet would respond to his summons. After all, what connection did he truly have to it? None, since he had declined to take the throne.

Another cry, so sharp it lasted but an instant, came from the shadows on the other side of the cavern. The awful pitch and terror of the sound could not have issued from a human throat, for such a cry could only mean one thing. Death.

Immediately, he started forward. Deirdre kept pace with him, her steps sure and unfaltering.

Together they moved into the darkness.

The earth began to shake. Far behind them, there came a loud roar. It was the awful sound of rocks shifting, falling, closing forever the way they had come. The air filled with dust and momentarily the light was entirely snuffed out. Egann saw

319

black, before, like in the blink of an eye, all became once more bright.

With one final shudder, the earth's movement ceased. Deirdre stood poised for flight.

"The rockslide was back near the entrance," Egann said, keeping his voice calm. Not for one second did he wish to betray to her the utter finality he had heard in that sound that if they did not find another passage out, they would be forever trapped under the earth.

She glanced around wildly, a fine gray powder coating her black hair. Egann could not help himself; he reached out and lightly brushed it away with his hand.

"We are in no immediate danger," he said.

Still silent, she nodded. The absolute trust he saw in her eyes humbled him.

"Come on." Fingers intertwined in hers, he led her forward.

Only silence greeted them as they reached the far, final dark wall. Silence and nothing else. The cavern appeared to be empty.

"This can't be all there is," Deirdre whispered as they came to a halt. "How could it end here like this, with no other path?"

"Nay." Though he knew not what kind of enchantment had been worked upon this place, he had no doubt some secret opening existed somewhere in the rock wall. Otherwise, their entire journey had been in vain. Which could not be the case.

"Help me," he said, releasing Deirdre's hand momentarily to begin exploring the bumpy stone surface of the cave wall.

Soon enough his supposition proved true. He found a hollowed groove at eye level about ten paces farther along the darkened stone. Here the wall, where ordinarily rough as sand, had been carved smooth, like a polished gem. Symbols of some archaic language had been carved there also, and Egann ran his fingers along their raised outlines, pressing hard.

As he did, the wall began to move. With a loud groaning and grating, the huge stone structure slowly slid to one side and created an opening. Tendrils of mist, dancing in a breeze that should not exist, drifted through, enveloping them in a foggy haze.

"Here," he called to Deirdre, turning to reach for her hand before he led her into the darkness.

"Where are you?" He heard her voice but could not see her. The mist had grown thick and soupy, its cold damp blurring his eyes and chilling his skin.

Without thinking he waved his hands in a quick spell, meaning to clear the haze, but nothing happened, not even a brief tingling in his fingertips. Cursing his fickle magic, he strode into the very heart of the miasma.

"I cannot see you," Deirdre called.

Morthar take this, he thought. Her voice came from a distance, as though she had gone on ahead of him. "Where are you?" he asked.

"Slowly I move forward." She sounded calm, which was good.

"I will come to you," he directed. He moved in a wide circle, knowing she was near—after all, there was nowhere else she could go in the cavern, except through the new opening his explorations had created.

His heart caught, then began to pound. Surely she hadn't—

"Egann?" Fainter now, her cry seemed to come from a greater distance.

Still the fog swirled around him, obscuring his vision. Then, with a loud groan, the opening in the wall began to slide closed.

His heart stuttered, then began to pound. Was Deirdre in the cavern on this side, or had she already entered the doorway in the wall?

"Do not move," he ordered, pushing away a brief flash of panic. He knew not what perils awaited through the opening in the stone, but he did not want Deirdre to face them alone.

This side? Or the other? From the sound of her voice . . . Praying he was right, he plunged through the narrow opening. An instant later it grated closed behind him.

The cloying mist began to disperse.

"Deirdre?"

"I am here."

As the haze cleared, he saw her. Slender and still, she stood with her hands clasped together, waiting.

"I knew you would find me," she said, her welcoming smile trembling around the edges.

Crossing to her, he pulled her into his arms, letting the soft warmth of her reassure him, not wanting her to know that for a moment he had doubted his own ability to find her, to keep her safe.

His brave Deirdre, so determined to hide her fear.

She buried her face in his throat, wrapping her arms around him to keep him close. He breathed in her familiar scent, so like springtime and flowers, and closed his eyes. Though each time he touched her the sexual pull seemed stronger, he merely brushed a kiss against the top of her head and felt content to simply hold her.

Deirdre pulled away first, wearing a lopsided smile that tugged at his heart. "We must go on," she said, her voice calm and certain. "For even if we could clear the first rockslide away, now that the stone door has shut behind us, the path we took here has definitely been closed."

Summoning a smile of his own, he reached out and captured her hand as he spoke. "No more shall we be separated." But he was not sure whether he reassured himself or her.

"Aye." She squeezed his fingers to show that she agreed.

The unnatural fog totally dissipated, and now the light was bright enough to show that they stood among the remains of an ancient castle. On the remnants of one wall, an archway bore an inscription carved in the stone, the raised letters still unblemished and easy to read.

" 'So, we shall be called Maccus,' " Egann read out loud. "This place belonged to them, long ago."

"What happened to make it fall into such ruin?"

"I know not. But 'twas here, long ago, that the Maccus must have come. Banished from Rune, this was their city, hidden by a stone door, built far from the prying gaze of both mankind and Fae."

"Now they have abandoned it." She sounded relieved. "I am glad, as I would rather not venture into a city full of Maccus."

"This makes no sense." Tugging on her hand, Egann stepped closer to the center of the ruined castle. "Unless things were different in years past, why would they live in a place where magic is unpredictable?"

"For their own protection," a voice rang out, gleeful and confident and full of an awful, terrible, madness.

Hearne.

Chapter Eighteen

"Magic is evil," Hearne continued, his twisted smile fitting the wild intensity of his gaze. "Only I am powerful enough to control it. All others who seek to use it should be destroyed."

Narrow-eyed, Egann studied his opponent, trying to gauge the advisability of simply running at the man, overpowering him with his fists, and yanking the silver-chain off him. Unless he could come up with a better plan, that was it.

"Something is wrong." Deirdre's fingers tightened in his, her low voice worried. "Look at the amulet. The gems sparkle brightly no longer. Even the silver luster has dulled and gone dim."

She spoke true. The ornament Hearne so boldly wore appeared to be but a pale imitation of the genuine talisman. It lay flat and lifeless against his chest, without a flicker of energy, without a single note of lament or song.

"Do you have no response?" Hearne's voice, full of contempt, echoed in the stone chamber. "Are there no words of defense, is there no denouncement you wish to make?"

"I care little for your beliefs, misguided or not," Egann replied. "I only want back what belongs to my people."

"This?" With a sneer, Hearne held up the silver pendant. " 'Tis but a worthless bauble now. You are welcome to it."

Yanking the chain over his head, he tossed the amulet onto the mossy rocks near Egann's feet. It landed with a heavy clatter.

Egann made no move to step forward and pick it up.

"Go ahead," Hearne taunted. "Take it, it's yours. Isn't this what you two have been searching for these many nights?"

"Not *this*." Egann indicated the thing on the ground.

"This dull necklace is a poor forgery of that which I seek. What have you done with the true Amulet of Gwymyrr?"

To his astonishment, the other man threw back his head and laughed. The loud sound echoed off the cavern's walls, rebounding several times until it finally faded away.

"Do you not recognize your people's own talisman?"

Though the mockery in the other man's tone infuriated him, Egann clenched his jaw and kept his voice level.

"This is not the Amulet of Gwymyrr. 'Tis naught but a bad copy, for no hint of magic resonates from its hollow shell. I say to you again, where is my amulet?"

Smile sly, the Maccus shook his head. Wearing an exaggerated expression of patience, he indicated the silver necklace that remained in the dirt near Egann's feet.

"I have drained the enchantment from the gems, taking the magic into myself." Hearne's eyes glittered, his entire body seeming to radiate with power. "Did you not hear earlier the thing's pitiful cries as it sought futilely to fight me?"

Egann and Deirdre exchanged a quick glance. The horrible shrieks they had heard had come from the amulet? Egann did not believe it. Judging from the stubborn set of her chin, neither did Deirdre.

Still, the amulet *could* sing.

"If you find magic to be so evil, why do you want it inside you?" Deirdre's softly voiced question drew the man's gaze. A chill ran down Egann's spine even as he saw Deirdre shiver.

"Only one should have such magic. I will be the one. I will be he who channels my people's power, as you are the one who channels yours." Hearne spoke in a voice that burned with anger and loathing. "I will destroy any who get in my way."

"Why?"

"Long ago, a great wrong was done my people by yours. But history always repeats itself. We shall again fight that ancient battle, and this time the Maccus are certain to prevail. We shall retake that which is ours by right—Rune. And all because of your Amulet of Gwymyrr." Again he laughed.

Was it true? Egann refused to believe in the certainty of the Maccus's remark. For too long had he heard tales of what would happen to one who wore the Amulet of Gwymyrr without right. Perhaps Hearne only *thought* he had drained it. Perhaps . . .

Then why did the ancient gemstones look so dull and empty?

With a quick motion, Egann stepped forward and scooped up the silver pendant. It sparked once, but it was a brief flash, a glimmer that quickly faded.

If Hearne had spoken true, Egann now held that which had been the focus of his and Deirdre's long search. He held his birthright, the precious repository of centuries of Faerie magic, three gemstones in a heavy silver setting. The spiral chain that he had once refused to wear around his neck now ran through his fingers. But was this truly the fabled talisman, the amulet whose song beguiled and enchanted and had once summoned him with such unrestrained joy?

If so, it was silent now; it no longer even recognized his touch.

A great sorrow filled Egann, then a rage such as he had not felt since the mortal had caused Banan's death.

"How dare you!" he roared. Closing his hands around the dull silver chain, he took a step forward. "You have no right—"

"I have every right." Still laughing, Hearne made several quick motions with his hands. "While all you have is a worthless necklace."

Knowing the other man's movements meant he invoked some sort of magical spell, Egann tried to summon enough of his power to counter it. Instead of the usual hum beginning in his veins again, he felt nothing.

"Some things," Hearne's voice rang out, clear and confident and strong, "require a sacrifice."

Beside him, Deirdre stumbled as the earth gave a violent shudder. "What is happening?" she cried, her voice full of shock and terror. "Egann, help me—"

With a cutting boom so loud that the mountain trembled, Deirdre disappeared. One moment she stood beside him, her hand in his. The next, she simply winked out of existence.

And Hearne too vanished.

While rocks fell all around and the dust rose to choke him, Egann stood in stunned disbelief. Instead of Deirdre's fingers, his hand now closed around empty air. Wherever Hearne had gone, he had taken Deirdre with him.

"He has not traveled far." Fiallan's voice sounded close in the small space. "There is another passage that connects this cave to the one where you met him earlier."

A white owl perched on a stone ledge—Fiallan's other form, the one he wore when he wished to observe in secret.

"Time is of the essence," came the sonorous voice as the elder continued. "Hearne was right about one thing—all too soon will history seek to repeat itself. Take the Amulet of Gwymyrr and go after him."

Egann opened his fist, staring at the now-worthless necklace of muted silver and dulled gems. Without its magic to assist him, he would not be able to follow much more quickly than a mortal could walk.

331

The central ruby began to glow like the smoldering ember of a hearth fire. Then, just as quickly as if doused by a bucket of water, it dimmed.

Fury burned in him, equally hot, at what Hearne, this interloper, had done to his people's amulet, the ancient repository of the Fae's magic.

"Your amulet," Fiallan said, reading his mind. "Only you can restore its power."

"Enough." Egann shook his head. "I seek to gather my strength for another attempt to follow them by magical means."

"Your magic deserts you here, under the earth," Fiallan warned. "To regain your power, you must first claim the amulet."

The rest, though unspoken, seemed to echo in the cavern:

And you must also claim your heritage.

King. And warrior too.

"What else is a king, but one who cares deeply?"

The question, like so many others asked of him by Fiallan over the years, was rhetorical.

"I have always cared greatly." Egann's response felt torn from the very depths of his soul.

"Yet you wished to walk away." The white bird, its pristine feathers glowing, watched him with an unblinking stare.

"I believed there would be another." And he had. He had even pictured such a one. Tall and fierce and kingly, he wore Banan's long-dead face.

"Another who could care more than you?"

"Nay!" Clenching his jaw, again Egann regarded the amulet. This time it was the sapphire gem, the one the current color of Deirdre's eyes that briefly glimmered. "One who could serve my people better. Can you not see? 'Tis because my people matter so much that I stepped aside. I could not give them less than capable hands to guard them."

"Banan had a choice." Fiallan's expression was kind. "You did not force him to touch the steel of the sword. You did not force him to stay with you, teasing the mortal."

"I did nothing to send him away."

"How were you to know the mortal would wake?"

"Enough!" Egann roared. "What is done is done, and many long years have I asked myself these very same questions. Let it rest, old one."

With a sad smile, Fiallan inclined his head. "Very well. What of the woman?"

The woman? My mortal Shadow Dancer? She whom I regard more highly than any other. In fact, she who—

"I love her." For a second, Egann closed his eyes. When he opened them again, he saw that the emerald gem of the amulet shimmered with green fire.

333

"To save her you must become king," Fiallan said simply. "And in doing so you will save our people."

For an instant, one shattering heartbeat, Egann heard the high, lovely sound of the amulet's song. Feeble and faint, nonetheless the notes seemed to welcome him, to invite him to take back what he had lost.

King.

He took a deep breath.

Warrior.

His stomach clenched.

Yet who else would take up the mantle of power, who else would step forward to save the Fae and Rune and the woman Egann loved? And, even were another man to do so, would Egann step willingly aside and let him attempt this, the most important rescue in the history of his people?

Nay. For too long had he refused to see those things he carried inside his heart: his love, his heritage, his birthright.

King. He, Egann of Rune. For the first time he felt the unshakable bond he and the amulet had always been fated to share. Finally, he accepted his destiny.

Acknowledging the truth of the Wise One's words, Egann lifted the heavy silver chain high.

In tandem, the gemstones glowed—bloodred, cobalt, and emerald.

Bowing his head, he placed the Amulet of Gwy-myrr around his neck. And felt the resonance of its power begin to vibrate in his veins.

King, the amulet seemed to whisper.

The white owl vanished.

A moment later, King Egann of Rune inclined his head and, with a quick motion of his hand, went after the woman he loved and would make his queen.

"Tonight, the full moon will rise." Hearne looked at Deirdre expectantly, his eyes glowing wickedly. "Soon you will dance."

Pushing away her simmering rage, Deirdre gestured at the hundreds of Shadow Dancers that were gathered in the surrounding immense cavern. "What of the others?"

"Oh, they will dance as well."

Though she had no desire to exchange words with this man, Deirdre had to know: "For what purpose?"

At his blank stare, she elaborated. "When I danced for the people of the cliffs, 'twas to ensure a fruitful harvest or to make sure the women would conceive. The magic of the dance was always used in that manner. It is the only way we can summon power."

His mouth twisted in a half-leer, half-smile, Hearne said, "So say you. But how do you know for certain if that is true?"

His words gave her pause. "Such is the way of those who dance in shadows. It has always been so."

"Then we shall have a *new* way." Hearne's smile broadened, stretching his face into a grotesque mask of lines that Deirdre found repulsive.

"And when you have finished the dance, you shall feel the kiss of the sun for the first time."

Uncomprehending, she could only gape at him. Then she collected herself and glanced again at the assembled crowd. The group seemed to swell by the moment as more and more Shadow Dancers joined it.

"The sun?" Though the pounding of her heart seemed to ring in her ears, she took great care to make her voice sound unconcerned. "Just me or"— waving a hand at the others—"all of us?"

"All of you." Hearne's dark gaze seemed to smolder with an unholy excitement. "Eventually. Once the curse has been lifted."

"How?"

"I am more than merely the leader of the Maccus." The confidence in his tone invited her to believe in him as well. "I will be the savior of your people."

Without thinking she blurted out her thoughts. "But you no longer have the Amulet of Gwymyrr."

His laugh was hard, cold, forced. "As I said before, that worthless trinket is no longer necessary. I have drained the power from its gemstones, and even now that power thrums inside of me."

Was this true? For one tiny moment she found herself actually believing the words of a madman. Hearne would be persuasive—if not for the strong sense of evil that stubbornly clung to him, especially now.

Yet she could easily understand why all the others had let themselves be led so easily to this slaughter. He had been lying to them, promising them everything they most wanted. And now he would use and destroy them.

"There is one small problem," Hearne continued. "I have informed the people of it already. They now believe one must die. One must give her life so the others might live."

A *sacrifice*. Her heart sinking, Deirdre knew then that the Maccus meant to use her as bait to bind the others to him.

"How?" she whispered. Straightening her shoulders, she lifted her chin to show him she was not afraid, even though inside she quaked with fear.

"After you dance, when your energy has deserted you, you will lie senseless on the ground. The sun will rise, and that bright orb from above will feed upon you, in fire and in light. The words will be spoken. Though you will die, your sacrifice will be enough to break the curse and let the rest of your people be free."

She would pretend she did not know the rest of his plans. "Why me?"

His expression turned sly. "Know you not that you carry *his* child?"

Stunned, she could only manage a wordless nod.

"A child of darkness and of light. Of Fae and of one who is . . . more than a mere mortal. Such a child could change the world."

Protectively, Deirdre cradled her stomach. All her life she had dreamed of feeling the warm caress of sunlight on her skin, or dreamed of dying after having given way to a new dancer. But not this way, not dying on the sacrificial altar of some mad prophet drunk with ill-gotten power.

What was worse, she knew with utter certainty that her death would not free her people in the way Hearne stated. Instead she would be the instrument that brought about their destruction. Around her they continued to gather: other Shadow Dancers with bright faces and hopeful smiles, avoiding her gaze, along with black-cloaked

Maccus with their burning eyes, simply staring.

Earlier, Hearne had used silver-tongued words to whip this group into a frenzy. Now they believed her death would win their freedom, that by dying, Deirdre would lift the curse that had haunted them for generations. They did not—could not—understand the true depth of his evil.

Setting her jaw, she looked up at Hearne defiantly. "I will not let you kill my babe. Or my people."

He pretended not to her the last part of her declaration. "Such a small sacrifice to make, for the greater good of your race," he cajoled.

"I will not lead them to death willingly," she warned.

Ignoring her, Hearne lifted his hand in a regal wave to the growing crowd. "After your body is reduced to nothing more than ash, I will lead the others forth, into the bright light of day, where they will feel for the first time the warmth of sunlight on their skin."

Deirdre recoiled. "All the Shadow Dancers will die," she whispered in horror, reading with certainty the truth in his smug expression. "You mean to lead them into the sun once you have killed me only so that they will all be destroyed."

"Your death will save them," he repeated with amusement. "And an archaic debt will be repaid."

But the undercurrent of insincerity that rang in the Maccus leader's strident tones was impossible to miss.

"This thing you mean to do—"

"Will do," he corrected. "For there is no one who can stop me."

With unshakable faith, Deirdre drew herself up. She straightened her shoulders, tossed her hair back, and met the madman's burning gaze.

"Ah, but there is. Egann." *One time*, "You have left out one important part of this historic moment. Egann of Rune." *Twice*, Expectantly, she cocked her head and adopted an attitude of intense listening. "Any moment now Egann—" *Three times*.

With a sharp clap of thunder, Egann appeared— an avenging warrior of Fae, bright and golden in the dim light of the smoky cave—wearing the Amulet of Gwymyrr sparkling with power around his neck.

Chapter Nineteen

The amulet felt hot against Egann's chest as he channeled its rising energy to confront Hearne. In the murky darkness of the Maccus's underground lair, his fury burned in him with the heat of a hundred fires.

He *would* settle this, and quickly. But first, he must ensure Deirdre's safety.

His gaze met hers, drawn across the smoky gloom like lightning to metal. Her lips parted, and he read his name on her silent mouth, hearing her wordless entreaty as clearly as if she'd shouted.

"My choice," she said. "I make it willingly."

Pain stabbed him, making his stride falter. She could mean to die.

"At last," Hearne roared at him, towering over Deirdre, a glittering giant tarnished by madness. "You are just in time to witness the changing of the world."

The instant Hearne spoke those words, the stone walls of the cavern began to shift with a great grinding of rock. The roof of the cave slid back, painful in its slowness, and the starry night sky became visible by inches.

Air rushed in—night air scented with salt and sea and sand. The murkiness vanished as quickly as if taken by a spell. The moon—full and ripe— bathed them in silver. The seductive pull of its fullness brought forth from the assembled Shadow Dancers a collective groan. Yet as one they re- mained huddling under a stone overhang, still in darkness, which apparently gave them protection from the moon's unfightable call. In the center of it all stood Hearne and the captive Deirdre.

Then Hearne moved back.

Deirdre, Egann's Deirdre, stood alone in the center of the stone bowl, glowing opalescent in the moonlight. Her glorious eyes closed, her face turned up to the silver moon, she began to dance.

About to move forward and pull her away, Egann halted. Though he had witnessed her dance only once before, he recognized in her movements a subtle difference. Her eyes flew open and her steady gaze locked on his. He realized what the difference was: The ripe moon, though seductive, compelled her not. Deirdre no longer danced for others. This dance was of her own free will; this dance was for herself.

And for him.

He could no more stop her now than he could have prevented Banan from reaching for that long-ago sword. She would dance or die trying, and he could no more block her than he could halt the sun from rising.

With every sinuous movement, every sweet sway of her hips, Deirdre called to him. She empowered him. The amulet against his chest recognized her intent and began to hum a low-pitched melody.

He felt as though a weight had lifted from his shoulders, and he knew then what he must do.

Moving forward, Egann paid no mind to the assembled crowd of Hearne's followers, nor to the madman himself. Every fiber in his body, nay in his *soul*, urged him onward, until he took Deirdre's delicate hand in his and began to dance with her.

The Amulet of Gwymyrr heated on his chest and began to glow. Its hum became louder, more melodious.

All around, the air filled with glittering shards of moonbeams mingled with magic . . . and moving as one the assembled Shadow Dancers took tentative steps into them.

A white owl circled in a flash of alabaster feathers, gave a sharp cry that might have been of joy or might have been a sound of predatory glee. Egann cared not. Touching Deirdre, he knew fully now the all-encompassing thrill of the Shadow People's Moon Dance. Intricately woven, each movement seemed part of an incantation, a spell spoken to a magic deeper than time and too powerful for mere words. He lost himself in it—and in her. Together they were joined, with only the touch of each other's hand to connect them, yet one with each other, with the moon, the sea, the stars.

They danced their love. No words passed between them, but he knew she understood his silent declaration. And he received it back, his love in equal measure, that final acknowledgment that in Deirdre he had found his one true mate, the only woman who could ever be his queen.

The power built, surrounding them with the visible thrum of energy, the amulet sparkling brighter each time their bodies touched. He could feel magic all around him, inside him too, as his blood pulsed through his veins and his strength increased with each heartbeat.

He became conscious of another spark, the flame of another life that burned inside Deirdre. In wonder and shock he gazed at her, seeing in the sweet curve of her ripe body the truth of what he had envisioned.

She met his startled gaze with a smile.

"Our child," she murmured against him. "Conceived by our love."

With her, moving, spinning, dancing, he rejoiced.

Now the amulet's song called another name, that of the woman whose life he shared.

Deirdre. Deirdre.

The musical sound of her name enthralled him. The touch of her skin, silky and smooth, bewitched him. Around each other they flowed and merged, until he no longer knew if the pulse that sounded in his ears was hers or his own. It seemed to go on forever, yet taking but an instant in the fabric of time.

Then, all at once, the dance ended.

Deirdre's fatigue seemed palpable as she sagged in his arms, sank to her knees with a quiet moan.

Blinking, Egann realized with growing horror that the moon had disappeared and dawn rapidly approached.

Nay, more than approached, morning was *here*.

A fiery ball of orange, the sun burst over the eastern horizon.

Deirdre lay semi-conscious, half in his arms, fully exposed to the onslaught of the deadly rays. He had always thought he would be the one to leave her, once his quest had been completed. He had assumed he would be compelled by his shame and anger into wandering the world, leaving her forever alone. Instead, it was *she* who would leave first, for when the sunlight touched her skin she would die. And he could not bear that.

His chest constricted. Nay, not if he could help it.

A laugh rang out, guttural and full of malice. Stepping forward, Hearne lifted his hands to the sunrise in gleeful supplication. He would now have his sacrifice.

All the Shadow Dancers who had been brave enough to venture beyond the protection of the stone attempted to retreat in horror. Stone walls slammed down, trapping them all in the open.

"Die." With one word Hearne mocked them. Waving his hand quickly, he began to speak harsh words of a magic so wrong and so old that the sound of his voice sent a terrible chill down Egann's spine.

As if to counteract such darkness, the Amulet of Gwymyrr began to sing. It was no lament this time, nor a welcoming song of joy, but a battle cry, pure and fierce and strong.

And Egann again knew what he must do. Somehow he must remove the curse.

Through the intricate motions of the dance, he had felt another power begin to build in him, familiar magic yet different, channeled through his Shadow Dancer and her dance, strengthened by the amulet. In Deirdre, too, some of the magic resided still. This would aid her, give her strength to face the ordeal about to begin, so with a gentle tug on her hand he awakened her.

Shakily she climbed to her feet, her serene expression showing no fear, only joy, even as the powerful golden rays of the dawn touched the creamy skin of her upturned face.

Hearne's voice increased in volume, the black and suffocating energy his spell created rushing at them like a wave of swirling darkness.

Egann lifted his hand and Deirdre's. He concentrated on the power inside him, focusing it on the talisman that seared against his chest.

With a howling screech, Hearne's spell attacked them. Unwavering in its song, Egann's amulet deflected the onslaught, enabling Egann and Deirdre to send it back—equally fierce, equally strong, upon Hearne and his Maccus followers.

Hearne became a sacrifice; he ignited. His followers, those who were used to sacrifices for their red and angry god, gathered around the furious blaze, quiet and uncertain now, yet seeming to accept the unexpected death of their leader with stoic readiness.

The Amulet of Gwymyrr, heavy and smoldering against Egann's chest, fell silent.

Finding the language from somewhere in his and Deirdre's shared consciousness, Egann heard himself speak the words to yet another ancient spell, one he had never before known yet now understood—one that should have been spoken eons ago. Finally, the ancient wrong would be righted.

The morning light continued to blaze down on them, purifying and bright.

Through this all, Deirdre stood tall, her hand still cradled in his, her face turned up in wonder, her lips curved in a bemused and welcoming smile as she accepted the amber kiss of the morning sun. She did not burn, or melt, or suffer. Rather Egann saw in her an attitude of rejoicing, even as she turned to look at him and her eyes changed color once more, this time to the warm tawny gold of the burgeoning day. Tears of joy streamed down her cheeks, even as she laughed out loud.

Seeing her unharmed, one by one the other

Shadow Dancers took tentative steps forward, toward her, toward the light.

With her hand still in his, Deirdre stood tall in the brightness of day and began to dance.

Epilogue

"Shall I call Fiallan?" Egann anxiously clutched Deirdre's hand as she let out a low moan.

"The babe is ready to be born," she gasped, arching her back and setting her jaw.

Though he knew the pain had to be fierce, Egann could not help admiring his brave wife, who refused to let him see how she suffered.

"Because I know you'll suffer too," she muttered. The sharing of their thoughts had become so common between them that neither thought much of it. Which was add because, even in Rune, the land of enchantment, such bonding between mates was rare and thus, greatly prized. But they were well aware of the great love they shared.

"Did I hear my name?" Grinning broadly, Fiallan appeared outside the doorway.

"Our child is about to enter the world."

"Come talk to me."

Egann shook his head. "I cannot leave Deirdre's side. She needs me." At his words both his wife and the wise man exchanged wry smiles.

"If you don't ease your grip on my hand, I fear my fingers will be broken," Deirdre added.

Recognizing that she spoke true, Egann released her hand. "I did not mean to hurt you." He dragged his hand over his face. "I did not realize that—"

"Go with Fiallan," Deirdre encouraged softly. "The babe will not arrive within the next few minutes. Send the midwife to me, and give me a few moments alone."

Understanding then that she needed to vent some of her pain and did not wish him to bear witness, Egann rose. Once in the long stone hall, he and Fiallan walked to its end and halted.

The wise man spoke: "The Maccus assemble with our people to celebrate the birth of their new prince or princess."

Egann raised a brow. "I thank Monk for that. He was one of the first of them to seek a way to make amends."

"He has done so, and Rune has welcomed him."

"All of them," Egann reflected. "Once Hearne was destroyed and his spell over them broken, they all seemed to deeply regret their actions under his leadership. The mortal world has both lost and gained, now that the Shadow Dancers hide in the darkness and dance no more to the light of the full moon."

Fiallan laughed. "Some of them have even married Maccus and come here to live. Unbelievable as it may seem, the great chasm between our people has finally closed."

"And the Hall of Legends has at last opened to you, as the legend said, in time of great need or great joy."

"Aye." Fiallan looked pleased. "Now that the ancient wrong has been righted, it has."

Narrowing his eyes, Egann regarded the man who had been mentor and teacher, prophet and seer, and, most of all, old father and friend. "Was this all part of a plan, Wise One? All of this?" He waved his arm in a broad gesture meant to encompass both Earth and Rune.

Fiallan only smiled a mysterious smile and said nothing.

"I visited Banan's resting place." For the first time in years, Egann was able to speak his brother's name without the sharp anguish of quilt and loss. "The rowan tree that grows there has become tall and strong."

"His spirit nourishes it." Fiallan lightly touched Egann's arm. "He would be pleased to see the contentment that creates such glorious magic."

"Even Weylyn has found happiness," Egann reflected, thinking of the great beast sheltering the smaller Cinnie. "Deirdre's small cat will grow into a sleek friend one day."

"Rune has welcomed back all of her lost children," Fiallan agreed.

A *lost child*. So too had he been, once. He thought of Deirdre's generous spirit and welcoming embrace, and smiled.

Six hours later their own child, a son with hair as black as his mother's, yet streaked through with bright ribbons of gold, was born. His eyes were the color of a sunny day, and they named him Banan.

SELKIE
MELANIE JACKSON

While the war to end all wars has changed the face of Europe, some things stay the same; the tempestuous Scottish coast remains a place of unquenchable magic and mystery. Sequestered at Fintry Castle by the whim of her mistress, Hexy Garrow spares seven tears for her past—all of which are swallowed by the waves.

By joining the water, those tears complete a ritual, and that ritual summons a prince. He is a man of myth whose eyes hold the dark secrets of the sea, and whose silken touch is the caress of the tide. His very nature goes against all Hexy has ever believed, but his love is everything she's ever desired.

SPIRIT OF
THE MIST
JANEEN O'KERRY

An early summer storm rages off the coast of western Ireland, and Muriel watches. From inside the protective walls of Dun Farraige, she can see nothing, yet her water mirror shows all. The moonlight reveals the face of a man—one struggling to overcome the sea.

He is an exile, of course. By clan law, exiles are to be made slaves. Yet something ennobles this man. The stranger's face makes Muriel yearn for both his safety and his freedom. She, who was raised as the daughter of a nobleman, has a terrible secret. And she can't help but believe that this handsome visitor—swaddled in mist and delivered to the rain-swept shores beneath her Dun—will be her salvation.

JANEEN O'KERRY

SISTER OF THE MOON

In the sylvan glens of Eire, the Sidhe reign supreme. The fair folk they are: fairies, thieves, changeling-bearers, tricksters. Their feet make no sound as they traipse through ancient forests, their mouths no noise as they weave their moonlight spells. And so Men have learned to fear them. But the Folk are dying. Their hunting grounds are overrun, their bronze swords no match for Man's cold iron. Scahta, their queen, is helpless to act. Her people need a king. And on Samhain Eve, she finds one. Though he is raw and untrained, she sees in Anlon the soul of nobility. Yet he is a Man. He will have to pass many tests to win her love. At the fires of Beltane he must prove himself her husband—and for the salvation of the Sidhe he must make himself a king.

_52466-X $5.50 US/$6.50 CAN

Dorchester Publishing Co., Inc.
P.O. Box 6640
Wayne, PA 19087-8640

Please add $2.50 for shipping and handling for the first book and $.75 for each book thereafter. NY, and PA residents, please add appropriate sales tax. No cash, stamps, or C.O.D.s All orders shipped within 6 weeks via postal service book rate.
Canadian orders require $2.00 extra postage and must be paid in U.S. dollars through a U.S. banking facility.

Name _____
Address _____
City_____ State_____ Zip____
I have enclosed $_____ in payment for the checked book(s).
Payment <u>must</u> accompany all orders. ❏ Please send a free catalog.
CHECK OUT OUR WEBSITE! www.dorchesterpub.com

MISTRESS OF THE WATERS
JANEEN O'KERRY

Planning to relocate to Ireland, the home of her forebears, after college, Shannon Rose Gray immerses herself in her studies. But when an old book reveals a mysterious scrap of vellum with musical notes and her name, she finds herself whistling a different tune in a different time. Suddenly in pagan Eire, Shannon finds the sexiest man she's ever encountered: Lasairian. Her senses ablaze with the beauty of the Beltane feast, Shannon finds herself enflamed by the virile Celt's touch. But there are things about Lasairian that Shannon doesn't know. Is her handsome husband everything he claims—everything she wants? And the Beltane ritual—has it made her the prince's mistress, or the queen of his heart?

___52309-4 $4.99 US/$5.99 CAN